Revenge on Ice

This is a fictional work. All the characters and incidents are the creation of the author's imagination.

Print layout, e-book conversion, and cover design by DLD Books Editing and Self-Publishing Services
www.dldbooks.com

Published by Ama Dablam, Inc
ISBN 978-0-9785353-9-1

Revenge on Ice

Linda LeBlanc

Sara/Ryker Mysteries Book 2

Ama Dablam, Inc.

Other books by Linda LeBlanc

Beyond the Summit
Everest Adventure and Romance

No Summit Out of Sight
The True Story of the Youngest Person to Climb the Seven
Summits

Four Teens on Everest

Sara/Ryker Mysteries

A Fair Knight Slain
Murder at the Renaissance Fair.

Revenge on Ice

Chapter 1

Sara stepped onto the patio to water thirsty plants after a week's R & R. Coffee steamed in her other hand as dawn streaked the sky in apricot and fire. The chief's 6:15 a.m. call shattered the calm. "Naked male found frozen in the Tidwell Meat Packer Plant. Get over there now."

Damn. She'd come home resolved to find the courage to call her father and stop wasting the few years they might have left. But a second murder in three weeks meant zero personal life, just the hurt. Dressed in ten, she hit the road.

Chief McBride paced the concrete outside Tidwell when she pulled in. His body looked heavily lived in. Deep walnut shell furrows stacked his forehead. His eyes had lost their spark.

"Who found him?" she asked.

"The butcher. I sent him home; he was shaking too hard to even sign his name." McBride jerked his chin toward the door. "Owner's fishing in Mexico. Can't reach him. No signs of forced entry. CCTV inside and out disabled. No prints. No footprints. This was a pro."

Her partner, Ryker, strolled up, a smile playing on his lips. "We have to quit meeting like this or people will talk."

She feigned amusement. "Another bizarre murder scene."

"Do we have an ID?"

"Not yet," said McBride. "CSI found no wallet, phone, or

clothing. Hopefully, the M.E. will discover dental work. Keep me posted. He opened his cruiser and retrieved a letter. Waving it, he called to Sara, "Almost forgot. This came right after you left. Postmarked Pakistan."

"Probably another fundraising appeal," Sara said. "I've donated to international hunger orgs and get overseas mail all the time." She pocketed it. Work first."

"Addressed to you at the station?"

She frowned. "Strange. I'll open it later."

A lean, balding medical examiner emerged through the side door with muffin crumbs on his coat. "No defensive wounds but ligature marks on wrists and ankles. A small puncture implies a drug briefly immobilized him. He would have awakened trapped inside. The cause of death seems clear. Hypothermia. Body won't thaw for hours."

"Did you find ropes?" asked Ryker.

"No, somebody cut him loose before locking the door."

"About how long ago?"

"Hard to tell. Cold kills slower than bullets and affects the time of death assessments. For now, I'd say before midnight. Go on in."

The cold bit through Sara's jacket. Inside was manufactured winter: bright lights, wet floors, the metallic sweetness of beef fat. Ryker rubbed his arms and tucked his hands into his armpits.

"Christ, it's freezing. Make sure the door doesn't lock."

A second meat cutter, face gray and jaw working, led them past hooks and rails to the back. Two massive sides of beef hung swaying slightly in the air currents. Between them, a man sat on the floor, knees drawn to chest, arms wrapped around his legs. Head forward. A naked knot of muscle and skin and frost, as if he'd tried to curl around the last heat he had left.

Ryker whistled under his breath. "I've seen freezer jobs but never one like this."

Sara crouched. The cold pressed through her knees. Frost

feathered the hair on the dead man's forearms. Ice laced the corners of his eyes. His white and blue lips were cracked.

"On Everest, I passed bodies sitting or lying frozen exactly as they died. I'm shivering. Let's go."

The door thudded shut behind them. Her breath looked like smoke in the morning heat as Florida sun punched through haze.

"What'd you see squatting?" Ryker asked.

"He'll be thirty-five in late October."

"You've suddenly become a facial expert?"

"He told us yesterday. It's Vance Miller. A local hero. This needs to stay quiet as long as possible. Everest didn't kill him. Somebody did and without mercy."

Chapter 2

Sixteen hours earlier.

Ryker rolled to the curb at Sara's place, glad she was back from a week's R&R. Three weeks ago, he'd first met her standing over a bloodied dead knight wedged in a dragon ride. Since then, she'd been an eclipse in daylight, impossible to ignore, way out of his league. While he chased New York crime lords, she'd been bushwhacking jungles and racing across deserts, not intimidated by snakes, gators, or poison dart frogs.

Sara moseyed down the driveway, her short ash-blond hair pillow-flattened on one side, green eyes not quite meeting his. In her late thirties, she was young enough to be his daughter if he'd knocked someone up at thirteen.

"Are you on a stakeout?" she asked.

He bowed with a full-arm flourish. "Au contraire, my fair lady. I bear the quintessential surprise."

"Still quoting your English-professor wife?"

"She and I always learned a new word every day. They keep her alive in me."

"And from age five, my punctilious dad made face a mirror and enunciate a new difficult word before I could go to school. It keeps him alive in me too."

Arms akimbo, she asked, "Sherlock, did you manage to stay out of trouble in my absence?"

"Since McBride hired me to stay here and work for him in Florida, I searched for better digs in case my daughter shows up."

"What? And vacate your lovely, two-star motel? Any word from her?"

"No. In that first conversation in years, Dulce swore she'll have nothing to do with me in New York. Memories of an absent police father and husband haunt the city."

Sara flicked donut crumbs off his collar. "Knock off the junk food if you want to look good for her.

He nudged the console. "Your turn. What does an adventure junkie do with a week off?"

"Go home to Colorado and climb a 14,000-foot peak."

His head shook in a double take. "For R&R? Without me to exercise your mind, it atrophied."

"Hiking the Rocky Mountains has always cleared my head. Coming from Florida at sea level, I was already gasping for air when I came to a steep talus slope. A misstep in the loose rocks would have sent me tumbling to my death."

"So you stopped."

"No, my dad programmed me to never give up. And he goes everywhere with me in my head.

Twenty minutes later, Ryker pulled into a packed lot.

"A rock concert?" Sara exclaimed. "Not our vibe."

"It's your thing, an Everest slideshow. The Reunion Heights hiking club leader took four members up in May."

Ryker ushered her to their reserved seats at the rear of a full auditorium. Colorful prayer flags hung above the stage. On the screen: snow-capped peaks and a red *Namaste*.

A tall, sun-leathered man with brown stubble crossed into the spotlight, a mic clipped on his lapel.

"Greetings, Vance Miller here to take you on a journey to the roof of the world. A year ago, four members of the Reunion Heights hiking club accepted the challenge of summiting Mount Everest with me. We trained hard for a year before attempting a high-altitude climb to 19,341feet on Kilimanjaro in Africa. Then in May, we left for what everyone once considered impossible.

"Meet my valiant team members. Without their physical and mental strength buoying each other, we never would have made it." He motioned to those in the front row. "Please stand and turn toward the audience when I call your name. Patrick O'Connor, Heath Pierson, Zoey Bennett, Tanner Brooks." After each one received loud applause, they all returned to their seats.

"Reaching the summit of Everest was the culmination of my dream. Eight years ago, I planned to climb the Seven Summits, highest mountain on each continent, before turning thirty-five. I barely made it. My birthday's the end of October. Although my wife is traveling for work tonight and can't be here, I want to pay homage to her enduring patience and support of me going off to climb those *savage* mountains, as she refers to them."

He clicked on a simplified world map of the Seven Summits. N America-Denali. S America-Aconcagua. Asia-Everest. Africa-Kilimanjaro. Europe-Elbrus. Australia-Kosciuszko. Antarctica-Vinson Massif.

A male voice from the back row yelled, "You're not done."

Shielding his eyes from the bright spotlight, Vance looked up. "Who are you?"

"Jason. Remember me? I'm here to steal your thunder."

Vance stepped forward to the front for a better view of the heckler. "Please be seated. You're interrupting."

"Your audience deserves the truth," he bellowed.

Vance ordered the guards to remove the troublemaker from the building. He clicked the next slide. "No roads. A short uphill runway, cliff at one end, mountain at the other, Lukla's one of the most dangerous airports in the world."

Ryker shuddered and asked Sara, "You flew into there?"

"Oh, yeah, white-knuckled from takeoff to landing."

Another click. "We landed at 9,383 feet, then hiked roughly thirty-seven miles to base camp at 17,598. Everything moves on the backs of two-legged or four. Eight hours a day. Seven days, with two for acclimatization."

Photos spilled: a crawling glacier, ladders over blue-black crevasses, a whiteout, lines of climbers above the Death Zone.

Listening to Sara's earlier account of her climb, Ryker had concluded climbers were batshit crazy. After watching this, there was no way in hell he would ever step foot on that mountain.

Sara's hands tightened in her lap. When a knife-edge ridge flashed—the cornice traverse—her eyes filmed. One tear slid.

Ryker bumped her shoulder. "Talk to me."

"That's where I came upon Michael six years ago. "Mask off, no oxygen left, dead-fish eyes, icicles on his nostrils, hair and lashes frozen. If I hadn't stopped and shared my precious oxygen, he would have died." She swallowed. "And I'd do it again."

Ryker knew he'd left her a few months later. That was six years ago, yet he still took up residency in her heart and head.

The audience clapped at the last slide of a child pressing her hands together and bowing slightly.

"Namaste," said Vance. "Come down and meet these heroic Everest climbers who will autograph pictures. Our newest club member, Beck Williams, is handling sales."

Ryker whispered to Sara, "Milking the crowd?"

"Let's see what he's selling."

A display of Everest photos occupied the entire rear stage. Visitors shuffled through a gallery of ice and snow that most of them would never experience.

"How many are you planning to buy?" Ryker asked Sara.

"I've got my own stockpile."

An elderly woman lifted a matted photo. "What's this camp with colorful tents on an icy hill?"

Beck shrugged. "No idea. I wasn't with the expedition and only moved here four weeks ago."

"Camp Three on Lhotse," Sara said, gently. "Fourth highest mountain in the world. So steep you stake your tent down."

"Dear me." She swapped for a hairy brown yak.

"Sounds as though you've been there," said Beck.

"Yes, six years ago but stopped three hundred feet short of the summit."

"I'd never go near Everest or do anything that insane, but I admire your courage."

"I'm with him," said Ryker.

"Thanks, you two. I've often questioned my wisdom."

As Sara chatted with the six-foot, long-haired cashier, Ryker saw Vance slinking behind a side curtain. This had to be worth spying on. He stayed out of sight but within hearing of Vance and Jason arguing.

"What are you doing here?" Vance asked.

"I got an anonymous letter advertising your Seven Summit speech. I checked into the Moon Bay Inn where we notarized our agreement."

Vance opened his hand. "So you brought the second key."

"Our contest isn't over. Messner's list replaced Australia's Kosciuszko, a Sunday stroll, with Carstensz Pyramid. And you haven't climbed it yet." Jason's lips spread in a malicious grin. "You're scared of the New Guinea natives with machetes, penis gourds, and feathers through their noses."

"That's irrelevant. I climbed the original seven, and you're one summit short without proof of doing Vinson in Antarctica. I win and will meet you at the hotel tonight for the second key to unlock my two hundred grand plus interest."

"Let's finish this the right way. Prove you're not a coward by climbing Carstensz and I'll do Vinson. First one done, wins

"Agreed." Knuckles popped in a handshake.

Ryker found Sara by the exit and relayed it all. "Two keys, two hundred grand plus interest waiting at the Moon Bay. They hate each other. I don't get it."

"It's a mountaineering thing, like Tour de France or Grand Prix. Very few finish. Speed records make headlines."

"Seven or eight summits?" he asked, starting the car.
"Depends on the list. Most serious climbers do all eight."
He backed out. "I've got a bad feeling about this."
"So do I. By morning, someone could be ice-cold."

Chapter 3

Ryker's breakfast arrived. As he shoveled it in, Sara said, "We need to question the four climbers before they hear the news."

He sopped gravy with a biscuit. "You honestly believe one of them killed him?"

"A logical conclusion."

"Made by someone who often listens to her gut."

"But identified the murderer in the Renaissance case."

She leaned across the table and sneaked a piece of toast from his plate. "Put the pieces together. It's brutal on Everest. Instead of shooting Vance in an alley, someone shoved him into a freezer. The female climber wouldn't be strong enough to haul his dead weight. Huddled on the floor between large slabs of beef, he's a shadow of the man we saw striding across the stage last night."

A shiver licked Sara's spine—the cold, thin air and the stare of death on an Everest ridge. She'd been there with Michael.

"Sara? You gone?" Ryker asked.

"No, I'm very much in the moment hunting a cold-blooded murderer."

She Googled Reunion Heights Hiking Club and found their calendar. "October tenth hike, level three to Marshall Pond. Meet seven a.m. at the trailhead. Trip leader is, Daniel Bennet . . ." She paused. "Wait, wasn't that the woman's last name?"

Ryker skewed his mouth side to side. "Good catch. Maybe you could be a detective."

She kicked his foot lightly under the table. "Smartass, get moving. It's seven thirty. Trailhead in forty-five minutes. Take your last sip and we're outta here."

"You got a buzzing bee up your butt?"

"Yeah, a swarm of them. We're heading for the woods and will commune with nature."

"You mean like talking to birds and animals. Have you seen your therapist lately?"

"You know I'd never go to one."

He grabbed two biscuits for takeout. In the passenger seat, he plucked off small pieces, crumbs falling where they may.

"Car talk. The long drive to Colorado and back, did you plan what to say to your father?"

"Moot. Our lives are on hold until we catch this degenerate who made a human icicle."

"A rationalization or is the intrepid racer afraid of him?"

She gave a swift look from the corner of her eye. "Tit for tat. Did you set a date with your daughter?"

He brushed crumbs off his pants onto the car floor. "No. You and I both failed the relationship class."

A brooding silence followed them to the trailhead. Ryker's foot jumped when he stepped on the ground. He lifted both pant legs. "These five-hundred-dollar Oxfords are calf leather with a goatskin lining and leather soles. I refuse to muddy them."

"You, who walked rat-infested New York streets?"

"They were my rats. I don't know what's in those trees."

"The trail's soft mulch following a river to the pond."

"They'll have to return this way?" The hard edges of his face softened like warm caramel. "Then we wait here."

"No, you begin an exercise regimen for your daughter."

He planted his feet firmly. "I'm not moving."

"Okay, relax here. Only six of Florida's forty-six species are poisonous. They warn before striking . . . usually." This was too much fun to stop. "And gators basking on the bank can hit thirty on short bursts."

He reached for the car door. "Got up too early and will nap in the back seat. Wake me when they arrive."

She jangled the keys. "Locked."

Ryker lunged but missed. He tried again, but she stayed just out of reach. He'd never catch her. "Coming?"

His face crumpled. "Reluctantly. Trusting you know what you're doing."

"Hydration's a necessity."

"You should've brought beer."

Two water bottles went from the trunk into her pack. She snatched his cigarette and ground it out with her shoe. "This too must end unless you plan to burden her with a sick old man."

A canopy of pines arched over the trail. Sara breathed in spruce and pine, a scent that once meant safety on hikes with her father. *Be strong on your own,* he'd told her. *I won't always be here.* At age ten, he packed a single suitcase and walked out the door, abandoning her to the emotional and physical abuse of an alcoholic mother. Nature became her only shield.

"What's that noise?" Ryker asked, pulling her back to the present.

"Woodpecker." She pointed high to a black bird with a red mustache.

"Leave. It'll come after us."

"It's not an attack bird."

"Wings flapping at my head unnerve me."

"Did you have a—"

"Yes, on my grandmother's farm when I was five. She sent me to collect eggs. A magpie swooped down and dive-bombed me the entire time I was crying and running to the house."

Ryker headed into the woods.

"Where are you going?" Sara asked.

"To water a tree."

"I strongly advise against it. Snakes hide in long grass."

"Then how—?"

"I'll turn my back and warn if somebody's coming."

"I feel like a homeless man in a New York city alley."

"Peeing is like yodeling in nature. Better than squatting."

Sara chuckled as Ryker sought a nearby bush. Zipped back up, he returned, smiling. "I feel better now."

"Your jaunt into the woods disturbed the neighbors. One of them is leaving the hood."

A thick-bodied snake slithered across the trail a yard behind him, its iridescent blue-black scales shimmering in the sun. He jumped away so fast he would have wet his pants if he hadn't just relieved himself.

"Relax. Harmless eastern indigo."

"I'm city born and not used to this outdoors, in-nature shit."

They continued along the river, listening to a mockingbird, until loud chatter silenced the song. Sara stepped onto their path. "Showtime."

Instead of walking around her, a tall man with short hair, a trimmed mustache, and a rounded goatee bumped into her.

"Hey, that was rude," said Ryker. "Apologize to the lady."

"She was in my way," he called over his shoulder.

Ryker's mouth tightened as he punctuated each word. "I said to apologize to the lady."

His feet churning up damp leaves and wood chips, the man spun around and marched back. "You talking to me?"

Ryker's hand clamped down on the man's wrist before he could think—old reflex, old rage that was born the night his father slammed his mother to the floor. With a sharp twist, he bent the finger back until the man's face contorted. "Show respect. Look her in the eye and apologize."

Larger than Ryker but in obvious pain, he mumbled, "I'm

sorry I ran into you. I was in a rotten mood and not thinking about where I was going. It won't happen again."

Sara motioned for Ryker to cool it. His rash impulses had gotten him into trouble working for the NYPD and interfered in their first case together. She touched his arm, firm and steady, her voice low enough for only him to hear. "You don't need to fight my battles."

She turned back to Daniel. "Are you the hike leader, married to an Everest climber?"

"Yes, I'm Zoey's husband. And you two are?"

"Detectives Sara Lansing and Ryker Harris. We're here on routine police business, looking for members of the expedition."

"What's going on?"

Ryker's tone conveyed his dislike of the man. "We're not at liberty to say."

Five minutes later, the other hikers caught up to their leader. Stroking his goatee, Daniel introduced the detectives to his wife, Patrick, and Heath.

"Vance introduced four Everest expedition members," said Ryker. "Where's the other one?"

"Tanner didn't show and left no messages."

His right hand buried in a pocket, Patrick said, "None of us know where he is."

Sara's eyes tracked the subtle glances of pack unity. "Then we'll speak with the three of you in private. Daniel, take the rest of your party to the trailhead."

He sneered. "I'm not leaving without my wife."

Ryker got right in his face. "Detective Sara of the Reunion Heights Police politely asked you to go wait in the car."

The three hikers stood whispering among themselves as the others left. Heath wore mismatched boots and laces; Zoey, well-endowed and flirtatious, twirled a strand of hair around a finger. Patrick's angular features gave him a sculpted look. His hand still in a pocket, he circled Sara and Ryker, surveying them.

"You didn't mention being cops last night."

Who was he to question the police? "We weren't on duty," said Sara. "We came to watch a slideshow."

He pointed at Ryker's shoes. "What're you doing out here?"

"To talk to you before you head home."

Eyebrows arched; glances shot back and forth.

Sara had often broken news of a death to family and friends, but it never got easier. She mouthed, *You do it*, to Ryker.

He squared his shoulders. "I'm sure Vance touched each of you personally, and his loss will be greatly felt. That makes me very sorry to report his body was discovered early this morning."

The forest seemed to gasp and hold its breath. Three faces paled as if the blood had drained from them.

A teary-eyed Zoey whimpered, "You're wrong. It's not him. Vance can't be dead. We were with him yesterday."

"I know how difficult this is," said Sara. "It will take time to absorb, but we've identified the body."

"What happened? Where'd you find him?"

Sara didn't want to upset them further by going into details. The onus fell on Ryker. He explained Vance had frozen to death in the Tidwell Meat Packer Plant.

"A little strangeness here," said Heath. "Police would not have sent two detectives unless they suspected foul play."

"I understand your concern," said Sara, "and I'm sorry, but we're required to ask everyone. Zoey, where were you after the slideshow and last night?"

Her tongue sliding over her lower lip, she eyed Sara up and down as if gauging her competition. "I was home having sex with the handsome husband you just sent away."

Heath next. He wandered off into the woods mimicking a mockingbird.

"You go get him," said Ryker. "I'm not going back in there."

"Heath," Sara called. "Where you were after the slideshow and last night."

His words rose and fell as if playing with each syllable. "I'm an artist and was in my studio all afternoon and evening."

"Can anyone corroborate that?"

"Only my parrot, Paco. I live and work alone."

"And you, Patrick?" Ryker asked.

"At our hobby farm, helping my wife care for our animals. It takes an hour to feed forty to fifty of them in the mornings and evenings."

Turning his back to them, Ryker whispered to Sara, "It's a little odd how he keeps his right hand in his pocket all the time."

"Noted. And Zoey seems unduly upset over Vance's death. I'll start with her."

Sara pulled a notebook and pen from her pack and handed them to Zoey. "Please record your phone, address, email, and employment. Then sign. We'll contact everyone personally."

Heath filled it out and passed it on to Patrick, who removed his hand to write. Three middle fingers were missing just below the first knuckles.

Handing it back to Sara, he said, "You'll need a much larger book than this. Many of those living in Reunion Heights won't mourn Vance's death."

Chapter 4

Sara filled her lungs and exhaled to a silent count of six before ringing Vance's doorbell. "His wife must be aware that he didn't come home last night," she told Ryker.

With a quirky grin. "Unless they're not sleeping together."

"You have a one-track mind."

"No, just been dealing with people much too long."

Sara envisioned the wife of a mountaineer as athletic and outdoorsy, not the slightly overweight woman in a business suit and carefully manicured nails who appeared at the door.

"Mrs. Miller?"

"Yes, I'm Celia Miller."

Sara and Ryker showed their IDs. "May we come in?"

Without hesitation, she opened the door and stepped aside, seemingly naïve about why two police officers would show up at her doorstep.

"Told you they don't share a bed," Ryker whispered.

Sara elbowed him.

Celia led them down a hallway lined with oil and watercolor paintings in elaborate frames. Each had a label card identifying the artist's name, title, date, medium, and dimensions.

"That's quite an extraordinary display," said Sara. "Are you an artist?"

"Oh, no, I'm not creative and wouldn't have time to paint if

I were. I own an art gallery catering to the rich and am too busy traveling to locate the finest paintings and sculptures. Last night was the grand opening of an important exhibit. My husband does the lighting and staging when new pieces arrive." She smoothed a hand over her skirt, composure practiced. "He's also in charge of the house and takes care of everything. It allows me to devote all my energy to work and gives him free time to hike, climb, and play pickleball."

Her face paled as she looked at Sara and Ryker. "Why have you come?"

"It's best to all sit down," said Sara. "We have news about your husband."

Celia slowly lowered herself onto a white leather loveseat, knuckles whitening on the armrests. Her eyes flicked to the floor before she steadied her voice. "Sorry, I came home exhausted after closing last night and went straight to bed. Vance must have come in later than usual. He's up and out of here before seven every morning to go play pickleball with friends." She flinched. "But his bag's still sitting by the door."

Sara tipped her head slightly toward Celia to give Ryker the message she'd talk woman to woman. She leaned forward in a warm, comforting gesture and watched her eyes for a reaction. "I'm sorry to report his body was found early this morning."

Celia's shoulders sank as resignation etched soft lines in her face. "I've lived with the constant fear of a knock announcing his death on an unforgiving mountain. But now that he'd completed the summits, I felt he was safe at home."

Ryker offered Celia a handkerchief to wipe sweat from her forehead. "It doesn't seem possible. He was always so strong."

"Death of a loved one has to be the hardest to endure," said Sara. "If you need time, we understand. But anything you know may help us."

"I'll do anything I can."

"Did he have any enemies?" Ryker asked.

"None that I know about. He was popular on the pickleball court. He spoke of many friends there."

"Where did he play?"

"On Beaumont Street."

"I know those," said Sara. "Didn't you play too?"

Celia averted her gaze. "No. I'm too clumsy."

"May we have a look at his room?" Ryker asked.

"You'll find nothing in the bedroom. He did everything in his office, second door on the left."

As they entered the office, Ryker whispered to Sara, "What on earth is pickleball?"

"Tell you later. Look for anything that will help."

Sara pried open a locked desk drawer and fished through a pile of papers. "Second mortgage on the house, utility bill long overdue, and huge Visa debt at twenty-four percent."

"He needed to win that contest." Then with a wry, told-you-so grin on his face. "Perhaps pickleball and hiking weren't his only pastimes."

"What has your aberrant mind conjured up now?"

"Just guesstimating."

He stopped in front of two walnut bookcases. "Something's stuck in between these. A cache. Our first clue."

"Quit postulating. Pull it out."

He withdrew a box of iridescent blue, green, purple, and red feathers. "Okay, Nature Lady, what bird wore these?"

Sara plucked one, turning it between her fingers. "I've seen these before." Her brow furrowed, then lifted. "The tail feathers clinch it. They're from Nepal's national bird—the Himalayan monal. They call it danphe."

"Quiet, here comes Celia."

She set tea, sugar cubes, and lemon slices on a small table with the calm precision of a hostess, not a widow.

After glowering at Ryker for dropping three sugar cubes in his cup, Sara thanked Celia for being gracious at such a difficult time. "Here's my card. Contact me with questions or information that could help you or us."

"One more thing," said Ryker. "Why did your husband keep these feathers?"

"I've never seen them. His climbs were private affairs."

"May we take them with us?"

"If you like."

Ryker crossed the room to a red statue of a chubby god with an elephant head, body of a man, and four arms. "What's that?"

"Ganesha," said Sara. "Pray to him when starting something new. He'll remove obstacles."

Finishing her tea, she spoke to Celia, "I'm surprised it's the only souvenir of Vance's many travels."

"He only went to climb and considered the rest a waste of money and a hassle to get home. That wasn't with his luggage. He must have bought it here."

"You have our condolences," said Sara. "Is there anyone we can call for you?"

"No, I'm used to being alone."

"Thank you for the tea," said Sara. She paused at the door. "I'm sorry, but we have to ask everyone where they were Sunday afternoon and night."

"At a friend's new gallery opening in Chicago."

Ryker handed her a card. "When ready, you need to identify his body at the address written on the back."

As they got into the car, he said, "I've seen widows before, and this woman didn't shed a tear. She served us tea and sweated instead of weeping."

"People cope differently. The first step is denial. She could fall apart once we're out of sight."

"Only because she may lose face with her uppity art cronies and have to hire a new houseboy. She didn't seem surprised to see us on her doorstep. Like she already knew."

"But Celia melted on the love seat and looked forlorn."

"Worthy of an Oscar."

"Motive?" Sara asked.

"To be determined."

"No means. She couldn't drag him. No opportunity. She was in Chicago."

Ryker's jaw tightened. "Or she wasn't."

Sara glanced back at the silent house. "She never asked how he died. Almost as if she already knew."

Chapter 5

Ryker said, "I learned one thing today, that you and Vance both failed Intro to Life 101. You travel to places most of us will never see but have no souvenirs."

"They would remind me of who I was and no longer am. Memories of racing in the rain with Michael are shrouded in fog. I can't go back again."

"The people you touched along the way? No remembrances of them?"

"You already declared that nobody will come to my funeral. A tactless remark—a gaucherie.

Gaucherie. The word stung his heart. It was the first one he and his wife, Lily, learned together. She'd died three years ago, but tears still nestled in his throat. Playing the vocabulary game with Sara helped dry them.

Sara's phone buzzed, and she put it on speaker. McBride's bark filled the surrounding air. "Where are you two? We've got a murder to solve."

Ryker moaned. "She dragged me into the woods at seven."

Sara shot him a look. "Since the expedition team gave us our only lead, I prioritized meeting them. Their leader's death barely fazed the men, and the woman looked stunned but not surprised. One didn't even bother to show up."

McBride cut her off. "Any suspects?"

"Too early."

"I might have one," Ryker added. "He and Vance argued yesterday about prize money. He'll bolt if we don't move fast."

"Then get the hell over there," The line went dead.

When they reached the car, Ryker said, "Let me drive. I have a Master's in car chases."

"But I have a PhD in catching bad guys on the hoof. So I'm taking charge."

He didn't stand a chance against this endurance racer, but he enjoyed giving her shit, and she tossed it right back. Their banter made the grueling job more palatable.

Stopped at a red light, Sara drummed on the steering wheel. "While I was collecting contact information, did you perchance notice any telltale body language?"

Ryker drew his brows together and puckered his lips as if in deep deliberation. "Restless, uneasy but nothing specific except for that gangly Patrick keeping his hand in his pocket. I thought he was playing with himself."

"Hah, that tells me where your mind is."

"Can't help it. It's been so long since I was with a woman."

"And will be a lot longer if you don't get with the regimen and quit drinking and smoking."

"But breaking a lifetime of habits is physical and mental torture subject to the international human rights law."

A sly curve tugged at the corners of her mouth. "So, take it to the international rights court."

The closest parking space to the Moon Bay Inn was a block away. Sara reached the counter ahead of panting Ryker and asked the clerk if someone named Jason was staying there.

"Sorry, but I cannot give out that information."

Ryker flashed his badge. "Sure about that?"

"Since you insist." He opened the register and ran a finger down the names. "Ah, yes, room number three twelve."

Ryker lowered his voice. "Don't even think of making a call to his room."

Sara goaded him into climbing three flights instead of taking the elevator. Out of breath, he leaned against the wall while she knocked. "Don't you ever slow down?"

When Jason cracked the door open, Ryker shouldered his way into a dimly lit room, a haze of cannabis clinging to the stale air. An open suitcase was sprawled across the bed, half-stuffed clothes spilling out like he'd packed in a hurry.

"Going somewhere?" Ryker asked.

Jason shut the door harder than necessary. "My business is done here."

Sara grimaced at the torn curtains, faded wallpaper, lopsided lampshade, and tired carpet that hadn't been vacuumed in weeks. "And what business is that?"

"Personal."

Ryker crimped the corner of his mouth. "A personal two hundred grand plus interest business?"

Jason froze mid-stride, and then masked it with a laugh that didn't reach his eyes. "How'd you—?"

Ryker leaned forward, forearms on his knees, voice low. "I heard you and Vance backstage. Not exactly a friendly chat."

"About climbing," Jason blurted out. "You got a problem with that?"

"No, but it's a whole lot of cash riding on a mountain race."

Jason zipped the suitcase and dragged it toward the door."

"Contest isn't over yet," he said.

Sara cut him off. "Think it is. Your competition isn't around anymore."

That stopped him cold. His head jerked up. "What? When was he murdered?"

Sara and Ryker shared a look. Neither had said murder.

Ryker tapped his thumbs together, eyes steady. "Funny slip, Jason. Real funny."

"You don't know what you're talking about."

Ryker held out a hand toward Sara. "He's all yours."

She stepped closer, her voice even. "You can't climb Vinson until summer there, winter here. Carstensz? Vance could have ticked that off anytime."

Jason's laugh was sharp. "Only if he had the guts to go to New Guinea. I made him agree to trek through the jungle, past tribes in penis gourds, instead of taking a helicopter. He wanted high stakes. I gave them to him."

"And you baited him," said Ryker. "Why this insane race?"

Jason leaned back in the threadbare recliner, its cushioning long gone, and draped his arms like he owned the place. "We were rivals long before Everest. College track. I won the blue ribbon senior year, but he got the girl. He never let me forget it. So we cut a deal. Five years to build our careers, and then first to climb the Seven Summits before thirty-five takes the prize."

"What prize?" Sara asked.

Jason slipped a key from his pocket and dangled it by the teeth. "Two hundred thousand earning at a high interest rate locked in a law office safe. Takes both keys to open it. Restricted cut. No locksmith in the world can duplicate it." The pride in his voice was unmistakable.

Sara scoffed. "So, you didn't trust each other. Why show up now?"

"I didn't fly down here for nostalgia. I came to protect my money."

Sara's eyes narrowed. "Protect it from what?"

He pulled a folded printout from the desk and waved it once before shoving it back. "Got an anonymous email about Vance's slideshow. Figured he'd use it to crown himself winner and cut me out of the pot. If he tried, I wasn't about to let it happen."

Ryker tilted his head. "Anonymous, huh? Somebody wanted you in that room."

"Doesn't matter who. I wasn't going to let him gloat."

Ryker picked up the suitcase and dumped it back on the bed. "Unpack. You're not going anywhere."

"Question his team. After hearing other climbers talk about Vance's negligence endangering them, I guarantee every member of that Everest climb has grievances. Vance looked out for one person only, himself. He was nobody's hero."

Ryker stretched his back. "We'll take care of it. Meanwhile, don't leave town."

Jason's smile faltered. "I'm not your suspect."

"Yet," Ryker said.

Sara had carried the image of Celia's dry eyes and making tea. Jason's shock was equally Oscar worthy.

Outside, Sara brushed a shoulder against Ryker. "Want to split up or grill them together?"

"Together. I'd miss you telling me how to run my life."

"I only do so to keep you healthy and to remind me of my failings." She gave him a friendly hip bump. "Come on, Patrick's missing fingers aren't the only thing that doesn't add up."

Chapter 6

The GPS took them down a two-lane road that twisted through stands of oak and pine. At their address lay a sprawling, wooded property hemmed in by a high metal fence with decorative finials. A heavy gate of solid steel blocked the driveway.

Ryker tilted his head, taking it all in. "Look at this spread. I want his job. What did he put down for employment?"

Sara flipped open her notebook. "Says he makes violins and other string instruments."

He gave a low whistle. "Sure, like there's enough fiddlers in Florida to pay for this. Must be a front company."

"We'll see." She pushed the gate buzzer.

A woman's voice crackled through the speaker. "Who is it?'

"Detectives Sara Lansing and Ryker Harris. We met with Patrick this morning and have a few more questions."

"I heard and have never seen him so troubled."

As the gate slid open behind dense foliage, Sara told Ryker, "Troubled because he's hiding something?"

"But he's not a suspect. You saw his hand. He can't grasp anything with it. Killer needed to haul Vance into a freezer."

The moment they stepped out, a quartet of geese charged, honking like airhorn blasts, necks outstretched, beaks ready to bite. A wire fence halted the imminent attack but not the grating noise. An unmistakable sign read Beware of Geese.

"Hah," said Sara. "Four-alarm security system."

Patrick sauntered down the driveway, waving his arm for them to stand back. "I'm the only one who can get anywhere near my geese." He rolled up his sleeve to display a purple spot on his forearm. "But even I have bruises."

Sara's gaze locked on his missing fingers. "And a greater injury there. Why'd you try to hide it this morning?"

He slid his hand into a jeans pocket and strolled back toward the house ahead of them. Before entering through the garage, she stopped him and asked, "Why are you so reticent to answer?"

His movement turned clipped, abrupt. "I was ashamed of not paying attention while using a power saw to build a rabbit hutch. A very costly, almost career-ending mistake."

A beeping truck backed up, and men in T-shirts unloaded folding chairs, cardboard boxes, and inflatable props. Patrick turned to direct them. "By the lake. Jail front goes on the left. Lanterns along the patio.

"I source parts from all over the globe to produce fine-tuned performance violins, violas, and cellos. Some sell for as much as a hundred grand." He opened his right hand. "They require a dexterity I no longer possess."

"What'll you do?" Ryker asked.

"Still oversee everything, but I'm training an assistant to do the intricate work."

Beck, yesterday's cashier, appeared with an inflatable pirate mannequin tucked under his arm. He set it beside the door and brushed off his hands. "Where do you want this one?"

"By the small pond. Give him a fishing pole.

He picked it up again and told Sara and Ryker, "Glad you stopped by. This place is a tropical paradise. Four months ago, Patrick and Ashley gave me a place after I'd lost my family and needed to be grounded somewhere. Couldn't ask for more." He gave them an easy nod and went back to helping unload props.

"Sorry," said Patrick. "I'll answer any question if you don't mind me working."

"No problem," said Ryker. "Earlier, you gave a hobby farm as your alibi. What is that?"

"Where you're standing. We keep animals because we love them, not for profit."

In an uncomfortable stance, Ryker drew his brows together. "Just how many animals are we talking about here?"

"Between forty and fifty, depending on the number of ducks that settle in."

Forty to fifty? Ryker mouthed to Sara as they went from the garage into the house past five dogs jumping and barking behind a two-foot gate. A hairless, wrinkled Sphinx cat sprawled across the kitchen counter with its own bowl and cushion.

Sliding doors opened onto a wooden patio the size of half a basketball court with tall cocktail tables. A fifteen-foot fabricated pirate ship sat anchored in a lake twenty yards away. Inflatable pirate mannequins lurked in the shrubs and hung from the roof. A warden, lantern and key in hand, stood guard over a plywood jail front with fake prison bars. The place looked less like a farm and more like the midway at a carnival, with plastic pirates scattered across the lawn like fallen soldiers, half inflated.

Patrick climbed a ladder to tie pirate flags above the door. "Be careful," Beck said and ran to steady it for him.

"If I fall, you can play the violin at my funeral."

Patrick's wife had a cascade of brunette and blond hair that framed her face, highlighting her sharp cheekbones. She walked onto the deck, her hand covering the phone. "Patrick, the caterer wants to know if same hors d'oeuvres."

"Spicier meatballs this year."

His arm around her waist, Patrick introduced Ashley to Sara and Ryker. "My beautiful wife is in charge of the menu and never fails. We have magnificent feasts."

"We're having a party Friday night," she said. "It'll be a

blast. Everyone will be there, and you're invited. But you must get into the spirit of things and come dressed as pirates."

"Thanks. We'll try to get here," Sara said, despite Ryker's disgruntled face and knowing he'll put up a fight.

The expression on Patrick's face said he wished she'd never come outside.

After she went back in, he said dryly, "I presume you came here to question me further, but I have much to do and little time. I need to feed the zebus now."

"We'll tag along," said Sara.

Ryker leaned into her. "Zebu. Some kind of bird, cat?"

"Cow. They're the beef on an African menu."

A barnyard sprawled behind the house, alive with clucks, bleats, songs, and the earthy tang of hay. Nubian goats stretched long necks over the fence, one catching Sara's shirt and tugging until she yanked it free. A trio of zebus crowded the gate, horns curved like parentheses, and loose skin with fatty humps.

"Friendly fellow?" Ryker asked, stepping back as the animal lunged toward the fence.

"Only when he's eating," Patrick said.

His left hand gripped a pitchfork, using his right palm to balance it, and tossed hay into their troughs.

Ashley's voice carried across the yard. "Patrick, I already fed them an hour ago!"

He stabbed the pitchfork into the dirt hard enough to make the handle vibrate. "I feel like a cripple in my own home." His voice dropped, bitter, before he straightened his shoulders and tried for a lighter tone. "Anything else you want to ask?"

"Did Vance have any enemies?"

"Not that I know of. He was decent. A leader."

"And Tanner who's missing now?"

"Smart guy, an architect. We invited them to dinner twice, got vague excuses, and gave up. He hovers over her. Something's going on with his wife that they won't talk about."

"Heath?" Ryker asked.

"I don't think he cared if he made the summit. He was there more as a tourist than a climber. He'd stop to look at the clouds, smell flowers, listen to a bird sing, or kick a ball with kids. Heath made us late all seven nights on our way to base camp. Then he'd spend more time with the kitchen staff and porters who didn't speak English than with us."

Patrick's tone deepened. "But upset him, you better duck."

"And why'd you go to Everest?" Sara asked.

"A wager to refute my older brother who always dismissed me as the lesser son since I built violins instead of bodies. He was a personal trainer for unfit, rich country clubbers."

Patrick lifted the damaged hand. "Souvenir of a poor bet."

Ashley called, "Patrick, the feed truck's here."

He turned to the detectives. "Sorry. Gotta keep the animals fed or they start plotting mutiny."

Back on the driveway, Sara and Ryker thought nothing of it when Ashley screamed at Patrick for leaving a gate open until they realized it was the dog gate. Barking canines rushed them.

"Run faster," Sara yelled. "It's more fun when you gasp."

They jumped into the car and rolled up the windows to escape the cacophony of five dogs barking, four geese honking, and three zebus mooing.

Ryker pressed the horn twice for Patrick to open the gate.

Sara said, "We just got more questions than answers. Ashley said everyone will be at the party. That has to include Vance's widow, Heath, Zoey, her husband Daniel, maybe Jason, a host of other suspects we're not even aware of. Drunk or stoned, tongues will loosen. They'll be wild cannons turning on each other."

As the gate slid open, she pictured Patrick's hand sliding into a pocket. Power saw? She'd seen injuries like that before and wasn't buying his story. He was hiding more than a hand and had a brother strong enough to carry deadweight to help a lesser son.

Sara's finger poked Ryker in the chest. "Friday night, you

and I are showing up here incognito as a pair of bad-ass sea rats."

"We're the last two people on this planet he wants to come. You saw his face. Ashley offered, so now Patrick has to ingratiate himself to avoid suspicion."

McBride's phone call rescued Ryker from further poking. Sara put him on speaker. An angry voice demanded, "Where are you?"

"Questioning a potential suspect."

His voice grew more strident. "Get in here and interrogate the two-hundred-fifty-pound butcher who discovered the body. He had the only key. Forensics found no sign of a break-in. Grill him about how the damn killer got in there."

Sara started the engine. "On our way."

McBride gave the usual two-finger summons to his office the minute they walked in. Interminable pacing had left a path on the floor. A line of sweat crept across his upper lip as he handed them a folder. "See what you can get out of him."

A man with disheveled hair, a neck like a pelican pouch, and enough insulating fat to work in a freezer sat in the interrogation room, waiting. When they both took a seat across from him, he shifted his weight uncomfortably and lowered his head, hands clutched tightly.

Sara opened the folder, slowly read the report, and sighed. "Well, Frank, it says that you've been working at Tidwell Meat Packer Plant for fifteen years."

He gave an almost imperceptible nod.

"So long that the owner entrusts you with the only key in his absence on a fishing trip." She turned her head sideways, trying to maintain eye contact when he tilted his. "Is that correct?"

"Uh-huh."

Leaning toward him, Ryker spoke slowly and deliberately. "You discovered the body when you showed up for work."

Frank drew back. "I came early, as usual, and saw nothing out of the ordinary. "His voice quavered. "And then there's this naked body just sitting there between two slabs of beef like he's trying to warm himself. I never saw anything like that before."

Ryker glared at him, his voice cold and exact. "Frank, how did that body get into a locked freezer?"

"I . . . I don't know."

"You have the only key."

He squirmed in his seat. "I didn't do anything."

"Somebody did," said Sara, her frustration leaking in every breath. "Who'd you give the key to?"

"Nobody.

"Then we'll book you as an accessory, opening the door for a murderer."

He trembled and gasped as if his throat had swollen shut. "No, no, no. I wasn't there yesterday or last night. We're closed on Sunday. You can ask my wife."

"But you know who was," said Ryker.

"No. I never saw him."

Him? Their first clue. "Who?" Sara asked.

"He had a strange-sounding voice, like in movies when the villain disguises himself."

"Where'd you hear it?"

"At the packing house Saturday night, while closing up. He came from behind and warned me not to turn around. So I didn't."

"What did he say?" Ryker asked.

"He kept going on and on about how cattle belch so much methane gas into the air it traps heat and causes global warming. He wanted the key so he could take pictures of all the cows and make posters telling people to quit eating beef."

Sara tipped onto the back legs of her chair and crossed her arms. "Are you saying some climate activist killed because of methane gas?"

"I thought he'd take pictures and maybe steal a carcass but never figured on him killing somebody."

She dropped back onto four legs with a thud. "Did you give

him the key?"

"Had to. If I didn't follow every direction, he'd take it out on my family." Frank looked up with moist eyes. "I've got a wife and four kids."

"What did he instruct you to do?"

"I was to put the key down at my feet and walk away without looking back. Then come to work Monday morning and find it on the office desk and the door unlocked."

"Why didn't you report this to the police?"

"I couldn't. He knew the names of all my kids and my wife."

Ryker slammed his hand on the table. "And who could this mystery person be?"

Frank looked about to soil himself. "Anybody who lives in Reunion Heights."

Ryker stood up and shoved the chair in place. "Our killer made good on his promise to leave the building unlocked." He snickered. "What a responsible fellow."

Sara gestured to Frank. "You're free to go but don't plan on leaving town. We may need to question you again."

Frank's legs and mind seemed out of sync as he stumbled his way out the door.

"Why'd you release him?" McBride asked Ryker and Sara in the hallway.

She sighed. "He's not the sharpest butcher knife on the wall but not dumb enough to kill in his own place."

"You have anything for us?" Ryker asked.

"The autopsy revealed no sign of fatal or defensive wounds, heart, or lung disease. The coroner verified the M.E. conclusion that hypothermia was the COD." McBride's chest sagged. "This case will drain me if it drags on too long. Go home. Sleep and be fired up for tomorrow."

Sara entered her two-bedroom house from the garage and set her keys in the laundry room. She nuked a bowl of mac 'n cheese, her comfort food, and curled up on the couch. The frozen stiff had taken priority over everything. To keep from brooding about the case, she used a knife to open the Pakistan envelope and found brightly colored, handmade paper.

"Dear Sara, by the time you read this, I will have flown to Pakistan to begin my ascent of K2, the second-highest mountain in the world. I will have thought of you and our time on Everest every step of the way. In the six years since we parted, I haven't been able to get you out of my heart and dreams. I don't know where you are or if you're with somebody else, but I need to hold you in my arms again. I left with too many words unspoken. I understand the need to settle past issues and heal the pain, but I want to try. I've tried contacting you through WhatsApp but got no response. Perhaps you don't have the app. Please download it and answer if you're willing to at least talk. If there's a path back, no matter how rocky or steep, I'll take it. Love, Michael."

"Michael!" His name leaped from her throat. "Why break all those years of silence with a letter now? Why'd you disappear, and where've you been hiding? Did you get married, go through a messy divorce, and now expect me to forget how, with zero explanation, you packed a suitcase and walked out the door the same way my father did?"

Sara looked at the month-old postmark. And nothing since then. Does that mean he never made it down K2? With doubt and fear wrestling in her throat, Sara's stomach warned not to try sending food its way. Mac 'n cheese went back in the fridge. Sara stomped to her room and withdrew a box from under the bed. She set her favorite selfie on the nightstand of sitting with him in their tent at 19,000 feet as he cradled her face in his hands and kissed her. They were shivering with cold but so terribly in love.

"No, I cannot allow you to hurt me again."

Sara wadded the letter in her fist and hurled it across the room. "I have better things to do like go solve a murder."

Chapter 7

Tuesday morning, Ryker was already at his desk with a coffee and Cinnabon dripping butter and frosting down his chin. A heart attack waiting to happen. Impossible man, totally untrainable.

Passing him on the way to McBride's office, she muttered, "Get off your butt. He's expecting us at seven."

Ryker wiped his chin with the back of his hand and gave her a crimped smile. "Yes, boss lady."

McBride closed the door behind them. "Have a seat."

She folded herself onto the hard, straight-backed chair. His body looked even more lived-in than before. He sat on the edge of his desk two feet from her, rubbing his neck with short, jerky strokes.

"Must've slept wrong," he said through shallow breaths. "I need names by tonight."

"We're working on it," Sara promised.

As they left the station, Ryker squinted against the early glare. "Now where at the crack of dawn?"

"Pickleball courts. Vance's morning crowd. New voices."

"What in the frigging world is pickleball?"

"The fastest growing sport in the U.S."

He scowled. "Why have I not heard about this?"

"Can't imagine why . . . a superb athlete like you?"

In a singsong voice, he mocked her, "A superb athlete like

you? Sorry, but some of us were busy keeping this country safe while you gallivanted around the world in adventure races."

"You're jealous. You never ventured out of the city."

The bickering lapsed into silence as Ryker parked beside a car with a license plate frame with Dink Until You Drop across the top and Pickleball along the bottom.

They walked toward six courts, half the size of tennis ones, ringed by chain-link. Pop, pop, pop echoed across the asphalt like a shooting gallery. Sunburned players in bright baseball caps waited in the bleachers, wiping sweat from their faces and necks, cleaning sunglasses, and commenting on the lobs and dinks on court number one in front of them.

"Everybody's just sitting or standing around," said Ryker.

"Waiting for an open court. Shouldn't take too long. Games only go to eleven."

"They look like giant ping-pong paddles," Ryker muttered.

Sara pulled one from the lost and found box and handed it to him along with a hard wiffle ball. "Try it. You might surprise yourself.

He snorted. "No way, not me, not ever."

She left him on the bleachers, scowling, and joined three women under a shade tree. "Hello, ladies. I was told Vance Miller played here. Have you heard what happened?"

"We're talking about it," said Margie, a name tag pinned on her visor. "He played more than pickleball."

"What do you mean?"

Roxie giggled. "He enjoyed touching women."

Judy, with a buzz cut under her cap, leaned forward. "Vance was a perv. He'd pat our butts, whisper how sexy we are, and say things like, 'If you miss the ball, I'll have to paddle you. And you'd like that, wouldn't you?'"

Roxie giggled again, her laughter as automatic as a hiccup. "He'd give this awful, lewd smile. None of us wanted to be on the same court as him. We'd move our paddles down."

Margie said, "I felt sorry for his wife at the Christmas party and wondered if she knew what a womanizer he was. To make polite conversation, I told her he was very popular here."

"How'd she answer?"

"Didn't. She was either in denial or didn't care."

"A bit pudgy too," Judy added with a little wiggle. "Maybe she was sexier when they got married."

"That's no excuse for screwing around," said Margie. "He was a lecher hoping one of us would bite."

"What did men think of him?" Sara asked.

"One called him an arrogant ass to his face for cheating on the score."

Judy said, "You should talk to Jeffrey. Rumor is Vance had to borrow money from him for Everest."

"Which one is he?"

"Left early."

"He ever get paid back?"

"Not likely. Don't think Vance had the money."

Sara gave her card. "Tell Jefrey to call me. We need to talk."

"Okay, but heads up. He's here by seven every morning."

Someone yelled, "Court!"

"That's ours. Gotta go."

Sara found Ryker on a bleacher, hunched forward, forearms on his knees.

"What do you think?"

"About what?"

"The game."

"Too noisy. All that pop, pop, pop."

"Maybe you should take it up."

"This body's not going out there making a fool of itself."

"So you rationalize not playing because of your weight?"

"Don't need to. Grossly uncoordinated works for me."

"Connect to your daughter by having fun, not working. You could play pickleball or go on a hike. Look at that guy on court two. He is heavier than you and hitting as hard as anyone."

"Obviously, a natural-born athlete, which I am not. What a waste of time coming here."

Sara urged him to get moving. "This was no fool's errand. Vance was a perv, a cheat, and owed money. We've got a slew of new suspects for McBride."

"Names?"

"Jeffrey, for one. He wanted his money back. He'll be here at seven a.m. tomorrow." She leveled a look at him. "And so will you."

Chapter 8

A dense sweet viburnum hedge bordered the long driveway to Heath's earth-tone stucco house. On the left, a two-car garage; on the right, a curved wall punctuated only by a row of narrow windows at the top. Center stage stood a massive metal bird, its delicate wing bones frozen mid-flight.

"Ah, the super sleuths have arrived," Heath's voice boomed from a loudspeaker. "Walk around back to my garden area."

"Damn, he's got a remote-control camera and is watching us," Ryker said, his mouth pulled tight.

"Maybe not the clown we tagged him."

He stepped aside to let Sara pass. "After you, Miss Sleuth."

They entered a riot of vibrant greenery. Heath was halfway up a papaya tree, bare feet gripping the trunk like a monkey, and dropping fruit with abandon.

"Basket, quick," he shouted. An oblong papaya plopped at Ryker's shoes. Heath twisted the stem, lifted another piece off, and let it go to Sara.

"If you wait until they're mostly yellow or orange, the birds eat them all. I share equally." He slid down the trunk and hefted the basket. "Now go inside for divine sweetness."

Ryker whispered to Sara, "Who put him in charge here?"

"Let him play it out."

A stone path wound past large metal sculptures, arcs of steel that seemed to ripple. Sara paused. "These are extraordinary. Did you make them?" her voice softening in genuine admiration.

"I capture the spirit of the wind. Even a breath moves them."

He ushered them into a cavernous studio the size of a tennis court, the ceiling soaring fifteen feet. Metalwork grinders, saws, drill presses, welders—all in ordered chaos.

"Metal sculpture is simply a matter of forming, cutting, and joining materials," said Heath.

Ryker ran his fingers along an arched piece with a bird's eye at one end and slender lines radiating in overlapping circles in a flurry of feathers.

"Finished by Friday," Heath said, racing up a steep, curved ramp. "It's going to Patrick's party."

"You see any stairs?" Sara asked Ryker.

"Nope, just him, a wingnut with a loose screw."

From the upper level, a blue and yellow parrot dive-bombed them, squawking a barrage of expletives.

Ryker flailed wildly and ducked his head.

"Paco, manners," Heath yelled.

"Goddamn bird," Ryker growled.

"Don't tell me you're afraid of birds, Detective," said Heath. "You have ornithophobia," he added with a grin.

Eyes locked on Paco circling overhead, Ryker said. "Zip it," to Sara. "Let's do what we came for and then get the hell out of this place."

"I think you're safe. Here comes Heath."

He'd changed clothes and put on socks, but nothing went together as if grabbed from whatever came out of a drawer first, regardless of color or condition. He seemed to notice the look on their faces. "Life's much too short to worry about whether one's clothes, socks, or shoelaces match."

But he seemed to care whether the two stories of his house did. Floor-to-ceiling windows flooded both spaces with natural light. He opened a sliding door and waved them onto a wide deck the length of the house.

A tropical forest enclosed his property. The pond, a hundred and fifty yards down the stone path, glimmered in the sunlight. A blue heron stood frozen in the shallow water waiting for its prey.

Resting his forearms on a wooden railing, Ryker suddenly leaned forward, pointing to a long, low body with a lengthy tail coming out of the water. "Is that a—?"

"Gator? Yeah." Heath laughed.

"It's coming toward your house."

Heath vanished into the kitchen and returned with a plucked chicken. "That's my buddy, George. We have an understanding. He's part of the natural world too and can hang out in my pond as long as he doesn't mess with birds or small animals."

Heath tossed the chicken. George lunged, teeth flashing, and swallowed it whole in one obscene gulp.

Ryker's angry voice tore out raw. "Wasn't that chicken part of your natural world?"

"Bought at the store, I saved a live one from being attacked."

A spontaneous smile danced on Sara's lips, one she could not have restrained if she tried. Before Ryker got himself all worked up trying to protect a female chicken that was already dead, Sara took a slice of papaya from a tray Heath had set down. Sweetness burst across her tongue. "Best I've ever tasted."

"Secret is letting the fruit ripen for a few more days." Heath popped one in his mouth and then eyed them. "So, what do you want from me?"

Still keeping an alert eye on the parrot five feet away, Ryker asked, "Did Vance have any known enemies?"

At once, Paco shrieked, "Vance bad. Vance bad."

"Quiet, Paco," said Heath.

"Vance—"

Heath's hand shot up, palm flat. "Stop." The bird fell silent.

The words ground between Ryker's teeth. "What in the hell was that all about?"

"Mimics what he hears on TV," Heath said cooly. "Didn't get it from me." He shifted his weight on the chair. "You were asking?"

"If Vance had enemies," Sara repeated.

"I can't speak of his life here. He cast me as a pariah. All I'll say is after the mountain, he wasn't someone I wanted near me."

"And your fourth member, Tanner?"

"I heard he disappeared. A good guy once but different after we came back."

"Patrick thinks you went to Nepal more as a tourist than a climber, that you didn't care if you made the summit."

"Who's he to judge? He made mistakes on the mountain and would be dead if this *tourist* hadn't given him oxygen."

"He also says you made the team late every night, stopping to smell flowers, kick a ball with kids."

"He'd rather time a porter's step than thank him for carrying his tent. And late for what? A mountain? Last time I checked, Everest didn't close at dusk."

"So you don't deny it," said Sara.

"Deny what? That I enjoyed being there? Someone had to notice we were walking through heaven. Patrick was blinded by a singular purpose to repudiate his brother."

"He lost fingers. Would he hold a grudge?"

"He's harmless. He can't even hold a coffee cup right."

Sara exhaled in a slow, even breath. "Patrick also intimated you have a temper."

"I will not go there."

"Then how about Zoey. Why'd she go to Everest?"

"Simple. To get away from that controlling husband who barely gives her the air to breathe."

"She doesn't appear too forlorn," said Ryker.

"It's all for show. Daniel works seven days a week, hardly recognizes her. Two morning hikes a week are his only off time. And you didn't see them coming hand-in-hand on the trail. He was fifty yards ahead."

Sara remembered walking behind Michael single-file and thinking what great calves he had. She'd yelled at him to stop. He turned and she kissed him, full of love. So Zoey had tried to get Daniel's attention by pursuing his only other interest, even though destined to failure.

She steered the talk lighter. "Where do you sell your art?"

"Don't unless on a commission. My pieces are portable. I place them here for a few days, funness for others."

Ryker cut bluntly. "Then how can you afford this place, pay for materials, feed George?"

"Sold my software company. Now I day trade. My office is downstairs." Heath pushed back his chair. "I've been offline too long and need to get back to work. Let yourselves out."

He raced back down the ramp, Paco flying overhead. When Sara and Ryker got down, Heath was at his computer in an office at the far end of the studio.

She said, "Thank you for your time," to which Paco replied, "Fuck you."

Ryker's cheeks burned crimson. His neck cords tightened. "If that whacko bird ever comes near me again, I'll kill it."

"Let's go." Sara hooked her elbow in his. "I noticed no TV up there or down here. Paco didn't pick those words from the air. Heath taught him and shut him up before he said more. Maybe he's not the nature lover he pretends to be."

As they reached the car, Paco's voice shrieked after them, harsh and clear. "Vance ate the bird."

Chapter 9

Aware that Heath might be watching them leave, Sara didn't enjoy being scrutinized like a suspect. "Turn and wave goodbye," she told Ryker.

"Not to him. He's either hiding something or addicted to the sound of his own wisdom," said Ryker.

"Patrick has rhythm and rules; Heath, excuses and poetry," said Sara. "Somewhere between them is the truth."

"Let's see which one cracks first."

"You drive while I look up Zoey's address for a house call on the last team member in town."

Navigation led them to a gated community of multi-million-dollar homes. He showed his badge to the attendant and asked directions to Daniel Bennett's.

"Three blocks that way. Left at the stop. You can't miss it."

Ryker parked on a circular drive made of stone pavers and stared at the two-story Mediterranean house with a slate roof. "Must be nice living in a mansion with a trophy wife. All three of these guys are wealthy."

"Climbing Everest's not cheap. Remember how Vance had to borrow from the guy at the pickleball courts. You need to be there before seven tomorrow to question him."

"Why me?"

"He's more likely to discuss money matters with a man."

"Speaking of which, I wonder how this one got so rich?"

"He's a surgeon in a solo practice. Works every day."

"So, Zoey went without him. Some marriage. Stay here. I'll see if she's home."

Ryker rang the bell. When a maid answered, he showed his badge and asked for Zoey.

"The lady of the house goes to the club every day and won't be home until evening. Wait a moment, and I'll get the address."

The luxury Royal Oaks club boasted a thirty-six-hole golf course and all the amenities, including a swim-up bar. The air shimmered with chlorine and suntan oil, the soft slap of flip-flops on hot pavers, and the shrieks of kids cannonballing into the pool.

Ryker spotted her first in a blue bikini on a white lounge, sipping a tall cocktail with a pink orchid floating on top. Would her perfect, lean body enjoy having lotion rubbed on her back?

"Zoey Bennett?" he said.

She slowly slid the straw in and out in a sucking motion and tipped her head slightly in a come-hither look. "How lovely to see you again, Detective Ryker."

What? This glamorous woman remembered his name. For once in his life, Ryker was at a loss for words. He could recite his wife's favorite John Donne love poem but might catch hell from Sara, saying it wasn't appropriate.

Fortunately, she saved him from an embarrassing moment. "We're investigating Vance's death and have already spoken to Patrick and Heath. Do you know of any enemies Vance had?"

"No, he was especially nice to me and my teammates."

"We heard rumors of expeditions having trouble with him."

Zoey's face flushed with an appealing glow. "Not ours."

"Patrick and Heath don't know where Tanner is," said Sara.

Zoey gave a one-shoulder shrug. "Me either. His wife went to Nepal with us."

Sara did a quick double take. "Nobody's mentioned that. Why didn't she stand up with him at the slideshow?"

"Because women don't count."

"You stood up."

"Vance had no choice."

"You were the only two women on the trip. On the plane ride, layover, or in Kathmandu, did you share the excitement of being in a foreign land, your hopes, fears, or perhaps even your marriages?"

"Nada. She seemed lonely, sad, and all bottled up. Knowing that sour feeling in her stomach, I didn't pry. All I can tell you is she stayed in Kathmandu when we left for Lukla Airport."

"Huh, interesting," said Ryker. "Your husband must have been worried about you being alone halfway around the world in a place where hundreds have died."

Zoey rolled her tongue around the tip of the straw. "I wasn't alone. Three men took care of me."

"Probably more than would have pleased your husband."

Sara intervened. "Why'd you want to climb Everest? It's not the latest rage or in-thing among the idle rich."

"Boredom and wanting people to learn there's more to me than my good looks."

"Then why flaunt them so blatantly?" Sara asked.

"Because it's the only thing I've ever been good at."

"Nonsense, you made it to the roof of the world."

Zoey stuck the straw back in the glass. "That's what Vance made us tell everyone. I never left base camp on the ascent day."

"Too scared?" Ryker asked.

"No, too sick. Five weeks, we'd climbed high and slept low, getting our bodies used to thinner air. The summit would only have a third of the oxygen we have here."

Zoey's shoulders slumped. "On the last rotation, we went to Camp Three for the first time. That night at twenty-four thousand feet, I got deadly altitude sickness and had to be carried down to the emergency medical tent in base camp."

Zoey looked at Sara. "I heard you've been on Everest and

know what it's like."

"Yes, and I didn't make the summit either. Don't mess with altitude. Why didn't you go lower immediately?"

"A whiteout. Sherpas couldn't take me down. They put me in this hyperbaric bag. The zipper teeth bit together above my head. I had no air, no light. A little plastic window fogged with each of my panicked breaths. I kept clawing for space that wasn't there and almost threw up. Claustrophobic hell."

"It beat the alternative of dying alone on a mountain."

Having come onto Ryker moments ago, Zoey looked like a frightened child fingering a towel thread in her lap. Missing the warmth of a woman in his life, he ached to pull her close but knew her performance was as calculated as the tilt of her head. His heart stalled. A flash of memory. His wife's laugh in a sunlit garden stabbed through him before he could push it down.

"Did anybody stay with you afterward?" Sara asked.

"No, I had my own private tent. Patrick and Vance shared one; Tanner and Heath, another."

"Vance's ego failed to mention your ordeal," said Ryker. "I wonder what else he left out."

Eyes still fixed on her lap, she said, "I don't know anything. I never left base camp after that."

"But you must have heard your teammates discussing what went on above."

"I've told you all I know."

Ryker studied Zoey's face, especially her eyes. He was good at reading people and sensed something communicated but not voiced. "Thank you for your time. The nightmares will pass."

As he and Sara walked to the car, she tucked a smile in her cheek. "Your lust is showing."

"Not lust. I just believe a thing of beauty is a joy forever."

"Now you're quoting Keats?"

He opened his hands and shrugged. "What can I say? My wife was an English professor."

"Yes, so you've told me, and she taught you well. But back to Zoey. She's a tease, lounging here all day, drinking, enticing men to rub lotion on her body, and sharing whatever pleasures they require. I don't think she understands the word *No*. Beware. Her seduction can be a ploy to draw you to her side if questioned later. And there's her husband Daniel, whose hot, quick temper you diffused on the nature trail. Jealousy ranks right up there as a murder motive.

Chapter 10

McBride called them back to the station. The desk clerk said, "Tread lightly. He's been holed up in his office all day with the door closed and blinds pulled. I haven't even gone in there."

"We have a bit of news to cheer him," said Ryker. When he raised his hand to knock, Sara warned him to tap lightly.

On quiet feet, they stepped into his office, stale air and no light filtering between the slats of exterior blinds. Sara traced the path worn by his constant pacing to open them. She looked back at McBride, slumped behind his desk, a scrap of confusion in her throat.

"Are you all right staying locked in your office all day?"

"Sorry, I didn't sleep well." He finger-combed some unruly hairs. "I just needed time to work without a lot of interruptions." His gaze moved across both faces, never settling, like a man searching for subtitles that weren't there. His voice wavered, off pitch. "What have you got for me?"

"We interviewed three of the expedition team," said Ryker. He threw his head back, smiling. "One of them, Zoey, is the blush of sunlight at dawn."

Sara gave him a look that could sour milk. "She's a flirt and he fell for it. She's not a suspect, but jealous husbands could be, including hers, whose aggression we've already met."

Ryker went on, "Heath's a whack job with a foul-mouthed

parrot that squawked, 'Vance ate the bird.'"

"Excuse my partner. Heath's a rare duck to be sure, blending creativity and an off-beat business acumen, but I saw no motive for murder."

Sara's fingers drummed on her thigh. "They are a motley crew. Patrick's missing the ends of three middle fingers, can no longer make violins, and lives on a farm with forty animals. But he's creative and industrious. He built a mock pirate ship in a lake off the patio and placed inflatable mannequins here and there for a pirate-themed party Friday night. Everybody must arrive in costume, and we're going."

"Are not," said Ryker.

"Are!"

"I'm not dressing up as some swashbuckler."

Sara patted his three-day stubble. "You're Blackbeard."

"Enough squabbling," snarled McBride. "Is there a motive prowling around somewhere in all this?"

"Nothing obvious," said Ryker.

McBride yawned and asked about the fourth.

"Nobody knows where he is," said Sara. "Tanner's at the top of my list. Present at the slideshow yesterday and then gone early this morning? He seems suspicious."

"Just because he didn't show up for a hike?" said Ryker. "Not everyone's a fitness junkie like you."

"It's the timing. You heard Jason say Vance's team could have grievances."

"And you trust that reprobate?"

She smiled at his use of reprobate. She'd best him with this one she'd been saving for months. "Call it my prescience."

He gave her a deferential, win nod. "Then we'd better find Tanner, the mysterious disappearing man."

"Go on, you two," said McBride. "No more clown shows."

Ryker sniggered as they got in the car. "Does your telepathic power foresee Tanner's address?"

"No, as a resourceful detective, I will find it."

Sarah googled the hiking club website on her phone again. Only those with a password could access the membership list, but the home page gave the president's email and phone number.

Sara called Kathleen Davis. "This is detective Sara Lansing. I'm sorry to bother you at such a difficult time. I know Vance's death has touched you all."

"I saw it on the news and still can't believe he's gone. Vance was a very active member. Why would anyone kill him?"

"That's what we're trying to determine. We spoke to three of the expedition team but can't locate Tanner Brooks."

"I'm not surprised. He hasn't come around much since they got back."

"Do you have his address?"

"I'm sure I must. I'll check my computer."

Hearing Kathleen sniffle, Sara regretted phoning but hadn't wanted to further upset the team members closest to Vance."

Her words broke apart, unfinished. "I hope this helps. I still can't . . . "

"I know it's been a terrible shock to everyone."

"I'll send it to your number."

"That's perfect. Thanks."

"I'm driving," said Ryker, "in case you experience another of whatever that word was."

"I admit looking it up months ago and saving it just for you."

Sara let the pressure drain away and relaxed for the first time all day as they drove thirty-five minutes to Tanner's in an upper-class neighborhood, wide tree-lined streets, a park with barbecue grills and a playground.

Ryker pulled into the driveway. "Pretty quiet here. Does he have kids?"

"How would I know? Ring the bell."

No answer.

"Try knocking," said Sara, "but not banging like a madman

as you're prone to do."

He rapped again. "Anybody home?"

"I'm going around back."

Tanner had young children, judging by the swing set. "No sign of anyone," Sara called to him. "Maybe dad is at work and mom took the kids to the park we passed a few blocks back."

"Check the neighbors first. I'll take the house next door on the left. You go right." Still pounding, he had zero noise filter. "Nobody here."

"Not at mine either. Everything's too eerily quiet. Did we miss an apocalypse?"

A woman across the street shouted, "Are you looking for somebody?"

"Yes, the residents of that beige house."

Jason was Ryker's target; Tanner was Sara's. She darted over ahead of him and displayed her badge.

The woman removed three pieces of mail and closed the lid. "Tanner Brooks, his wife, and two daughters, ages three and four. Lately, we watch them so frequently that my husband and I feel as if we're their parents."

"Why so much?"

"She accompanies him when he travels for work. Then the two climbs on Kilimanjaro and Everest took four and six weeks each."

"But his wife wasn't on either expedition, was she?"

"No, she stays in each city to study its history and culture."

"Leaving young kids, she sounds more like a scholar than a parent," said Ryker.

"She's a very loving person and knows they're well taken care of. Her two girls and my two are inseparable. He brought them over last night to get out by six this morning."

Out by six? A quick shake of Sara's head, like resetting a thought. "When did they set the departure date?"

"About ten days ago and said they'd be gone over a month."

Premeditated murder. Behind her back, Sara held one finger up to Ryker, implying a first-degree indictment.

"What does Tanner do?" Ryker asked. "I'd like a job where I can escape weeks at a time."

"He's a well-known architect hired to design homes built into a customer's natural setting. He's good about calling the girls and checking in with his office once a week. But I'm worried about them. Since they've been back, he and his wife have stopped coming to the weekend barbecues. She also dropped out of our women's coffee group. We meet every morning after the kids leave for school and the men are gone."

"What do you talk about?" Sara asked.

"Everything relating to our children starts the discussion. Then topics like unsatisfactory sex and poor communication. One husband lost his job; another had an affair with his twenty-year-old secretary. We also talk about gardening, recipes, health, and beauty issues. Our guess is she quit coming because of a serious illness. and they've gone for treatment unavailable here."

Sara took out her notepad. "What's his wife's name?"

"Well, that's the thing. Back from Nepal, she changed it to Karamia, meaning beloved peace."

"There's no harm in doing that. I didn't get yours."

"Barbara."

"Nice to know you. We've talked to the other team members but not Tanner. I have no cause for a warrant but would like to go in his house and see if there's anything that might explain the timing of his departure."

"They're good people and must have a reason."

"I'm sure they do, but it's my job to follow up on everyone."

Barbara let out a long, heavy sigh. "I guess it wouldn't hurt. I have to go water the indoor plants, anyway. Let me round up the children. I can't leave them here alone."

Four kids under the age of five burst from her house and ran circles around Sara. She broke out laughing and shouted, "You're like the silly geese I met yesterday. They came at me like this." Wobbling as if running on webbed feet and honking loudly, she chased four giggling girls across the street into Tanner's yard.

"They're quite the handful," said Barbara as she unlocked the door. "I only come in once a week."

"I appreciate your help."

Sara and Ryker checked the kitchen, living room, family room, three bedrooms, and baths. Nothing stood out. If Tanner's wife were that ill, someone had taken over the housekeeping. The door to a fourth room remained closed.

"Mind if I take a look?" Sara asked.

"No, go ahead. I don't think it's ever used."

Sara stepped in. The blinds were drawn. The only furniture was a floor mat and a low table. "Apparently not."

Barbara led her and Ryker down a hallway. "Tanner's office is in here. He enlarged a photo of himself on the summit, framed it, and hung it on the wall over there."

"I'm sure he was very proud. It's quite an accomplishment. Not everybody makes it to the top." Sara noticed a picture hanger seven feet off the floor on either side. "What was up there?"

"Long pieces of painted cloth he brought back from Nepal. There was a large circle in the middle surrounded by Buddhas."

Sara googled *thangka* on her phone and clicked on images. "Did they look like these?"

"Yes, exactly."

"What happened to them?"

"I don't know. I rarely come in here. I hear the girls coming. I'll tell them where we are."

After she left, Ryker asked, "What did you show her?"

"These thangkas."

"And they are?"

"Not one of your wife's daily vocabulary words?"

"Give her a break. She was a university literature professor, not a world traveler like you."

"They're scrolls with a Buddhist deity in the center, sacred images around it. Genuine ones painted on silk by Tibetan monks can sell for hundreds of thousands into the millions."

A laugh sputtered out, half nervous, half disbelieving.

One of the girls appeared in the doorway holding a furry hat with bunny ears. "I want to put this on the elephant."

"It's their dressing game to see who can make him look the silliest," said Barbara. She searched the room. "He's not here, honey. Your daddy must have moved him to another place."

Sara brought up Ganesha images on her phone. "Is this their elephant?"

"Yes, that's him."

"Why's he got a human body and elephant head?" asked one of the girls.

"Well, that's a very interesting story. Want to hear it?"

"Yes," all four kids yelled at once.

"Me too," said Ryker.

"Legend says that Pavarti, the goddess of beauty, wished for privacy while bathing." Sara looked each girl directly in the eyes. "Wouldn't you?"

Barbara's daughter said, "One time, my cousin tried coming in while I was in the tub. I screamed at him to leave."

Sara nodded. "Good for you. Now Pavarti asked her son to guard the door and not let anybody inside. His father, Shiva, the god of destruction, had been away at war so many years that the boy didn't recognize him. He told him to stop right there." Sara drew her brows together and lowered her voice. "Shiva did not like this stranger telling him he couldn't go into his own house. He took his trident and sliced the boy's head off, not knowing it was his own son."

A chorus of, "No, not his own son?"

"Well, you can imagine how upset Parvati was. She ordered Shiva to replace the boy's head with that of the first animal he came upon." Sara leaned forward as if to reveal a secret. "Guess what it was."

"An elephant!" Four giggling girls yelled, "An elephant!"

Sara opened her arms to them. "Oh my, you're all much too clever to fool." She tousled every girl's hair. "Anyone else thirsty besides me?"

"Yes," they shouted and scampered back across the street.

Ryker hugged her shoulder. "You would have been a warm, fun mother."

"I would like to have been everything mine wasn't."

"From what you've told me, that's a pretty low bar."

"No kids is the one thing I regret but, it's too late now."

She kept her voice low so Barbara and the girls wouldn't overhear. "Their fingerprints will be all over the glasses. Collect them discreetly. Matching them to ones on Vance's Ganesha will prove he didn't buy it here. He stole it and no doubt lifted the thangkas too. The man was desperate."

Having finished their apple juice, the girls rushed into the family room, surrounding Sara with giggles and excited chatter. In the kitchen, Ryker picked up each glass with a napkin and placed them in a paper bag. "We'll return these ASAP," he told Barbara. "We're just testing a theory."

As he and Sara got back into the car, she said, "For the kids' sake, I hope Tanner had nothing to do with this."

"Me too, but jumping out of town on a planned departure date sounds like something is rotten in the state of Florida."

She gave a lopsided grin. "Now you're quoting Hamlet?"

"I can't help it."

"I agree the timing sucks, but nobody we've questioned has a clear motive, means, or opportunity. I'm exhausted. Let's both go home."

On the way, Sara pictured the joy and wonder in the girls' faces and voices. How she longed for that. She'd spent most of her childhood sitting alone in a booth in smoky bars while her mother got wasted and picked up men for the night. To relieve the boredom, she'd roll pieces of napkin into spit wads, lay her cheek on the table, take aim, and flick them at blotto customers staggering by. Most didn't even notice. One four-hour miserable afternoon, she stockpiled artillery and dumped hundreds on the seat of a red convertible in the parking lot.

Sara shoved her past back into the shadows. Right now, it was Tanner's absence that screamed the loudest.

If he was innocent, he had a hell of a way of showing it.

Chapter 11

Ryker and Sara met with McBride at 6:45 a.m. Wednesday. His eyes were shadowed, and his lids drooped as if he hadn't slept in days. A damp patch darkened his collar, although the air in the office was cool.

"You look exhausted," Sara said.

"Indigestion. Couldn't sleep."

He flipped a pen back and forth, the plastic clicking with each rotation as it slipped between his fingers. He fumbled once and cursed, stooping to grab it off the floor. He straightened, and a sharp intake of breath was all he could manage. "What do you have?"

"A pickleball player loaned money to Vance," said Ryker.

"Did you question him?"

"He wasn't at the courts, and no one knew his last name. I left my card with instructions to call if he shows up."

"Get back over there and find out what for and how much." He shifted again, tugging at his collar as sweat trickled down his temples. McBride turned to Sara. "What's your agenda?"

She leaned across the desk toward him. "I'm troubled by the Tanner disappearing act. The morning after the murder, he and his wife hightailed it out of town at six a.m. and will be gone over a month. They set the departure date and time ten days in advance with a neighbor who babysits their daughters."

"Where'd they go?"

"All she knows is Tanner's wife often accompanied him on trips and stayed in Kathmandu while he climbed. It's interesting that she's been a recluse since their return and changed her name from Ruth to Karamia. The neighborhood women's coffee klatch thinks she's gravely ill, and they've gone for treatment."

McBride stifled another yawn, his jaw cracking as if it hurt to keep his eyes open. "I'll have someone check flights, buses, and trains that left early Monday morning. Is that all you have?"

Sara gave a crooked smile. "Then there's Patrick's fictitious story. A power saw would have cut clean across. His fingers are slightly different lengths."

McBride wiped sweat from his forehead, blinking hard as if the room had tilted for a moment. Resting against the back of his chair, he asked, "What's that got to do with murder?"

"He's lying. I want to know why. I'll visit ERs and talk to the doctor who treated him."

"They see a thousand patients a month. Nobody will recall a non-life-threatening accident."

"Patrick left Nepal at the end of May and would have been jet lagged a few days. The accident had to occur shortly afterward to have healed so well. That gives me a short search window for who or what nibbled Patrick's fingers."

Ryker stretched his arms over his head. "While you're racing down a rabbit hole, I'll catch Larry the loan shark."

**

When Ryker arrived at the courts, Judy, Roxie, Margie, and a fourth player had just come off and paddled up for the next one.

Judy cocked her head, studying him. "If you came to play, you can't go out there in those clothes and shoes."

Who was this woman in shorts and sneakers to tell *him* how to dress? "These are five-hundred-dollar Oxfords."

Judy smiled. "I meant you'll fall in slippery leather soles."

Ryker didn't relish doing a faceplant in front of everyone

and embarrassing himself. He inhaled a deep breath and held it twenty seconds to regain his composure. "You're right. Of course they would. I'm dressed for work, not play. Did you give my card to Jeffrey with instructions to call?"

"We did." Margie pointed. "He's on court six in the green shorts and white top."

"Thanks." Ryker lifted the gate latch to enter.

Roxie giggled. "You can't go across there during a game."

"I'll walk behind them."

"No, you have to go outside and around to the last court."

In an irked tone. "Got it."

Flowering shrubs along the court fence obscured his view of the players. Suddenly, a gate opened. Green shorts and white shirt sprinted across the street, jumped into the car, and backed out, tires squealing, before Ryker could catch it.

He'd bragged to Sara that he had a Master's in car chases, but the situation didn't warrant one. Green shorts had too large a head start, and chases endangered innocent bystanders. Back to the women.

"It's ludicrous that none of you know his last name."

"Hey, I'm lucky to remember first names," said Roxie.

Ryker looked at Margie. "And you're sure he got my card?"

"Yes, and said he'd call." Hands akimbo, she asked, "Are you married?"

What a cheeky woman asking such a personal question. He was the cop. "I'm in charge of interrogations here."

"Well, are you?"

"No," escaped before he could catch it. Now he knew how he makes others feel.

"Then you should take up pickleball. It's very social and a good way to meet active women."

Who would whip his ass. "Nobody'd be interested in me?"

"You're a single, decent-looking male with a full-time job," said Judy. "You'd be surprised at the attention that you will get."

These women were ganging up on him. "In my defense, I don't know how to play."

"We'll teach you," said Judy.

Struggling to find a plausible excuse, he wished they'd go back on a court. He pretended an interest in the game until a man in his fifties tripped and fell while going for a hard-driven ball. The small hairs on Ryker's neck stood on end.

"No worry," said Judy. "As wide as he is tall, he rolls over and gets right back onto his feet."

An amusing image. "Do many players fall?"

Roxie giggled. "It's been known to happen now and then."

Not to me, Ryker turned away and marched to his car. He would not be bullied by three women.

**

Sara called three ERs to see if a doctor had treated a power-saw injury to a man's hand in early June. Desk clerks said they were understaffed and too busy with post-Labor Day accidents to pore through hundreds of old records. Maybe next week. They took her name and number in a memo that would surely be buried in a pile of papers. Labor Day already passed? The seven days off had warped her sense of time. McBride would stress out and be all over her if she didn't come up with something. Better make the hospital rounds in person.

Sara walked into the closest ER and showed her badge to the admissions clerk. "I'm investigating a murder two days ago and need to speak to anyone on call in early June."

She crossed her arms over her chest and gave Sara a once-over. "Are you the same woman who called me an hour ago?"

Sara drew her breath in slowly. "Yes."

"And did I not take your name and number?"

"Yes, but maybe sometime next week is too late. There's a killer on the loose, and I need to find him before he adds to his body count." She pressed both hands flat on the counter and gave an accusing glare. "Surely you wouldn't want to be responsible for another death by not allotting me a couple of minutes."

"I'll get into trouble for this."

"But you may save a life."

"Okay, I'll call for an orthopedic surgeon." She clicked the intercom. "Paging Doctor Johnson. Come to the lobby."

A doctor in his forties, wearing blue scrubs and eyes gentle enough to soothe any female patient, came to the desk. "What do you want, Rose?"

"This detective insists on talking to somebody."

He tapped a pen on the counter. "I've got patients waiting in three rooms."

"I understand, but I'm trying to catch a murderer and have to chase down every lead, no matter how slim. Did you or one of your associates treat a power-saw injury to a hand in early June?"

"Not that I recall."

"Review records?"

"I don't have time now."

"It's very important. Will you please ask anyone who might have been here then?"

"Only if you promise to leave."

Sara stepped out of the way of six people waiting in line to register. Friends, family, and patients occupied every seat in the lobby, some nodding off. Guilt nagged her. Her Patrick fixation could waste a doctor's valuable time.

Doctor Johnson returned. "I asked the entire staff. No one is aware of such an injury, but it was three months ago. Thousands of patients have come through here since then.

"I'm sorry for intruding and truly appreciate your help in such a busy time."

Sitting in her car again, Sara considered the options. Burden the already stressed employees of a hospital. Allow McBride to fret and remain sleepless until the case is solved. Her compulsion to always finish what she begins prevailed.

Five hospitals later and no leads, she slunk into the station, sat low out of sight, and wrote the day's report. She peered over the top of the monitor. Why hadn't McBride laid into her yet? His blinds were drawn, and the door was closed. Huh, not his usual demanding self. A welcome relief.

She typed the conclusion that her Patrick O'Connor premise was a dead end and headed for the break room.

Her phone rang. "Hello, this is Detective Lansing."

"I'm Doctor James and heard you've been inquiring about a power saw injury. I'm not aware of one, but I amputated parts of three middle fingers with severe frostbite. I remember because we don't see that here in Florida. The patient had just returned from Everest. If he'd had gradual warming and decent medical care the first few hours, the prognosis might have been different."

Aha, she knew it. "Did waiting until he came home before seeing a doctor diminish his odds of recovery?"

"No, the drastic decision to amputate is generally delayed a few weeks. What appears to be dead tissue may heal and recover over time. I agree he made a prudent choice in seeking treatment here, not in Nepal." Doctor James paused. "You're investigating a murder. Is he in some kind of trouble?"

"The investigation is ongoing. I suspected he'd lied to us and wanted verification. Thank you for calling."

"My pleasure. Let me know if you need anything else."

Sara called Ryker. "Did Larry the loan shark squeal?"

"The weasel ran off the court and into his car before I could reach him. He deliberately avoided me."

"And Patrick deliberately lied to us. No power saw injury at any of the hospitals, but a doc just phoned. He amputated three frost-bitten fingers on a patient returning from Everest."

"Holy crap. The other three climbers and his wife knew he was lying and went along with it."

Sara sighed. "If the saying goes, It takes a village to raise a child, maybe it took a cabal to commit a murder."

Chapter 12

Sara was adding Patrick's amputation to her report when a horrified scream and mass confusion tore through the station. She sprang from her chair and raced into the hall. "What's going on?"

A middle-aged female clerk was trembling in an emotional earthquake. "I've worked twenty years for Chief McBride. When he didn't pick up the phone or answer the door, I asked the desk officer to check on him." Her voice grew thick with emotion. "He was bent over in his chair. A dispatcher called for an ambulance."

Sara's pulse roared in her ears as the front door swung open and two EMTs ran a gurney down the hall to McBride's office. A brush of wind as they passed, wheels squeaking on the tile floor.

She drew a quick, shallow breath and touched the arm of a distraught clerk with tears streaming down her cheeks. "Bonnie, the best way to help is to stay out of the way and let them work."

A long three minutes later, the EMTs had loaded McBride into an ambulance. "He had a heart attack and would be dead if somebody hadn't found him in time. We're taking him to Saint Joseph's."

A flush of tears building in her throat, Sara called Ryker. Before she got a word out, he launched a tirade against Larry the loan shark for ditching him.

"Hush! Listen! McBride had a heart attack. They're taking him to Saint Joseph's. I'm heading there now."

"Oh, shit. I'm not far away. See you there."

Ryker had arrived first and met her with two cups of coffee. "You'll need this. They just took McBride in to run multiple tests. There's nothing we can do but wait."

"It's my fault for not realizing something was wrong when he holed up in his office and kept having trouble breathing."

"Now *you* hush and listen! You chewed me out for piling guilt on myself. So knock it off."

"Touché."

"I know nothing about him," said Ryker. "All I've witnessed is this angry, impatient man shouting orders at us to hurry up."

"You've only seen him under the gun with a lot of pressure. It's taken a major toll on him."

"Does he have anyone to ease his frayed nerves?"

"Not since his wife died of ovarian cancer three years ago. He's done nothing but work and go home to an empty house. Married officers invited him for the holidays, but he remained alone. He has no children. Both parents and an older sister who lived in Canada are dead."

"So basically, he has nobody."

"He's a mother bird with wings spread over chicks to protect them. For twenty years, the citizens of Reunion Heights have been his chicks. When that drug lord campaigned to become mayor, McBride ran against him." Sara slowly rotated the coffee cup between her hands. "You saw how stressed he was. And now a second murder in three weeks? It's too much."

"No wonder he constantly paces."

"His only companion is a dog named Ozzie. I've never seen him but know McBride's devoted to him."

Sara and Ryker jumped up when a doctor came in two hours later. "Tests, including an echocardiogram, EKG, MRI, and chest X-ray confirm. Mr. McBride had a myocardial infarction. His arteries were blocked ninety-five, ninety-seven, and ninety-eight percent."

"Can you put stents in?" Sara asked.

"When all three arteries are involved, we've had better luck with bypass surgery."

Sara gasped, sucking in air too heavy to breathe. "No, this can't be happening to him."

"Timing is crucial. The sooner we restore the blood supply, the less damage there will be to his heart muscle. He consented to proceed with surgery and is being prepped now."

"How long will it take?" Sara asked.

"Three to six hours. Someone needs to stay here if a problem arises."

"He's been under a lot of stress with a nasty election and two murder cases. Could it have caused the attack?"

"Quite possibly. I need to scrub in now. I'll tell him you're both here and will report back when we're finished."

A fragile peace settled in as Sara drew both hands down over her face and around her neck. "Whew, I never want to ride that coaster again. Despite how annoying McBride can be, I really care about him. He's the closest thing to a family I've had here."

"Even though your father's only forty minutes away."

She leered at Ryker. "Do not go there. Not now. It's major surgery. Things can go wrong. Complications with anesthesia."

His voice steadied. "I'm not minimizing the risk. His attack sent a vital message that I don't want to end up like him with only a dog to love and wrap my arms around."

"But your daughter—?"

"I haven't heard another word from her."

Ryker lowered his head and peered up at Sara with those sad basset-hound eyes he'd used on her before and won. "I don't want to die alone, but this rusty old clunker leaks oil, has a battery that doesn't start, and wears threadbare upholstery. I need help with that online dating site you talked about."

Sara cast a doubtful look.

"Give me a break. I'll quit smoking and drinking and lose

weight, but not all at once." He pushed off the seat and reached for her cup. "Right now, we need more coffee."

After seeing McBride and listening to Ryker, the image of dying alone loomed in her head. The two most important people in her life had abandoned her. Did shielding herself from her mother's abuse render her incapable of giving or receiving love? Could she offer Michael what he sought now?

Ryker returned and handed her a fresh cup. "All we can do is wait."

"I can't. I have to walk."

Sara adopted McBride's anxiety, pacing the length of the corridor back and forth, counting steps to keep her mind off him."

"Would you sit down and relax?" Ryker ranted.

"Would you get up and walk off the Cinnabon?"

After thirteen thousand steps on her pedometer, two more cups of coffee, and a bathroom break, the doctor came through the door and removed his surgical cap. "Everything went well, but his blood pressure is way too high. He'll need to make some lifestyle changes. He's awake in room three fourteen. You can go see him now but don't stay long. He needs to rest."

As they rode the elevator, Ryker said, "To put him at ease, let's say we have several suspects and expect an arrest."

"You mean lie to him?"

"We could have some."

Sara turned her eyes to the ceiling. "When pigs fly."

McBride's attack had reduced an imposing figure to a pale man in a hospital gown with an oxygen tube in his nose an IV in his arm.

Sara asked, "How do you feel?"

"A bit woozy."

"Are you in pain?"

"No, thanks to that bag hanging up there."

"The doctor said everything went well and you can go home within a week, depending on how you're progressing."

"Till then, who'll take care of Ozzie?"

McBride, who was always so hard-nosed about sticking to a case, asks about his dog before the suspects?

Ryker stumbled his way out of pet sitting. "I can't. When I came down on a temporary assignment, I got a motel room and still live there. No pets allowed."

Sara never had a pet as a kid, not even a goldfish or hamster. The closest she'd come to owning a pet was tossing a ball for the neighbor's beagle.

She feigned a smile. "I'll be happy to keep him at night."

"Thank you."

Panic attack. "What does he eat? Where does he sleep? How do I know when he needs to go outside?"

"I'll text a list later when I'm not so groggy. My phone's in the drawer next to my keys."

"Thirsty?" Sara asked, got a nod, and then held a plastic cup with a bent straw to his mouth while he sipped.

"Thanks, but don't try pacifying me with water. Where are my suspects?"

"Jeffrey, the moneylender, saw me coming and took off so fast I couldn't catch him."

"Try again first thing tomorrow morning. And your hopeless endeavor, Sara?"

Her hands curled into fists she didn't 'realize she'd made. Sometimes, the man made it difficult to care so damn much about him. "I struck out at every hospital looking for anyone who had treated a power saw injury three months ago."

He beamed with an I-was-right expression.

She wiped it right off. "Patrick told us a bold-faced lie. A surgeon called who amputated three frost-bitten fingers from a patient who had recently returned from Everest."

"Why'd he lie?"

"After spending all morning on this, I'm dead set on finding the truth during a pirate party at his place Friday night."

Arms folded over his chest, Ryker stated, "I am not going."

"Oh yes, you are and in full costume," ordered Sara.

McBride motioned for someone to adjust his pillow. Seeing a proud man needing help for the simplest task was disheartening. Sara asked, "You need anything?"

"Yes, pick Ozzie up at the house, take him home, and bring him to me in the morning. The nurse said he could come but not stay overnight."

That was just terrific. She wasn't trained to be a dog sitter. As they left the hospital, she told Ryker, "You're coming with me. I don't know a damn thing about dogs. Surely you had pets when Dulce was growing up."

"We did, but I was too busy working to have anything to do with them."

"No wonder she's angry at you." Seeing the solemn look on his face, she hooked her elbow around his. "Sorry, I didn't mean that. It was a low blow."

"But duly deserved. As for a dog named Ozzie, I doubt he's part of the K-9 squad. If you're worried, treats work. I'd start with them."

She shopped at a grocery store for the brand on McBride's list and had them in hand as she unlocked the house. A small tan terrier with a bushy muzzle and pointy ears greeted her.

"Here you go." She tossed two milk bones inside to lure him away from the entrance. "You're probably not used to guests and wonder who's this strange woman throwing things at me? We have to be friends a couple of nights and will get along if we both obey the rules. I give you food and water. You tell me when you need to poop."

Ozzie followed her into the kitchen. She located everything except his bed. To her great relief, it was in McBride's room, and she wouldn't be expected to share hers. Sara put his leash on, led him to her car, and told him to jump in. He didn't move. She patted the seat. "Come on. Get in here." She tried dragging him in by the leash. Ozzie dug his heels in and would not budge.

He gave her the stink eye and then stared straight ahead to confirm they weren't on speaking terms. "I'm too tired to play this game." She picked him up, set him on the passenger seat, and slammed the door.

When they got to her place, Sara opened the passenger side and gripped his leash to prevent him from running off. "We're here. Get out and I'll feed you."

His furry little cheeks and nose up in the air, he ignored her.

"Cut the attitude, you stubborn little—"

Sara picked up a limp, deadweight hound and carried him into the house. She set him on the kitchen floor and filled his water bowl.

"There, drink up while I follow this recipe for a better steak dinner than I'll ever eat."

Ozzie wasn't having any part of it. He sniffed through the living room to the front door and back again, the way he'd seen McBride pacing. Then he lay in front of the door, his back legs splayed flat on the floor behind him.

"Dinner's ready, your highness."

Not the slightest tail wag.

"If you don't eat, my boss will throw a fit."

Nothing.

She set the food bowl in front of him. No dog could resist the waft of a meat aroma.

Thirty minutes passed. "You miss him, don't you? I do too." She carried him to the couch, sat beside him, and petted his back.

No response.

She phoned Ryker. "All those years as a family man, you had to learn something. How do I pet this dog?"

"An impercipient nature woman who doesn't—?"

"Shut up, Sir Logophile, and tell me how. I'm desperate."

"This is hearsay, not my experience. They like to be rubbed behind their ears and on their hips. Smooth and gentle."

"Thanks, I owe you one."

As Sara massaged behind his ears, Ozzie nuzzled her hand. "I got a letter from my ex-husband. After walking out on me six years ago, he now wants to see me? He was my first love and broke my heart into so many pieces it never healed. I spurned the affection of the falconer at a Renaissance fair who offered all a woman could ask for. I'm angry and frustrated with Michael but don't want him to have died while climbing a mountain."

When Sara's hand slid off his hip, Ozzie's paw pulled it up. Sara lifted him onto her lap and rubbed his entire back. Leaning forward, she whispered, "He wants me to download WhatsApp and write him, but I'd have nothing good to say." She paused, trying to decide what to do, and got another reminder to continue petting. "Okay, I admit memories of him swarm so thick at times there's no room to breathe."

She glanced at Ozzie. "You're not much help. Tell me what to do."

He climbed onto her lap and snuggled into her. As she gently stroked behind his ears, he laid his paw on her other hand. She drew him closer, and tears blurred her eyes. "This must be what love feels like, Ozzie. Do I dare take the risk again with a man who already broke my heart?

Chapter 13

Thursday morning, Sara drove to the hospital. In the passenger seat, Ozzie sat up straight, his head whipping back and forth, not missing a thing. "If people were as attentive as you, it would make my job a whole lot easier."

She parked in the hospital lot next to Ryker's car. How'd he beat her here? To maintain hospital rules, she leashed Ozzie but doubted he'd do a runner. "Let's go visit that cranky man we both care about."

From the hall, she heard Ryker and McBride chatting, but all conversation ceased when a little tan terrier entered.

"Someone's here to see you," said Sara.

McBride wiped his eyes and sucked a tear back inside as she lifted the dog onto the bed and unclipped his leash.

"He missed you last night and wouldn't eat a steak dinner, but he did this morning, must've sensed you'd be together soon."

"Any problems?"

"No, he's sweet, but hospital rules say no sleepovers."

Ryker smiled at Ozzie, curled on McBride's lap. "So you're the vicious attack dog I've heard about. Take good care of this man. We need him healthy and happy."

"What'll please me most," said McBride, "is you getting on the job and nabbing that pickleball suspect. Find out if Vance stiffed him. I've seen people murder for less."

"That's my plan."

"And I'll call Vance's wife," said Sara, her fingers drifting down Ozzie's back. "You two take care of each other. I'll be back this afternoon."

**

Remembering Jeffrey's usual parking spot, Ryker stayed close but not enough to draw attention. He liked stakeouts, a chance to chill without feeling lazy. From his trunk cache, he grabbed a bag of potato chips, a soda, and a chocolate-covered donut. He was his own man. Sara's voice be damned.

Thirty minutes passed and no sign of Larry the loan shark. A game ended. Players walked back toward court one to paddle up. They came in all ages, and physique didn't separate winners from losers. Some were pencil thin; others, overweight. After never playing any kind of sport, why would he want to now? He licked the frosting off a donut, rolling his tongue along the side.

"Get rid of that," he heard Sara shouting in his head. "You went to pot after your wife died. Is this what you want for your daughter?"

He chucked it onto the back-seat floor, hung both arms over the steering wheel, and pondered what to do now. He knew the answer. Contact Dulce.

Where was that damn loan shark? If he would just show up, Ryker could legitimize going after him instead of phoning her. Guilt lizard. If Larry wasn't here in another thirty seconds, Ryker would have to make the call.

Twenty-eight, twenty-nine, thirty. He clicked Dulce. His chest rose with a tight pull of air, pulse climbing with the rings.

"Hi, this is Dulce. Leave your name and number. I'll call you back."

His frame softened, easier talking to a machine. "It's your father, sweetheart, and I miss you terribly. I hope you'll forgive me one day. I loved your mom with everything in me, and you just as much."

He spoke of regretting having missed her tennis matches, graduation, Christmases, always for work. The night her mother died, he'd been called to a bridge where a teenage girl wanted him by name. He saved her life but lost his wife and daughter.

His fingers clenched around the phone as another memory flared—his father striking his mother with a fireplace poker and her falling onto the brick hearth. Dark blood pooling across the floor, a coppery smell, and the sound never left. Blaming himself for not being strong enough to stop his father, he swore that night to protect women.

Needing air, he spoke again into the phone. "I've left New York ghosts behind. Let's start over in warm Florida. We could try new things like pickleball or going on a hike."

Then movement. Jeffrey had just pulled in and was heading for the courts. "I need to go, sweetheart. I love you. Call me."

Ryker leaped from the car, sprinted after Jeffrey, and seized the back of his shirt.

Jeffrey shook free. "Who the hell are you?"

"Detective Ryker Harris. I need to ask a few questions."

"Sorry, but I'm late already."

Feeling cocky with what little he knew of the game, Ryker said, "It's drop in. Come and go whenever you please."

"I'm meeting my partner to practice for our tournament."

"He can wait. There's a park bench over there. You could've saved us both time by calling the number on the card I left.

"I had nothing to say."

"That's for me to decide."

Jeffrey stomped to the bench and sat with one leg crossed over the other knee, bouncing his foot. "What do you want?"

"You know or wouldn't have dodged me the other day. Why did you loan money to Vance?"

"Because he needed it?"

"You can sit here until dark, come down to the station, or cooperate, and then hit balls with your partner. I'm asking again.

"Why, when, and how much?"

He gnashed his teeth and spat out, "A hundred grand a year ago to save his skin."

"Why from you?"

"Because I have money, and all his other wells were dry. I own a successful strip mall with a coffee shop where Vance hung out. At twelve percent, I'd lend to my own brother."

Jeffrey's phone buzzed. "Yeah, I'm here in the park being interrogated by some cop. I'll head over now." He picked up his bag and stood. "If you're done, we're next in line for a court."

"Not yet. How much had Vance paid back?"

He held his hand up, the thumb and index finger touching. "A big fat zero."

"One last question. Where were you Sunday afternoon and evening?"

A brash expression on his face. "At a doubles tournament in Rupert, Florida. I'm done talking."

After Jeffrey stormed off, Ryker phoned Sara. "Larry the loan shark showed, and we had a brief chat. Vance borrowed a hundred grand at twelve percent a year ago, zero paid back."

"Means and opportunity?"

"Claims he was in a pickleball tournament in Rupert. I'll ask around to verify."

Ryker spotted Judy waiting for a game. "Hi, again. I talked to Jeffrey. He claims to have played in Rupert last Sunday. You know anything about that?"

"I've heard him brag about winning here and there, but I don't track him. We're not close friends."

"How late do tournaments run?"

"I don't know but think usually daytime. I'm not into it. I play for fun, not glory."

"Thanks for your help again."

"Bring better shoes and clothes next time," she teased.

Walking back to the car, Ryker called Sara. "I'd add Jeffrey to a suspect list. He's a rich snob, and the tournament alibi may not hold up."

He paused. "Hold on, a note's pinned under the windshield wiper that reads, 'Whoever killed Vance did the world a favor.'" Seems he pissed off more than a few people who thought ill of him, but not enough to murder. I'm heading to Rupert to verify an alibi."

**

The afternoon heat pressed on Sara's shoulders as she parked near the dead climber's house. She tucked her fingerprint kit inside a bag and was headed up the sidewalk when two figures partially hidden by shrubbery caught her attention. Dominant stances and arm movements implied an urgent discussion, but she couldn't identify the actors. Sara felt like a lion crouched low and creeping through tall grass to sneak up on unsuspecting prey.

His back to the street, he hugged Celia and then kissed her, more than a friendly peck on the cheek. Sara crept low, the lion stalking its prey, as the Seven Summits rival passed her.

Shuffle the dec and start over. Having won the contest by default, why was he here with Vance's widow? Did she send the autonomous letter alerting Jason to the show? And if so, why?

Sara rang the bell twice, giving Celia time to collect herself.

The haughty art dealer flinched at the sight of her "I wasn't expecting you again."

Sara stepped inside without waiting for permission. Better to apologize than ask. "I came to answer insurance questions you may have."

"Thank you, not sure what happens in this situation, I was afraid of being left on my own."

"In murder cases, companies pay the full amount as long as the beneficiary wasn't involved. It's called the slayer rule."

"Thank goodness." Celia fidgeted with a large gold hoop dangling from her left ear. "Anything else?"

"When here earlier, I noticed you have a Ganesha statue. In

Nepal, the popularity of this elephant-headed god struck me. I'd like to see him again. May I?"

"Yes, of course. If you don't mind, I was in the middle of something and need to finish. You know where his office is."

Finishing something to do with Jason? Once Celia was out of sight, Sara lightly spun powder over every statue surface and found two prints on the underside of one elbow that someone had missed when wiping it clean. Gotcha Ganesha. She lifted it on a piece of clear tape and pressed it onto a card ready for the lab. If they matched Tanner's kids, Vance had stolen Ganesha along with two thangkas, possibly worth tens of thousands of dollars.

She found Celia in the kitchen making tea. "Like some?"

"No, thank you. I have to get back to work." Sara paused at the door. "By the way, I saw Jason leaving as I was coming in."

Celia's face blanched. "Uhh, yes, he stopped by to offer his condolences since he's in town. The three of us went to college together. Jason and I dated for a while."

How considerate. He'd won the blue ribbon in college, but Vance got the girl. Was Jason after both prizes now, and was murder involved?

Chapter 14

When Sara arrived, Ryker was sitting at McBride's bedside. Ozzie's head lay in the chief's lap for serious ear rubbing.

"How are you doing?" she asked.

"Better than yesterday. The nurses take good care of me. He opened his arm toward the nightstand and asked her to get the paper from it. "I was still groggy when the night nurse came in and said a man had called to leave a message for the police chief."

"The press must have leaked I'm here."

"Twenty years on the job. People care about you."

"She's right," said Ryker. "Seventeen calls in the last three days. Everybody wants to play detective like at a mystery party."

"Any follow-up on them?" McBride asked.

"Four or five. All dead ends."

"Maybe we'll get lucky." Sara sat at the end of the bed. "A clerk at the Havenwood Motel claims to have information about the murdered man." She folded the paper. "Never heard of the place."

"Probably not the haunt of your racer types," said Ryker.

"You two have nothing better to do than babble?"

"We identified six or seven suspects but don't have enough to bring anybody in."

Sara rubbed Ozzie's hip, making him wiggle. "Don't worry. Get 'em all drunk at tomorrow's party, and they'll squeal like pigs on each other."

"I want results now. Go question this clerk and report back to me."

"I'll drive," said Ryker. "The motel's forty-five minutes out of town. Did this desk character give any hints as to what he thinks he knows?"

"None, and no telling how credible he is. We need to humor McBride. Stress over these last two cases may have landed him in that hospital bed."

"We're wasting time on a wild-goose chase."

As Sara got into the car, she wrinkled her nose. "What's that smell?" She peered over her shoulder, picked up a soggy donut from the back floor, and held it in Ryker's face. "What's this?"

"Stakeouts demand food."

"An apple or carrot sticks, but not artery-clogging donuts."

"It energizes my brain. Stakeouts also offer quiet time for navel gazing." He pulled out of the parking lot. "I made the call."

"What call?"

"To my daughter Dulce."

Miracles can happen. Sara turned to catch a smile or frown.

"I got her voicemail."

"How disappointing." She leaned over the center console. "Promise me you left a message."

He attempted a Southern drawl. "Why yes, ma'am, I most surely did."

Sara laughed at his lame imitation. "If you hadn't, I would have smacked you in the head.

"It's only been two hours, and she may never call back."

Carolina sapphire cypress trees lined the motel's driveway and entrance. Ryker went in first to the desk. "I'm looking the clerk who phoned the Reunion Heights Police."

"That's me, I'm Lewis," said a heavyset, bearded man in his late fifties. "I've worked this desk for ten years and know our regulars. At my sister's wedding in Arizona last weekend, I hung out to see the famous Grand Canyon." He opened the photo app on his phone. "Look at that. It's amazing. You ever been there?"

"No, I have not," said Ryker.

Lewis shared a selfie standing in front of the south entrance. "Very nice," Sara said.

Impatiently drumming on the counter top, Ryker raised his voice. "Lewis, why'd you call us?"

"When I got home and saw the news headlines, I recognized the murder victim's photo but not the name Vance Miller."

"What're you talking about?"

Lewis laid the reservation book open on the counter and turned it toward them. He ran his finger down the list, pointed to Steve Campbell, and declared proudly, "This name matches that face. Steve's been coming here for years to the same room, pays cash, and never stays more than a couple of days. I record all check-in and check-out times."

Ryker's mouth twitched with a repressed grin. "Welcome to my city world, Sara."

Lewis pointed to tabs on some pages. "I stuck these on days he was here and noticed a six-week gap."

"April and May when Vance was in Nepal," said Sara.

"Can we photograph each marked page?" Ryker asked.

"The last entry was on Sunday. He checked in at six and out at nine."

Sara gave a quick thumbs-up. "Look at the times. We could be at the crime scene. Do you have CCTV for both that day and night?"

"Yes, in the back office. I'll set it up."

They followed Lewis into a room with a coffee maker, small fridge, microwave, and shelves of CCTV footage. Hovering over his shoulder, they watched Vance exit the motel, turn right, and then step out of camera range.

"What's over there?" Sara asked.

"Nothing but lots of bushes and trees."

"Did he have any regular visitors?" Ryker asked.

"None that registered. But there's a back door that can only be accessed with a motel fob."

"So a guest could enter if opened from the inside?"

Lewis nodded. "A CCTV covers the back door, but not the entire rear parking lot. It caught what looks like a woman in a hooded jacket, exiting the building at eight forty-five and then turning left out of sight."

"Have any idea who it is?" Ryker asked.

"No one else registered near his time, but he could have let her in the back door."

"Copy both footages from five to ten o'clock onto a USB. We'll wait outside."

With an alluring smile, Sara strolled past Ryker, rolling her hips in a sensuous motion. "Follow me, Vance, my brave Everest climber, for a romantic tryst in the shrubbery."

"You're delicious." He opened his hands in surrender. "But sadly, I cannot. I'm faithfully married to my beautiful wife, Celia. I come here only to meditate while she's away on business."

Sara snickered. "Now that's a mental picture I can't get out of my mind."

They found a black sedan parked beneath flowering bushes. The sheer volume of bird droppings covering the roof and hood made it obvious the car had been parked there for several days. Ryker called the station to run the plate.

Five minutes later, he said, "It's registered to Vance."

"Then tell them to send CSI and a tow truck."

They waited in the motel lobby while Lewis downloaded the CCTV. With a playful crease on his forehead, Ryker said, "Your come-hither look was unscrupulous coercion to make me join that dating site."

A satisfied grin. "That was mission."

Lewis entered from the back office looking equally pleased. "I hope this helps find who murdered our long-time customer."

"I'm sure it will," said Sara. "We also need to speak to the person at the desk on Sunday night."

"My niece. She's just a mile from here. I'll get her over."

A girl around nineteen or twenty showed up fifteen minutes later, smacking gum. "What'cha want, uncle?"

"The detectives would like to ask you some questions about Sunday night." Lewis showed her the registration book. "Do you remember this man, Steve Campbell?"

"I don't learn their names. I just ask people to sign in and pay. Then I give 'em the room keys."

Sara brought up a photo of Vance on her phone. "Did he look like this?"

"That was five days ago. I don't memorize faces."

"Did anyone else come in around that time?"

"People always coming and going. If they don't need me, I leave 'em alone and play games on my phone. Can I go now?"

Sara nodded and then told Lewis, "I know she's your niece, but that's a pretty low bar for relief help."

When the CSI team showed up and asked to see Vance's room, the clerk explained it had been cleaned and rented to four others since then.

"Vance's car is over there under some bushes," said Ryker. "We didn't touch anything."

The lead CSI man said, "We'll take over from here. Is there anything else we need to know?"

"Follow me," said Sarah. "There's a back door that could have been used by someone of interest. Dust for prints. From the outside, it can only be opened using a key fob. If someone opened from the inside, there could be prints around the door or knob."

As she and Ryker got into the car, Sarah said, "Speaking of prints, the lab confirmed the ones off Ganesha in Vance's office match those of Tanner's kids. I think it traveled from their house to Vance's, and two thangkas went along. The cloth scrolls roll up for easy transport and storage."

"Why bother with souvenirs?"

"One possibility is that Vance had access to Celia's catalogs, evaluated the scrolls' worth, and stole them himself. She could have been oblivious to his debt and known nothing about it. Or they were cohorts. He'd steal and she'd sell on the art black market. A third possibility is she sold them after his death."

Sarah rolled down the window for some fresh air. "By the way, how was your trip to Rupert?"

"He and his partner entered the tournament, but it ended at five thirty, early enough to make it back here by seven."

"So he kills Vance but doesn't get his money back?"

"Man like him, whose self-esteem is rooted in money, ain't gonna forgive a hundred grand, even knowing he'll never get it."

Sara laughed. "Maybe Vance's loving wife will pay up."

"Hah, only with a butcher knife at her throat. Speaking of Celia, what are the odds she knew about his debauchery?"

"Let's see how the widow reacts to news of his mistress."

Chapter 15

As they pulled in front of Celia's house, Sarah said, "The last time I was here, she and Jason were in the backyard. He hugged and kissed her."

"On the lips? Not a sympathetic, commiseration peck on the cheek?"

"Nope, full on mouth to mouth."

"Remember how he talked of needing two keys to open a safe holding two hundred grand plus eight years' interest? With Vance dead, Jason wins the contest. Is he cozying up to Celia for the other key?"

"They dated in college," said Sara. "What if Jason murdered Vance for the money and to win the girl he felt he deserved?"

"Or she knew about his mistress and orchestrated the entire scenario to get Jason's key," said Ryker. "She played him with an anonymous letter about Vance's summit announcement."

"Could Celia have grabbed Jason by the short hairs strong enough for him to murder for her?"

Ryker ran his nails up and down over his forehead. "You can't believe what I've seen men do for women. You females are the superior half of our species."

When they reached the house, Sara said, "Tap lightly on the door and fake a smile when she opens."

Seeming less than thrilled with them on her doorstep, Celia cringed. "Why are you here again?"

"I have a few more questions," Sara said, stepping inside. "I'm curious about the Ganesha piece. When did Vance buy it?"

"Why I . . . I can't remember the exact date. It was too long ago but sometime after he got back from Nepal."

"Short as in two weeks or long as in three months ago?"

"Oh, only weeks maybe. Why?"

"A Ganesha is missing from the home of one of his team. When I was here the other day, I tried to lift fingerprints, but the statue had been wiped clean except for one spot on the underside of its elbow. That print matches one of Tanner's children. Have any of them been here?"

"Vance and I kept our lives separate. I never met this man Tanner, his children, or any of the expedition."

Sara wrote Patrick's address on the back of her card and gave it to Celia. "There's a party here Friday night where you can meet everyone and show support for your husband. It's a pirate theme. Everyone will be in costume."

Shifting from one foot to the other, Ryker bunched his lips in a faux smile and asked, "As a high-end broker, are you familiar with thangkas?"

"Certainly, but that's a niche market, not my line of work."

"Would you be able to evaluate their worth?"

"I suppose so after some research. Why are you asking?"

"Two are also missing from Tanner's house and may have traveled with Ganesha."

"Are you accusing me of stealing them? What an offensive insult."

"I apologize," said Sara. "We heard your husband had some financial difficulties and might have tried to sell them."

She dismissed them with a backhand wave. "It's time for you to leave. I have important work to do."

Ryker headed for the door but turned. "Important work like

scheduling your next business travel? A successful woman like you must keep meticulous records. We don't care about your financials but want a list of the last three months' travel times."

Her mouth flattened into a tight, unwavering line. "Why on earth do you want those?"

"To compare with your husband's nights at the Havenwood Motel," said Sara. She wasn't normally this blunt, but the woman appeared to have little regard for him. Celia had barely shed a tear upon hearing of his death. And then there was Jason.

"You despicable woman smearing a man's reputation whose life was brutally taken from him."

"I merely asked about dates. You jumped to slander."

Ryker intervened. "Go get the books. If you hesitate, we can get a warrant."

Celia's body stiffened, the thin line of her mouth pinching tighter. She pivoted on her heel and stormed off.

"That wasn't exactly subtle," said Ryker.

"You pride yourself on being able to read people. What did you see? Sorrow for her loss or anger that we want something?"

"Anger. And I'm about to piss her off even more."

Celia returned and shoved a ledger in Sara's hands.

"Then there's the question of Jason," said Ryker.

Celia pulled back abruptly.

"We interviewed him and know about the prize money he'd lose due to climbing seasons. With a high interest rate, it could be a tall stack of bills. The problem is you need two keys to get it. I'm sure Jason has one, but where's the other?"

"I saw you two kiss in the rear garden yesterday," said Sara. "Did Jason show up here for more than condolences?"

"I know nothing about prize money and have no idea where Vance would store a key."

"I presume there's a safe deposit box with the second one. Shall we take a look?"

"Not without a search warrant. Now get out of here."

"Whew," Ryker said as they exited. "Lady's got a temper."

"Neither of us said anything about Vance meeting women at the motel. Celia went straight there. So, yeah, she knew what a perv he was. There was no heart-throbbing, sensual love in their marriage, no until death do us part. She openly professed it was transactional."

"Here's my take on it," said Ryker. "Knowing he cheated on her gives Celia an excuse to get rid of him, seek Jason's help hauling dead weight into a freezer, and collect Vance's share of the prize. She figures his key is somewhere in the house but needs Jason's too. Celia notifies him that Vance will declare himself the winner at a Sunday slideshow. They kill him that night and place the blame on expedition members."

"Possible, but we have zero proof. The burning question is who or how many women shared his little hideaway? We need to compare her travel schedule with his motel visits. I'm done for the day. We've questioned every potential suspect and won't get the CSI report until late tonight or tomorrow morning. If you come over, I'll help you with the online dating site."

"I hate going home to an empty place with no one to hold at night. But putting myself on a dating site risks being turned down by hundreds of lonely women. I have a greater chance of winning the Nobel Peace Prize."

"Not if you do it right. Go home, get cleaned up, and put on your best shirt and slacks. We'll need to take a picture or two."

"Can't I use older photos before I got so heavy?"

"Absolutely not. When you meet in person, women will see you lied. That's no way to start a relationship."

"But my most charming smile could simply win them over."

"Sorry, a lie is a lie. You won't get any second dates, and the whole thing will be a waste of time."

**

He showered, shaved, combed his hair, and then stood in front of the mirror, naked. It took three years after his wife died to gain this much weight. How long to lose it? Forever without Sara's endless nagging that pisses him off, but he needs her motivation. Without it, he'd never have the courage to go through the dating ordeal and would end up alone like McBride.

Ryker reached Sara's at seven with a six-pack. He set five in the refrigerator and opened one. A finger to his lips. "Hush, do not say it. This is courage in a can."

He squatted to pet the dog staring up at him. "And some of us need all the help we can get."

Taking the first sip, he surveyed the living room. "You still have nothing on your walls and shelves. No family photos or memorabilia of the adventure races you and Michael did in weird places all over the planet. It's like you have no past."

"I'm a minimalist."

"That's a gross understatement."

"It's my life to lead the way I choose."

He dropped onto her leather couch and set his beer on the coffee table. "Then let me do the same."

Sara moved his bottle from possibly spilling on her laptop. "You're lonely and want a woman in your life, not just an Ozzie. The promise of one may inspire you to—"

"Be somebody I'm not." He belched. "Sorry about that. Go on and get this tribulation over with."

When Sara opened the site, Ryker guffawed and pointed to the first question. "Am I to choose whether I'm a man, woman, or other? What other? Like an alligator or hippo?"

"Smartass."

He clicked Man, added his name, email, and location.

"Birthdate?"

"July 8, 1965."

She smacked him on the head with a National Geographic magazine. "Quit sabotaging yourself. What year?"

"Okay, you win. 1974."

His profile read: Single male, age fifty, average build,

widowed, non-smoker, non-drinker. Interests: Pickleball, hiking.

"You're lying."

He reached for his beer. "Doesn't everyone on here?"

"You'll find out."

"Time to post a photo," Sara said. "Where are the pictures you brought?"

Grimacing, he withdrew three from his pocket and handed them over.

"When were these taken?"

"A little while ago."

"Two decades ago."

"What's a woman going to say when she expects to see *this* and *you* show up?"

"By then, she will have fallen for who I am, not how I look."

"Come into the kitchen. Stand against the white wall."

"A mug shot? He made ridiculous bodybuilder poses, stuck his tongue out, and lifted his shirt, baring his stomach.

"Quit acting like a thirteen-year-old."

He ran both hands through his hair, straightened his collar, and smiled for ten photos."

A devilish grin. "Pick the best, frame it, and hang it on your empty wall."

"Dream on."

Three beers in his belly when they'd finished, Ryker said, "I'm leaving the rest for the next time you invite me over."

"I'll guard them with my life." She walked him to the door. "I hope you find what you're looking for, but be wary. All is not as it seems."

"I'm too good at reading people to be fooled."

She closed the door behind him. Naïve and too needy. I'll do a background check on anyone you date more than twice.

Chapter 16

Friday morning, Sara took Ozzie back to the hospital. When the dog immediately nestled in McBride's lap, his eyes netted with wrinkles. "He's happy. You're taking good care of him."

"Ozzie's a sweet, nonjudgmental listener who tolerates my dining and sleep habits and bathroom hours. I'll miss him when they let you go home."

"That might be as early as this Saturday or Sunday."

"What might be?" Ryker asked, entering the room.

"Going home. But only if he doesn't argue with the nursing staff and agrees to follow post-op instructions."

"And if all goes as planned tomorrow," she said, "we'll have a confirmed suspect for a welcome-home gift."

McBride searched her face as if trying to discern whether she was telling the truth or merely trying to cheer him up. "How's that possible?"

"Patrick invited us to a party at his hobby farm. All potential suspects will be there, and free-flowing booze might loosen their tongues." Sara averted her gaze from him. "But there's a small caveat. He requires all guests to arrive dressed as pirates. Will the department pop for costume rentals?"

"For her, not me," Ryker blurted out. "I'm not going."

McBride's eyes narrowed, his brows drawn tight. "You will both attend in full regalia. That's not a request; it's an order." He nodded at Sara. "And I want every receipt."

"Understood. I know the perfect shopping place. She took Ryker's arm. "Come on, Blackbeard."

He shook free. "Is this a mischievous plot to make me feel as uncomfortable as possible?"

"No, dress up, they said. It'll be fun, they said."

Sara strolled jauntily to the car. "Get ready for a circus; this party will be a blast."

Grumbling under his breath, Ryker kicked a pebble across the parking lot.

She gave him a whimsical smile. "Oh, come on. Get in the mood. What was your favorite Halloween costume as a kid?"

"Didn't have one. My dad forbade trick-or-treating."

"Why?"

"He called Halloween a pagan holiday, inviting the devil."

"That had to be tough when everyone else was celebrating. But you must have gone to parties."

"We lived in a small community. The son of the town drunk wasn't welcome in people's homes."

"And friends weren't welcome in mine. I was too ashamed to have anybody see my mother slumped down in a chair, drunk or high on drugs." Sara climbed into the driver's seat. "We both had shitty childhoods, so party on!"

"I hate to burst your euphoric bubble. A pirate party's not Halloween."

"But I still get to dress up."

Sara parked at the town's largest costume shop and reached across the console to tug Ryker's cheek. "Spread those lips into a smile and pretend you can hardly wait to be a pirate."

She dragged him through the door by his shirt sleeve and told the salesman her companion wanted to dress as Blackbeard, the bloodthirsty, most feared man on land and sea.

He scratched the back of his head. "Not sure what we've got. There's been a run on pirates this week for a Friday shindig."

As the salesman went to the back room, Ryker glared at her. "You're gonna owe me for this."

He returned with a bushy black wig that hung below Ryker's shoulders and down the sides of his face.

"Perfect," Sara said and tied on an enormous black beard that covered his entire chest down to the waist.

Ryker bristled. "You done messing with me?"

"Go look in the mirror."

After viewing himself side to side, he yanked the wig and beard off. "I'm not wearing these. I don't even recognize the person looking back at me."

"That's the point. We're going incognito to avoid being tagged as cops." She turned to the salesman. "What else?"

"Black boots, shirt with balloon sleeves, waistcoat, tricorn hat, and cutlass."

"You've got it, Blackbeard. My turn now."

She chose black knee-high boots, red breeches, and a long red waistcoat over a loose-fitting white blouse.

As they got into the car, Ryker muttered, "We'll be a pair of cockamamie cops."

"No, cutthroat marauders out to nail a killer. Do what you must at home and then come to my place in two hours to dress. I need to pick up a few things first."

The party couldn't have come at a better time. It would echo Agatha Christie's bringing everyone together in a confined group but rougher around the edges. Ryker wasn't a gentlemanly Poirot but had an uncanny ability to work people. He'd have to be on his game 100%. Any sign of a police presence would torpedo their chances of snaring someone vile enough to lock a naked man in a freezer.

Standing at the bathroom mirror, Sara took a controlled deep breath before applying a black temporary dye to her ash blond, shoulder-length hair and long bangs. Saturating each strand, she massaged it in, let the dye sit for thirty minutes, rinsed it in cold water, and blew it dry. The stuff had better wash out. Now for the fun part.

With a black makeup pencil, she drew a broad line from her nose, arched over the brow to her temple, and back down along the cheekbone to the start. She darkened the entire orb, including eyelids, and added a fake scar on her cheek. A gold ring hung from each ear under a broad-brimmed hat with a red plume.

Ryker arrived at the front door, costume in hand. He jumped back a step and shivered when she opened it. "Holy crap. All that black on your face makes you look like a cadaver. You're too creepy. Get away from me."

"And good evening to you too, matey, won't you step into my parlor?"

Crouched and slowly stepping backward, using her hands and a low voice to beckon him. "Come with me."

"Hurry and get this over with."

In front of a full mirror, she handed him the long, shaggy wig and tried not to laugh when he pulled it too far over his forehead, burying his cheeks in hair. Werewolf came to mind.

She drew a heavy mustache arching from his upper lip to his chin and widened his brows to come together in an angry V.

She stepped back to admire her work. "A sword in your belt will attest to you being the most terrifying pirate on the seas."

He finally grinned. "Yeah, that's been my life's ambition."

"Enter separately. Suspects seeing us together might deduce our identities and undermine my masterful cosmetic job." She gave him fake pistols to wear across his chest and slipped knife into her belt.

"Ready to catch a murderer, Blackbeard?"

**

Sara drove Ryker to the hobby ranch. A parking attendant dressed as Captain Jack Sparrow waved a cutlass and directed her to the end of a long line of cars on the right-hand side.

"I'll drop you at the gate," she said. "Be careful getting out with two flintlock pistols strapped to your chest. Earbud ready?"

He tapped his ear.

"Good and play it cool. No heroics. Just observe."

"Aye, aye, me matey."

"I'll park out of sight and wait ten minutes to make it look like you came alone."

As Ryker strode up the long driveway, Patrick's four geese charged the fence, honking furiously. Blackbeard spread his arms and stomped toward them. Wings beating wildly, they scattered to the safety of their pond.

He swaggered, chuckling to himself, "Scourge of the seas."

At the entrance, an eight-foot orange banner with skull and crossbones read Beware of the Pirate in red caps. A barefoot skeleton in breeches, sailor shirt, and tricorn hat held a lantern, casting an eerie glow on the web-shrouded, foggy path to a patio illuminated by ten tiki torches, pulsing with rock music and fifty costumed buccaneers.

Patrick, magnificent as Captain Hook, wore a red tricorn hat, a ruffled white shirt under a red velvet waistcoat, and a gold-trimmed cuff with a silver hook hiding his injured hand. Black leather boots and black breeches fastened below the knees.

Ashley was clothed in a laced, corseted dress with off-the-shoulder sleeves. A striped red and black striped skirt matched a red bandana with strings of long, dangling beads

Ryker passed a tall cocktail table where pirates raised their steins, chanting, "Grog, more grog."

Facing a long sweltering evening buried in a heavy black wig and beard. He rationalized needing a drink to blend with the crowd.

Beck was tending bar next to a sliding door entrance into the house. Lowering his voice to disguise it, Ryker ordered a rum and cola and scanned the crowd.

Cheers erupted, and all eyes turned as Heath and Paco made a grand appearance. Dressed as Long John Silver, he hobbled onto the patio using a crutch to support a convincing wooden leg. Its boot didn't match the one on his other foot. Red shoelaces on the left went with his shirt; blue ones on the right, with his pants. Perched on his shoulder, Paco squawked a loud, expletive-laden greeting.

Heath stepped aside as two men wheeled in the giant, metal bird sculpture Ryker and Sara had seen at his studio. "Lads and lassies, I offer my latest work," he said as they installed it in the center of a large garden. "It captures the spirit of the wind." A gentle push on the flurry of feathers set the bird in motion.

"Well, blow me down! Would ye look at that!" shouted an old salt, and everyone cheered.

"What's that noise?" Sara asked through Ryker's earbud.

He moved to a more private location. "Heath's showing off his art. You on the way in here?"

"I'm almost to Jack Sparrow. Seen anyone else?"

"Patrick and Ashley. The libidinous Zoey's still at large."

Sara laughed. "You must've been saving that word since the country club."

"Aye, only the best for me matey."

Monitoring that red, yellow, and blue fowl sitting on Heath's shoulder, Ryker instinctively ducked when the parrot circled his head before settling on the sculpture. After ordering Paco to stay, Heath began dancing alone in the middle of the patio. Despite Long John's wooden leg, his arms and body moved in perfect harmony with the music. He was in his own world as if no one else existed.

Seeing Sara enter with dyed hair and heavy black makeup around her eyes, Ryker wouldn't have recognized her and hoped nobody else did. Through her earbud, he asked, "Do birds have a sixth sense about who hates them? Staring at me with his beady little eyes, Paco flapped his wings as if threatening to fly into my face."

She laughed quietly. "Your ornithophobia's showing. Calm

down and do the breathing exercise I taught you."

"Aye, aye."

Ryker inhaled through his nose and exhaled from his mouth, counting to four, then five, and six until his pulse slowed and confidence returned. He was unflappable.

As he neared three men whispering among themselves, he told Sara, "This place might be rife with leads."

A robust pirate with a bulging belly said, "I didn't know if Patrick would throw a bash this year after losing three fingers."

A pirate dressed in red. "I heard it was only at the middle knuckles. Captain Hook's a damn clever costume. Hides it well."

Bulging belly said, "His hand is useless. Close yours and try picking something up with nothing below that joint. Impossible."

The third horned in, "He must have been drunk while using the power saw. Patrick's usually so diligent."

"Patrick doesn't drink."

"He came back from Everest not right. In med school, I did a study on the effects of high altitude on the brain. It can damage cells involved in motor activity and cognitive functions."

"He seems fine," added the pirate in red.

"But may not have been so soon after returning."

"Vance would have commented on anyone being ill."

"Not to any of us. And now he's dead. The *Reunion Heights Sentinel* reported he was murdered, but police made no arrests."

"It was a hit job," said Bulging Belly.

"Ordered by who?"

"Anyone he owed money to. A guy at work plays no-limit poker. Vance was a big better and so far in debt he'd do anything to save his skin. Word on the street is that a few of his poker pals threatened him."

"I came to drink and have a good time, not talk of corpses. Raise our steins to the hosts, Patrick and Ashley."

Ryker slipped away and spoke to Sara's earbud. "I just heard Patrick's friends talking. They believe his power-saw saga. One blames altitude for motor loss."

"Altitude and deep cold froze them."

"Another claims Vance's death was a hit job by somebody he owed money to. He was in deep gambling shit and would do anything to save his skin."

"Like claiming the Seven Summits prize, while fully aware of the eighth mountain."

Ryker scanned the other guests, looking for Zoey, Celia, and Jason. Suddenly, a hand slid up his arm, fingers twining in his beard. Adrenaline rush. He spun around in a fight-or-flight mode and met a bosomy woman in a red tube top, bare midriff, curve-hugging shorts, and fishnet tights. With full lips and sultry dark eyes, she asked, "Is Blackbeard as daring in bed as he is on the seas?"

His beard trapped sweat coursing down his face as he nearly dropped his drink. Was this beauty coming onto a former NYPD officer, or was it just the mystique of sleeping with a renowned swashbuckler? He froze, speechless for the first time in his life.

Patrick shouted, "Fire in the Hole." A bright flash and loud boom blasted from the ship's cannon. Partygoers rushed to the pond, sparing Ryker from the embarrassment of responding to the seductress tantalizing him.

He ran with the crowd and saw Zoey sitting waist-deep in the water with her arms resting on a low stone wall. Chin on the back of her hands and wet hair streaming down the sides of her face, she was a Greek siren luring sailors to death. Her ample lips invited a lingering gaze. Two beguiling wenches within minutes? His pulse kicked up. The first aroused his interest, but Zoey he could not resist.

Her tongue lightly ran across her lower lip in a playful smile. "Good evening, Blackbeard."

Oh, thank god, she didn't recognize him. He could embrace her sexuality from a safe moral distance without tarnishing his reputation. But Sara called, ending the fantasy.

"Celia and Jason entered fifteen minutes apart like we did. Neither bothered to wear a costume. She's in a plain baggy dress, and he stuck a cheap patch over one eye."

"You encouraged Celia to come meet the team that climbed with her husband, but what's Jason doing here?"

"Playing some kind of game, but we don't know the rules yet. Zoey's the only one unaccounted for."

"She's here and was already lounging at the pond before I arrived. Since you're driving and we're off duty, I'm going for more grog. Blackbeard has to maintain his image."

Heading back to the patio, Ryker passed a man wearing a red bandana and a white shirt open to the waist, flaunting his six-pack. He strolled to the pond, spoke to Zoey a moment, and then stepped aside as she lifted a shimmering blue mermaid tail and fluke onto the stone wall, her ample breasts barely covered by a crop top.

A sharp blink to clear Ryker's vision. How in the hell did she get into the pond wearing that thing?

Six-pack kneeled and caressed her tail from the fluke to the curve of her hips. She twined fingers through the black curls on his forehead and leaned in for a kiss. Ryker closed his eyes a moment, imagining the touch of those sensuous lips.

Then a shout boomed like thunder, each word cracking like lightning. "Get your goddamn hands off my wife."

The threat shocked Ryker back to reality. His body coiled, every instinct screaming to step in. Daniel's aggression on the nature trail showed he had no anger filters. Ryker rocked from one foot to the other, poised to attack.

Sara's text buzzed. "Get a grip. Stay out of it. We came to observe, unseen."

Daniel reached the pond, grabbed the man's collar, and spun him around. "You prick, stay away from my wife."

"The name's Jack. And get your hands off me." He shoved Daniel stumbling backward. "Open your eyes. I'm not the only man she's seduced and won't be the last 'cuz Zoey's not getting enough pleasure at home."

Daniel's jaw twitched, fists whitening.

Throwing his arms in the air, Jack laughed. "A whore's not worth fighting over. I'm going for a drink."

His body shaking, Daniel stormed after him, grabbed a sword from the costume table, and raised it high.

"You'll never call anybody a whore again."

The music stopped. Heath quit dancing solo on the patio. Ryker's muscles tensed.

Chapter 17

Jack sprang out of the way. "What the hell! Who are you coming at me with a sword? Are you insane? A red-bearded pirate with a string of skulls hanging around his neck handed him a sword.

"Defend yourself, man. This guy's a lunatic."

Jack deflected Daniel's blow and did a sweeping strike back. Blocked, he thrust his blade again. Daniel dodged, spun around, and attacked with greater fury. Their blades locked. They stood face to face within inches, hurling verbal threats before striking again. Steel shrieked against steel, sparks snapping in the humid air. Gasps rippled through the crowd like a wave.

The clashing steel sent a tingling sensation along Sara's spine. How could this be happening?

"Ryker," she said through his earbud, "stop them. Now. But keep your badge out of it."

He ducked a swinging blade, grabbed Daniel from behind, and held him in an armlock.

His face bone white, Patrick marched over to them. "Cool down. Both of you. Too much grog. Jack, hand the sword over to Beck. Go join your friends."

His arm stiff, Jack pointed to the plywood prison. "Not till you lock him up."

Patrick surveyed the pirate audience. "Has the jury reached a verdict yet?"

Ashley quickly assumed her role. "Yes, your honor. We find Daniel guilty on all counts and sentence him to thirty minutes in jail."

The crowd applauded and whistled. Holding Daniel's hand, Patrick bowed as if the entire incident had been choreographed.

On the way to jail, Patrick stopped at the buffet table. "Put some food in your stomach to soak up the rum and enjoy the rest of the evening."

Ryker returned Daniel's sword to the table next to Sara, who was pretending an interest in paste-on tattoos. He chuckled. "Good luck with enjoying the evening, Daniel, when your wife's a mermaid and pirates are chugging beer."

"You should know. I saw you lingering around Zoey at the pond. But good work. Blackbeard's so convincing even Patrick didn't recognize you. I chose a skull tattoo and am done here."

To get their party back on track, Ashley placed a speaker outdoors for background music while Patrick handed out lyrics for sea shanties to all who were interested.

Palm facing down, Ryker shook his hand back and forth in a not-singing message to Sara. Heath took a copy and stood at the rear of a crowd. Celia remained close to the house, but Jason wasn't in sight.

Patrick began, "Mateys, close your eyes and imagine you've been at sea for endless months and are forlorn, heartsick."

"Disconsolate," Ryker whispered in Sara's earbud.

She moseyed toward the bar. "Lugubrious. I win."

"Ah, but tonight I'm the victor. Not one, but two luscious, steamy, sensual women came onto me."

"Yeah, I get it. They were hot. You didn't—?"

"No, but they certainly aroused my attention and buoyed my confidence in meeting women."

He'd monitored the voluptuous wench in a red tube top and watched her licking her lips while tracing an invisible line on Daniel's mouth and chin. It was a prison break, and he followed her into the woods. Pay back, Zoey.

Waving the lyrics, Patrick said, "Is everyone ready to sing? Nothing lifts our spirits and nurtures our souls more than music."

Sara mentally totaled the cost of the landscaping, fences, house, three expensive cars in the driveway, patio, pond, animal enclosures, feed, and veterinary bills. He'd made a fortune off instruments, but what was his destiny now?

Patrick, the shantyman leader, signaled Ashley to begin the first tune with fiddles, harmonicas, and flutes.

> Oh it's all for me grog me jolly, jolly, grog
> It's all for me rum and tobacco
> I've spent all me tin with the lassies drinking gin
> Oh across the stormy ocean I must wander

A chorus of eighteen drunken voices and Paco singing his own tune couldn't drown out the terrified screams rising from the goose pasture. All heads turned as Patrick's lyrics scattered and his frustrated yell echoed, "Some idiots must have ignored the Beware of Geese sign."

Ryker told Sara, "Celia just rushed into the house and pulled Jason out before Ashley got there."

"We'll unravel their game later. There's a more imminent danger now. I'll go. You stay here and keep tabs on them."

**

Sara followed Patrick, the singers, and a few stumbling drunks to the four-foot spiked fence allowing access by gate only. A couple in their thirties had blundered into dicey territory and provoked the geese guarding their turf. Cornered with no escape route other than the gate fifty yards away, the man was yelling and waving his arms, agitating the geese even further.

Ashley caught up to the gawking bystanders. "Patrick, do something. You're the only one who's ever been able to get even close to them. But don't go in wearing this thing. It would appear strange and alarming." Untying the gold-trimmed cuff and silver hook, she dropped them on the ground.

The geese hissed, defending their property against invaders whose skeleton costumes featured stark white skullcaps and faces painted white with blackened eyes, noses, and mouths.

"Get them away from us," yelled the woman.

"And do it now," said Ashley.

Patrick took a deep breath and entered tentatively, trying to calm them down with open hands. A brown goose honked a loud warning. When Patrick moved closer, a gray one charged and bit the curious, injured hand. Emboldened, the other two rushed him, wings spread and honking, bills open ready to bite.

Slowly stepping backward, Patrick made it to the gate and called for reinforcements.

"You don't need them," said Heath. He discarded his crutch and removed the artificial wooden leg. "I'm going in."

"What the hell do you think you're doing?" Patrick asked.

"Resolving your predicament."

Quietly mimicking a goose call, he strolled to the center, sat cross-legged, and folded his hands. Seeming perplexed, all four geese lowered their heads and stared at him without moving. The intruders inched around the perimeter and slipped out the gate. Sara closed it behind them.

The birds moved nearer to Heath as he clucked a softer and more soothing noise.

A guest standing beside Patrick asked, "Did you know he could do that?"

"You mean sound like a goose? No, but during club hikes, he imitates every bird song."

Heath's slow movements and gentle murmuring coaxed the geese to inch forward. No one left. Even the drunks fell quiet. The only sound was the soft huff of feathers as the birds pressed a little closer.

When the brown one allowed Heath to gently stroke its neck

and head, the other three sought attention too. He lifted them one at a time into his lap for snuggling and petting.

Standing in awe, a crowd of tipsy buccaneers brought their hands together in silent applause.

Sara told Ryker, "You should see Heath down here. "He's a bird whisperer and might cure your ornithophobia."

"I'm never going near Paco again."

"Just a suggestion."

Grog and music calling, the crowd meandered back to the patio. Sara was the last to leave Heath and four geese vying for his attention. While racing around the world, she and Michael had encountered dozens of unknown species and wished somebody like him had been there to educate them.

Michael wouldn't get out of her head and quit torturing her with memories, yet she couldn't resist opening WhatsApp for the fourth time in two days and found nothing. She blinked away a tear. The world clock showed Pakistan's current time was four a.m. the following day. If lying injured in a hospital bed, he'd be asleep, not texting. Unable to stand the uncertainty any longer, Sara found his original note and clicked Reply.

Laughter and clinking glasses meddled with her thoughts. Sara found an empty bench by Heath's sculpture. Paco kept his mouth shut long enough to answer. "Why haven't you written since Pakistan? If you truly care, let me know you're safe after K2." She paused. He had signed his, Love, Michael. She typed, Love, Sara, quickly deleted Love, and clicked Enter.

With an iced tea from the bar, she sought the elusive Ryker who was nowhere in sight. Damn, had he taken advantage of the free booze and swilled a few too many?

Sara squeezed past a pirate quartet hanging on each other's shoulders and singing the same drinking song again.

Sipping tea, she watched Celia standing guard at the sliding door. When Ashley started to enter with an empty hors d'oeuvres tray, Celia fell against the wall and slid to the ground, holding her chest and breathing hard, her face contorted in pain.

Ashley screamed, "Is there a doctor here?"

Someone answered, "Yes, but he's down at the pond."

"Go get him."

Beck brought a cool rag from the bar. Ashley wiped Celia's forehead and held her hand, reassuring her help was on the way.

Sara wasn't buying Celia's stellar performance. Hmm. No sign of her accomplice or Sara's partner. She sneaked into the house. "Ryker, you in there?"

"Yes, follow five yapping dogs locked in the bedroom and turn right at the end of the hall to Patrick's office. Jason has been rifling through desk drawers and file cabinets."

"What's he looking for?"

"We're about to find out."

When he and Sara entered, Ryker slammed his hands on the desk. "What are you doing in here?"

Jason's mouth jerked into a contemptuous smile. "None of your goddam business, Blackbeard."

"That's no way to speak to one of Reunion Heights' finest detectives," said Sara.

"Bullshit."

Ryker moved the fake pistols aside to pull his badge from the heavy waistcoat. "Detective Harris, Reunion Heights PD. Want to try again?"

Jason's face hardened, the muscles twitching with repressed fury. "I came for what's mine."

"And that is?" Sara asked.

"The second key to prize money." His hands trembling, he added, "I earned fair and square."

"But why here?"

"I've searched everywhere else. Patrick and Vance shared a tent on Everest, so I thought . . ."

"That Patrick stole it?" Sara asked.

"No, that Patrick hid the key for Vance as a precaution."

"His death the night you realized you couldn't possibly win is quite a coincidence," said Sara.

"Doesn't mean I killed him."

Ryker took Jason's arm and escorted him from the office. He tried wrestling free. "I know my rights. You can't arrest me."

"Oh, but I can for unlawfully going through Patrick's desk. I suggest you leave before he charges you with trespassing."

Jason nodded at Celia and exited the house. She slowed her breathing and told the doctor and Ashley, "I feel much better now. I came to meet my husband's team and celebrate his life with them, but it's too soon. I'm still grieving and just felt a little lightheaded."

"You're lying," Sara whispered, "and have now been added to the list of murder suspects along with Jason."

Ashley announced, "She's okay, everyone, just a little dizzy spell." She tried to enliven the party. "It's karaoke time. Who wants to sing? A karaoke machine and microphone await you by the metal sculpture. Here's a list of instrumental recordings."

"Singing in front of a crowd would be my worst nightmare," said Ryker.

Sara agreed. She filled a plate with fresh fruit and cheeses and moseyed to where Patrick was watching the cornhole games governed by a naked skeleton wearing only a hat.

She heard the man next to him ask, "Why aren't you over there singing with your wife?"

"I was the shantyman; Sara runs the karaoke machine."

As they continued chatting, Sara noticed Heath coming from the patio with his wooden leg and Paco yelling obscenities at the first person brave enough to take the mike.

"Either shut that bird up or get out of here," said Patrick.

"I brought the silver hook you left at the pasture. It's an apt costume. Well done."

Instead of a thank you, Patrick's reply stunned Sara. "You humiliated me with the geese in front of all the guests."

"Is your ego more important than their safety? You blew it. I stepped in to remedy a dangerous situation."

"And made me look pathetically incapable of tending to my own animals. Ashley and I go to great expense and time nurturing each of them. But you're a psycho about birds. You went ballistic enough over that pheasant incident to kill Vance."

Patrick's accusation hung in the air like a sonic boom. All conversations died; even Paco went silent, his head cocked.

Anger pulsed in every line of Heath's face. "You want to repeat that?"

Patrick stepped closer, his hook flashing under the string lights. "You heard me."

"You self-righteous bastard. Are you calling me a murderer? How about you losing your livelihood because of him and lying to the police?

"Heath, don't," said Ashley.

Sara started toward them, cutting through the stunned circle of guests. Every muscle screamed, *not here, not now.*

Before she reached them, Beck slid smoothly between the two men, a tray of glasses balanced on one hand, a genial smile on his face.

"Gentlemen," he said, calm as still water. "The night's too fine for fighting. How about another round instead?"

Patrick froze, torn between rage and embarrassment. Heath took a step back, fists trembling at his sides.

Uneasy laughter rippled through the crowd as Beck set the tray on a nearby table and returned to the bar. Music stuttered back to life.

Across the patio, Ryker murmured into Sara's earbud. "You see? Agatha Christie would've wrapped it up by now."

"We're not characters in a Christie novel. Ours doesn't end at the party."

Chapter 18

No longer on center stage, Celia and Jason wanted to escape. Ryker escorted them to the parking lot. "You're both a person of interest and advised not to leave town until we have concluded the investigation." As they got into their car, he asked, "Is that clearly understood? If not, I'll hunt you down, and you won't like the ending."

Back on the patio, he saw Sara standing near the bar. She spoke through his earbud. "I just overheard Heath and Patrick argue and accuse each other of being the murderer."

Ryker's insides rushed out of control. "You're joking. What instigated that?"

"Geese and a pheasant in Nepal. We need to grill all three on the spot while they're in finger-pointing mode. You get Zoey. I'll collect the other two. Meet us in the privacy of Patrick's living room."

"Tell Heath he can't bring Paco into the house."

"I'm sure Patrick and Ashley wouldn't mind."

"If that bird comes, you'll question on your own."

Thank god, he could finally get out of this frigging costume. Ryker shed the wig, beard, and mustache and asked Beck to keep them behind the bar. They were due back tomorrow by three.

His skin still itched from clinging to beard glue. He wanted nothing more than a shower and a quiet room but knew Sara was like a pit bull gripping his pant leg. He stopped at the restroom to clean his face and fix his hair before going to Zoey.

Floating on her back with her ample breasts above water and slowly swishing her tail, she had an entourage of suitors in the lake. He wandered closer. "Zoey, Sara and I need to speak to you, Heath, and Patrick in the living room."

"Back off, buddy," a man yelled. "The lady's busy."

"It's all right. I know who he is." She swam to the side and pulled herself onto the low wall.

The silky mermaid's tail seemed to ripple in the light. Ryker stammered, "Uhm, do I need to carry you?"

She replied with those titillating eyes, "Not if you help me get out of this suit."

His voice rose an octave. "I'm always ready to serve."

She held onto her shorts as he worked the tight tail down her legs and off her feet that were laced together.

"You have a gentle touch," she said.

He inhaled three quick breaths through his nose to begin Sara's breathing exercise. "I try. Shoes?"

"Behind the ship if you'll get them for me."

As they walked to the house, the cannon fired for the fifth time with a blast of light and loud boom. Ryker thought anyone clever enough to rig a cannon is capable of premeditated murder.

The air inside the house was thick with leftover rum and sweat. Glass doors muffled laughter from the patio. No one dared sit back; every breath seemed to wait for the next accusation.

Patrick, Heath, and Sara sat around a marble coffee table.

"Welcome," said Sara.

Zoey's lashes fluttered in a slow blink of appraisal. "You did something to your hair. So unbecoming. I hope not permanent."

"Why, thank you, Madam Mermaid."

Sara bent forward, arms resting on her thighs. "Patrick, why have you been lying to us about your hand?"

Avoiding eye contact, he flicked a cracker crumb from his

sleeve and straightened a ruffled cuff.

"I spoke to the surgeon who amputated your fingers."

A tremor shivered through his frame. "What happened to patient confidentiality?"

"He didn't state a name."

"Then it wasn't me."

"Frostbite on someone recently returned from Nepal?"

Tiny lines gathered at the bridge of Ryker's nose. "She doesn't believe in coincidences."

"When you told us Vance was dead, I wanted nothing that would implicate me."

Ryker glanced at Heath and Zoey. "You've both known all along that he was lying but never said a word."

They shied away. Then Heath nodded at Patrick to begin.

"It's a long story that started in Kathmandu. "We arrived at four p.m. to the chaos of horns blaring, incense curling from temple doorways, monkeys on the power lines."

Sara settled comfortably on the couch and folded her arms. "Go on. We have all night."

"We checked into our hotel in the Thamel tourist district. With an eleven-hour jet lag, the four of us ate in the dining room, but Vance left and didn't return to our room until midnight."

"We were supposed to fly to Lukla at ninety-three hundred feet the next morning," said Heath, "but he told us fog grounded all flights until the following one. We had a free day to explore on our own."

"That was fine by me," said Zoey. "I shopped till I dropped in this awesome, hip city."

"And she made us accompany her," Patrick grumbled.

"Married men are used to their wives dragging them from store to store," said Heath. "I refused and followed Vance instead to a Western Union office outside the Thamel. I saw him pick up a big envelope of cash."

"Was he aware of you?" Sara asked.

"No, I'm sure he wasn't. I also followed him to a store where he purchased five boxes of oxygen bottles and regulators to be delivered at the airport in the morning. No problem there."

Heath looked back at Patrick. "Your turn."

"Late afternoon, I returned to my room shared with Vance. While cleaning, the maid service found a poker chip and placed it on the desk."

Ryker mulled over the conversation about Vance being a compulsive gambler and receiving death threats. Jason accused him of playing for high stakes, and Jeffrey loaned one hundred grand to save his skin.

"You think he lost money the first night in town and wired for more?" Ryker asked.

"I'm certain he was low on cash," said Heath. "When we arrived at Lukla, he claimed the delay had reduced the number of available Sherpas. We'd be one short of our agreement. After dinner, I asked our sirdar about the idle men I'd noticed at the airport who seemed to want work."

"Your who?" Ryker asked.

Sara explained, "A sirdar's the head Sherpa over porters, the cook, etc. He knows the mountain and usually speaks English and can discuss logistics with the expedition leader."

"So, Heath, what did your sirdar say?"

"That he'd hired the number of Sherpas Vance requested and now had to let one go without the expected job. Working as a porter was the sole livelihood for this man's family with three kids. When I questioned yesterday's flight delays, he said there were none." Heath paused and drank from a canteen. Screwing the cap back on, he said, "I concluded this was a scheme for time to get enough money wired to finish the expedition."

"Why did the sirdar let Vance get away with not paying a porter he'd hired?"

"Confronting him, Pemba could lose his wages too. Vance never parted with money unless forced to. At the end when we all gave Pemba the customary tip, Vance handed him a note with his phone and address, saying it was far more valuable than rupees. If he came to the US, he could stay at Vance's house."

"In the meantime, said Patrick, "the other porters divided the load among themselves without extra pay. "It's only forty miles from Lukla to base camp but takes eight days from ninety-three hundred to seventeen hundred and sixty feet. We were already one behind."

"Pemba repeated *bistari, bistari*," said Zoey. Eyeing Ryker, she placed her right ankle on her left knee, tightening her shorts. "It means go slowly," she added drawing the word out. He tried keeping his eyes on Patrick, but they ventured back to the silken skin under his fingertips as he removed her tail.

"But Vance kept pushing to get there in six," she continued. "I had a constant headache and couldn't sleep."

"Nauseous too?" Sara asked.

She nodded.

"He wasn't giving you enough time to acclimatize. You had mild altitude sickness. How about the rest of you?"

"I was exhausted but otherwise okay," said Patrick.

"Me too," said Heath, "but Tanner developed a short fuse. We'd been passing these awe-inspiring walls in the middle of the trail. They were beautiful and constructed of sacred prayer stones engraved with Buddhist mantras. Vance thought it was amusing to scribble charcoal over the symbols and piss in several places on each wall as if marking his territory. That was it for Tanner. He blew up and slugged him in the face, knocking him flat on the ground with a bloody nose."

"Who are you to talk?' said Patrick. "Instead of using a fist, you went berserk over a pheasant in an obscene tirade filled with expletives. No wonder your parrot has such a foul mouth."

Ryker dragged his hand across his forehead as if to wipe the frustration. "You're arguing about a bird?"

Heath gripped the armchair. "Not just any bird. Danphe is

the most exquisite pheasant in the world."

"What's that got to do with Vance?" Sara asked.

"The first time I heard its song, Pemba explained the male is very shy and rarely seen. I quickly mimicked the call, and it worked. For half an hour, he seemed to follow me up the trail, his voice growing louder and closer with each reply. At our lodge for the night, I went outdoors onto the patio and waited patiently before calling to him again. Then moments later, there he was sitting across from me on a bare branch as if to say, *Here I am in full display of my resplendent glory for your eyes only.*"

Heath had been shifting from one hip to the other. Then his movements turned clipped, abrupt. He shoved the chair back hard enough to rattle the coffee cups and turned toward the door.

A shout ripped from his throat. "Sorry, but I can't do this anymore."

The room fell silent except for faint music from the patio and laughter fading to a dull murmur waning in the night air. The door shut behind Heath with a hollow click that sounded final.

Patrick leaned back against the cushion, his face hollowed by exhaustion, his hook glinting in the lamplight. Zoey lounged in a white linen chair like she owned the place, one leg draped over the other. The air shimmered faintly with her perfume and the suggestion that everything she touched was curated for effect.

The air between them thickened with things unsaid.

Sara felt the fine hairs on her arms lift. Whatever happened on that mountain hadn't stayed there. It was alive here, circling the room like thin air and unfinished guilt.

Chapter 19

Sara scanned the empty chair where Heath had been. Through the window, she saw him sitting on the patio, shoulders slumped, a silhouette under the torches. Paco perched motionless on his shoulder, both man and bird cloaked in silence.

She asked Patrick and Zoey what had been so disturbing that Heath couldn't talk about it.

After a long throaty sigh, Patrick began, "The lodge owner served chicken, potatoes, and carrots for supper. Pemba seemed uneasy, encouraging us to eat and go straight to bed. Tomorrow would be a seven-hour day of climbing an extremely steep hill. We had almost finished when Heath noticed the meat on Vance's plate differed from ours. He looked up at the owner, eager to clear the table."

Zoey said, "When questioned, the poor old man bowed and admitted Vance had ordered him to cook the danphe."

"Heath totally lost it," said Patrick. "It took both Tanner and me to restrain him physically. So, he struck with venom spewing from his mouth. Then going outside to cool off, he discovered danphe feathers dumped in the trash."

"Hmm, Vance didn't toss them all," said Sara. "He stashed a green crest and iridescent feathers between two bookcases in his home office. If you're done talking about birds, I'll find Heath and bring him back in."

She slipped outside. The air smelled of damp grass and the faint sweetness of spilled rum. "It's time to come back in," she said. "Patrick and Zoey aren't finished."

Stroking Paco's wings, he said, "Give me a minute. He hates goodbyes."

"Make it quick. We all have ghosts waiting."

Sara returned to the living room. "Heath's coming back. He needed to cool off."

Ryker stood at a window, watching their reflections instead of their faces. He gave a curt nod. "We all do."

Patrick sat forward on the couch, twisting his wedding ring. He didn't look up. "You think any of this helps? Digging into things better left on the mountain?"

"It has already followed you down," said Sara. "You can't bury what never froze."

Zoey's mouth curved faintly, not in a smile but something close to defiance. "Then I hope you brought a big enough shovel, Detective."

Heath entered and sat cross-legged on the couch. Sara said, "Patrick and Zoey told us about the danphe. It's inconceivable anyone would do that."

"I might have beaten him to death if Patrick and Tanner hadn't pulled me off."

"I understand," said Sara. She turned to Patrick. "It's time for the truth about what happened up there."

"It's a long, complicated story. I have guests outside. Can't we do this another time?"

"Ashley has everything under control. We want all three of you in here now."

Patrick rubbed his hands together as if trying to warm them as he reflected on the cold. "We'd spent five weeks climbing high and sleeping low to acclimatize. All the expeditions had finished rotations and were in base camp waiting for the window to open."

Ryker threw his arms in the air and dropped them in his lap.

"Seriously, a window on Everest?"

Sara pushed her palms forward in pause mode."

"Relax. Jet stream buffets the summit with hundred-mile-per-hour winds. Monsoon from India pushes it off. You have a three-to-seven-day window before it rains and snows."

Patrick said, "Expeditions were studying weather forecasts, but the models didn't agree."

"Same here," said Ryker. "Ours get it wrong half the time."

"Hundreds of climbers going up at once cause a traffic jam and bottlenecks," said Sara, "all for fifteen minutes of glory on a summit the size of a large table. Waiting in line for two to three hours, some have died from exhaustion, running out of oxygen, frostbite, or altitude sickness."

Patrick clasped his hands between his legs, eyes fixed on the floor. "Our troubles began with the prospect of waiting in line. Vance staked his credibility on having done six of the seven summits and on his ability to assess weather. Ignoring Pemba's warning to wait for a better forecast, we sneaked out in the dark, left Zoey at base camp, and went ahead of other teams."

Sara drew her knees to her chest. "I dread where this story is going."

"Not to a good place," said Patrick. "We did fewer rotations than other teams and weren't prepared for the thin air at twenty-three thousand feet in Camp Three. I crashed and felt pathetic compared to the Sherpas hauling our supplies and an arsenal of seven-pound oxygen bottles."

Heath, cross-legged on the couch, said quietly, "None of us had used oxygen before and didn't know what to expect. Pemba explained that at rest, a bottle lasts ten to twelve hours. Climbing, you cut that in half. The soft, steady hiss of our regulators was normal. A louder hiss meant a leak. Ignore it, you die."

Zoey looked at Ryker and Sara. "Remember that I got so sick at Camp Three, Sherpas had to haul me down to base camp. They zipped me into that plastic bag thing called a hyperbaric chamber. Claustrophobic nightmare. I was done."

"Be glad," said Patrick. "It only got worse. At a low flow rate, my oxygen lasted seven hours, not twelve. I needed a fresh bottle but couldn't get one. When an icy breeze chilled us on the way to Camp Four, Pemba said a storm was coming. We had to return to Camp Two. Vance argued we'd lose at least one day and be forced to wait in line with hundreds of other climbers. He demanded we move on to Camp Four, but Pemba warned wind and snow would prevent us from leaving for the summit that night."

Ryker asked, "Couldn't you just climb the next day after the storm?"

Sara answered before Patrick. "No, you start late at night to reach the summit at dawn. Most deaths occur on the descent. You want to go down in daylight."

Anger pulsed in every line of Heath's face. "Vance declared himself the expedition leader and Pemba the hired help. Patrick, Tanner, and I didn't know who to trust. We had just climbed up the steep ice from Camp Three and didn't relish going back to Camp Two. Vance was a known entity; Pemba, a mystery. We went with what we knew."

Patrick said, "By the time I staggered into Camp Four, my bottle was nearly empty in less than five hours. Heath and Tanner had the same issue with theirs. We were all using the same Poisk bottles, but Vance didn't have any problems. Was it operator error? Had we set flow rates incorrectly? Everyone hydrated and slept, intending to leave for the summit at ten p.m."

With a wistful smile, Sara said, "I remember that feeling with Michael, lying in our tent, thinking tomorrow we'd be on the roof of the world. I miss the excitement, the challenge, and the anticipation of achieving something great. My favorite quote is, 'Getting to the top is optional. Getting down is mandatory.'"

Ryker shifted, uneasy. "Sorry, but just sitting here listening to you people makes me want to have a beer. I've decided you're all certifiably deranged, including my partner."

"Everest does strange things to people," said Heath. "It's like staring into a mirror that only shows what you want to hide."

Patrick glared at him. "Or maybe just kills the unprepared."

Zoey smiled without warmth. "You two make it sound like a religion."

"No, it's more the power you choose, whether you come to conquer or to be seen," said Heath. "Power's a funny thing. The mountain strips it away until you look inside and discover who you really are."

With a scoffing laugh, Patrick asked, "And who are you?"

"To be determined."

Next, Patrick turned on Zoey. "I think you want to conquer and have power over that controlling husband of yours."

Her presence dimmed, as if fading.

"Wrong." Heath reached for her hand. "I think you desire the attention of that emotionally detached man more devoted to his work than to you. That's what the pool incident was about." He looked into her downcast eyes. "Am I right?"

Zoey nodded.

"Well," Ryker interrupted in a dry tone, "you all sound like a therapy group of adrenaline junkies."

Zoey's smile returned sharp and her armor back in place. "We prefer to think of ourselves as survivors."

"You don't survive on philosophy," said Patrick, "but on knots that hold."

"By seven p.m." said Heath, "gusts rattled the walls. Then at eight, the storm hit. Winds hammered our tents for nineteen sleepless hours. Vance's plan to reach the summit first backfired as other teams arrived the next afternoon."

Sara shook her head at the men. "Why'd you ignore Pemba? He lives there. Right?"

Patrick rubbed his forehead. "Vance thought he knew better. We took our chances."

"And lost, stranding yourselves in the death zone too long."

As if witnessing a horror movie, Ryker's jaw hung loose, unmoving. "Death zone?"

"Above twenty-six thousand feet, your body slowly begins to die. Try to stay less than twenty-four hours, forty-eight max."

"But they were using oxygen," said Ryker.

"Doesn't make it safe. Just buys time."

"We left at nine," said Patrick, "and reached the balcony rest stop to eat power bars, hydrate, and take in amazing views. But in only four hours, my gauge showed almost empty."

"So did Tanner's and mine," Heath added. "Thank god, the indomitable Sherpas lugged bottles up and cached them. Pemba had watched us struggling with each step and said we had to turn back. With the extra night in Camp Four and thirty minutes on the balcony, we'd been in the death zone for thirty-five hours. Six or seven more to the summit, fifteen minutes on top, and six to descend. The risk of pulmonary or cerebral edema was too great."

Sara wrinkled her nose. "And yet, there you went."

"Vance said after coming this far and with Everest in sight, he wasn't turning back. His life depended on that summit."

Sara closed her eyes and shook her head. "Those geese are brighter than you were. Hypoxic, brains not working, thinking you're gods."

Heath stretched his legs out. "We all connected new bottles at the balcony even though the gauges read only three-quarters. Vance said to just lower the flow and add a bottle to our packs."

"I left the balcony a few minutes sooner than Vance, Heath, and Tanner," said Patrick. "An eight-man team quickly clipped onto the fixed ropes behind me, separating us. The queue of a rope-linked chain of climbers inched slowly forward one by one. I'd been in line for two hours when the piercing hiss of my regulator grew louder. In a bottleneck after the South Summit, it died."

Patrick got up and walked to the window to check on Ashley

in charge of a karaoke singer doing Sweet Caroline, Paco joining in on the verses. Patrick glared at Heath over his shoulder.

Heath shrugged. "What can I say. He says what he hears."

"Finish your story," Sara demanded.

"Panicked, I grabbed the spare. Empty. I desperately gulped the thin air, my lungs starved, greedy for oxygen. Nauseous and dizzy, I stayed clipped on the rope. The speed of the queue was controlled by the slowest person ahead. On a narrow ridge of deep snow and boulders, I couldn't concentrate on what to do next. It became a confusing battle between body and mind, with my brain no longer speaking to my legs as if they belonged to someone else. No coordination, I stumbled and fell but don't remember anyone picking me up."

"I found you thirty minutes below on the descent," Heath said. "You'd unclipped from the rope and were teetering on the knife-edge of a cornice with a ten-thousand-foot drop. You'd taken the right glove off to caress Ashley's face and kept mumbling how much you loved her and would be home for supper tonight."

"Hallucinating?" said Ryker. "Lucky you didn't end up in a padded room."

"He's fine," said Sara. "Mountain madness fades away as the brain gets more oxygen."

Patrick looked at Heath. "I'm sorry for the unwarranted, harsh words earlier. My bruised ego over the geese usurped the better part of me. Without your spare bottle, I would've died." His left thumb wound the wedding ring. "I still have nightmares of not getting back home to Ashley."

Heath's voice softened. "We're all part of an interconnected existence, each dependent on the other. I needed help too. My hose froze, shutting off all the oxygen to my mask. Like you, I couldn't breathe. A stranger behind me, a Korean climber, punched the valve with a solid right hook and freed it."

The hand gripping Sara's stomach relaxed its fingers. "The

smallest acts decide who lives and who doesn't. The line between them gets awfully thin up there."

"What about Tanner?" she asked. "No one mentioned him."

"He had the most harrowing experience," said Heath. "His regulator froze. The pressure blew it out, shooting all his oxygen into the air like a giant plume. Certain he would die alone on the mountain, he was weeping for a widowed wife and fatherless children when Pemba reached him. Sharing his own mask, he got Tanner down safely. But he was never the same. Nobody knows where he disappeared."

"The timing's suspicious," said Sara. "Would Tanner have a motive for killing Vance?"

Heath leaned forward, secretive. "We all do. In Kathmandu, while Patrick was at the hospital, I did a little digging and found something I'll relate later. Neglected too long, Paco may start a rebellion."

Zoey closed her legs, voice brittle. "Maybe some things are better left unspoken."

Patrick looked up sharply. "Or left undone."

Silence stretched among them like a rope drawn too tight.

Sara's gaze moved from one to the next. Patrick sat rigid, twisting his wedding ring; Zoey's polished veneer cracked, eyes on the door; Heath unreadable. These weren't just witnesses to a death. They were fragments of a single, splintered truth.

Chapter 20

Saturday morning, Sara's alarm went off at six for her daily run, but she was too beat mentally and physically. Back by ten, she'd barely managed four hours of restless sleep. Voices in her head kept repeating Heath's admission that they all had a motive for killing Vance, Zoey's statement that some things were better left unspoken, Patrick's comment, *or left undone.* She'd promised McBride a suspect but might hand him a cabal. The word alone made her skin crawl. A cabal meant secrecy, shared guilt, and pacts made in darkness. If all four had blood on their hands, who struck first and who only watched?

Ding! She shot bolt upright. What was that? Ding! There it was again and coming from her phone. A notification. WhatsApp message from Michael.

Her throat dry, she clicked open. "My dearest, Sara. Sorry, I couldn't reply sooner. No internet on K2. I made the summit and had you with me all the way, but I missed snuggling and sharing our body warmth in the bags zipped together on freezing nights."

What did he want from her? Click Reply. "It's been more than a month since your first letter."

"I didn't know your current situation or if you'd ever speak to me again. I checked WhatsApp three times a day hoping for an answer. When none came, I feared I'd lost you forever."

"Then why write today?"

"I'm gambling on another chance."

A text from McBride popped up at the top. "I'll be out of here at ten. Bring Ozzie to the hospital ASAP."

"My boss just texted me," she wrote. "I have to go. Bye."

Thank goodness for an excuse to exit a conversation that left her tongue tied. She needed time to reflect on the words *snuggled* and *body warmth* that aroused sensations buried long ago.

Ozzie met her at the door, head tilted as though he sniffed a change in the air.

"No worries. I'm just a little off balance. Michael texted me. Your buddy is going home." After packing his food, bed, treats, and toys, she crouched and rubbed him from his ears to his tail. "Love you, Ozzie."

Ryker's sedan was already parked under a dripping oak, windshield glinting in early sun. He'd swigged enough grog for a nasty hangover and must've shaken it off faster than any sane liver could manage.

"The hospital corridor reeked of disinfectant and wilted flowers. Sara's boots squeaked across the linoleum while nurses wheeled a pale man past them on a gurney. On a leash, Ozzie led her to the room and barked to be lifted onto the bed. McBride's eyes watered as he hugged him.

"Your clerk will look after you as long as needed. I think she's got a crush on you."

A twinkle in his eye. "Bonnie has visited me every morning with berries, nuts, and whole wheat rolls."

"Good nutritious food. You're in loving hands." Sara pulled a paper from her pocket. "Here's the costume receipt. I dropped them off on the way over here."

McBride's eyes widened. "Christ, it had better be worth it."

"It was," said Ryker. "Deeply in debt, Vance cut corners and pushed the team too fast into the death zone." He opened an arm toward Sara. "She knows more about this shit than I do."

"Zoey had altitude sickness and washed out. The three men didn't have enough oxygen. Patrick removed his glove too long and lost parts of three fingers to frostbite. Heath was also sick. Tanner's bottle blew up. We haven't found him yet."

McBride's shoulders dropped. "I haven't heard any motives strong enough to justify an arrest."

"Vance killed and ate Nepal's national bird," Ryker added.

"You're telling me a Sherpa came here and took revenge?"

"No, just saying Heath's a bird whisperer and flipped out."

"He did some snooping in Kathmandu before they left," said Sara, "and claims to have discovered something."

"Like what?" asked McBride.

In a frustrated tone, she admitted he hadn't shared it yet.

Ryker raised his hand before McBride could speak. "I'm not done. Zoey's flirtation with men enrages her husband. Jealousy's a common motive for murder."

Sara gave him a sidelong look. "What are you implying?"

"Nothing tangible but many years as a cop taught me not to dismiss anything. I also caught Jason fishing around in Patrick's office for the key to a hefty sum of money he won in a climbing contest with Vance."

"He's my prime suspect," said Sara. "He only won because his competition's dead. He and Vance's wife are colluding."

McBride slapped the bed. "You two will give me another heart attack. Find this missing Tanner, question the bird lover, and see what Jason's up to."

"We'll get on it as soon as we take you home," said Sara.

"Leave now. Bonnie's coming at ten to drive me."

"Hah, I knew she had a crush. We're off to interrogate."

Sara asked Ryker to drive. Michael had caught her off guard with no chance to process his message. How will she feel seeing him again, or he her? Will he still be her soul mate, the man she fell passionately in love with, or had time altered who they are? The biggest question. Could she forgive the pain and give her heart freely, or had her emotional defenses made it impossible to ever love or be loved again?

"We're here," said Ryker. "You've been unusually quiet. Is everything okay?"

She rubbed her forehead and raked both hands through the sides of her hair. "Just tired. I couldn't sleep last and this case has sucked my brain dry, incapacitated."

He parked in Tanner's driveway. "You go in. The neighbor lady and her kids know and trust you."

"It shouldn't take long."

Ten minutes later, Sara got back into the car and reported, "Barbara still doesn't know where Tanner is. He calls his girls at random times but checks with his staff every Monday at ten."

Sara Googled the address. His office was on the eighth floor of the same building as her father's Financial Management on the seventh. She felt numb all over as the elevator passed his floor.

"Sure you're all right?" Ryker asked. "On our last visit here, those goons from the Renaissance case blackmailed you with threats to expose your father and send him to prison."

"It was a gut-wrenching Catch-22."

"You and your dad haven't spoken in six years. We made a deal. You'd reconcile with him and I with my daughter."

Sara leaned on the console, tilted her head, and looked up at him. "And how's that working out?"

"Better than for you, who's not even trying."

"Well, I got this. Tanner's receptionist agreed to let us in at nine-thirty to prep for tracing his call."

Next, they drove to Celia's as promised to return her ledger. In the backyard, she and Jason didn't appear to be engaged in a romantic tryst. He was pacing and yelling at her; she, waving both arms at him.

Sara and Ryker sauntered toward them. "Excuse us, Celia, we're returning your ledger."

Her smile looked painted on, too bright for the morning, too brittle for innocence. Sara had seen it before on women balancing fear and fury, unsure which mask to wear. Jason jutted his chin and shoved both hands in his pockets.

"There are a couple of things I'd like to go over with you in private," said Sara. "Perhaps Jason could give my partner a tour of your property."

Celia dismissed them with a backward wave of her hand and then asked Sara to join her at the picnic table.

Sara laid out two pages, side-by-side. One listed the dates Vance checked into the Havenwood Motel. The other showed a direct correlation to Celia's travel days.

"Were you aware of your husband spending time there?"

Celia squirmed in her seat. "I suspected something and lied about going out of town one night. I followed him to the motel and waited, hidden in the rear parking lot. When Vance opened the back door for a lone woman to enter, I took a picture and left."

"Did you confront him about it later?"

"No, the photo was my insurance to be claimed as needed."

"Too late now. Somebody already did."

Sara pointed to an empty space on Celia's calendar. "At the slideshow, Vance accounted for your absence as traveling for work. Your alibi was attendance at a friend's new gallery opening in Chicago." Leaning across the table toward her, Sara waited for a response. "Nothing to say? Shall I do an internet search for that night?"

Celia chewed a piece of dry skin on her lower lip. "That's unnecessary. There was no opening."

Sara straightened back up. "So where were you?"

"With Jason. He'd won their competition and came to me to ensure Vance had the second key for them to open the box."

Sara's mouth split in sheer amusement. "You didn't know where it was and still have no idea. Vance didn't confide in you."

"Jason and I will go to court with his death certificate."

"No judge will look at it until we've solved the murder."

Sara gathered the papers and called to Ryker that she was ready to leave. They took a leisurely walk back to the car, giving him a chance to clear his brain of a minor hangover in fresh air.

"If Jason ever gets his hands on the money, do you think he'll give Vance's half to Celia?" Ryker asked. "Or is he simply using her to find the key?"

"She thinks she's entitled to it. If they're cohorts, they timed the murder after the slideshow to divert guilt onto the expedition team. While we're busy investigating the members, Celia and Jason could find the key, take the money, and run."

Crowing, Ryker flapped his arms. "Only they ain't got it."

Sara laughed. "If your daughter could see you now." She finished watching his grin fade and then said, "Next, we need to rendezvous with your favorite suspect."

The morning sun had climbed high enough to bleach the world flat and colorless, as if the day itself were holding its breath. Sara buckled her seatbelt and felt the weight of Michael's message, her estranged father, and the tangled web of motives pressing against her chest. It was time to pull the next thread and see what truth Heath will finally set free.

Chapter 21

Ryker was flustered. They'd come to Heath's, and he didn't want to step inside any building housing Paco. "I don't speak the same mountain language as you two. I'll wait in the car."

Sara walked around to the driver's side, opened the door, and mussed his hair. "Now it looks like you nested with a bird."

Grinding his teeth, Ryker got out of the car. The earth-tone stucco house had no front doorbell. They waited for his camera to spot them.

"Welcome, super sleuths," came over the loudspeaker. "I'm in the workshop."

He met them at the entrance, holding a welding helmet and gloves. "I've begun a new sculpture, a Nepal danphe." His voice dimmed. "I hated Vance for what he did to that extraordinary bird but not enough to kill him if that's why you're here."

Ryker hung back with his arm outstretched, palm forward. "Please keep your parrot away from me."

"He doesn't bite."

"I can't stand wings flapping around my head."

Heath raised his arm parallel to the floor and called Paco. The bird landed and squawked, "Welcome, super sleuths."

Even Ryker cracked a smile." A talking menace."

Heath crossed the studio and climbed the ramp to his upper level. "Join me for coffee, tea, or papaya?"

Sara whispered to Ryker, "His hair's messier than yours. He must do his own."

"Who wants what?" Heath asked.

"Coffee's fine for us both," said Sara.

They carried cups onto the patio overlooking his garden, large metal sculptures, and the alligator lake. The parrot hopped onto a table beside Ryker. He tried shooing him away, but Paco rocked back and forth, chirping an unintelligible song.

"I don't like him. Get him down."

"He's trying to make friends," said Heath. He gave Ryker a handful of sunflower seeds. "Offer him one."

"He'll bite me."

"No, I swear by all my sculptures."

His fingers shaking, Ryker held it toward the dreaded beak. Paco quickly split the shell open and ate the seed. "More seed."

One corner of Ryker's mouth curled into a smile. "This is sort of fun as long as he keeps his wings tucked in. "Like a doctor, I swear to first do no harm."

Heath leaned back and clasped his hands behind his head. "I imagine you're here to learn what this ace gumshoe ferreted out in Kathmandu."

Sara shot a warning look at Ryker to hold his tongue. "Yes, anything you can tell us would be most helpful."

"Perfect." Heath bounced forward, hands free to gesture. "Something didn't smell right about our extra day in Kathmandu. While Patrick and Tanner shopped with their wives, I followed Vance to Western Union and to the store where he purchased the oxygen bottles. I didn't think too much of it at the time."

He rose and headed indoors. "More coffee, anyone?"

"Please," said Ryker.

Heath returned with a full pot and a plucked chicken. "My gator, George, will be coming up the walk soon for lunch." He sat down again. "After learning Vance lied about the flights being canceled and not enough Sherpas for hire, I didn't trust him. I returned to the bottle store after our climb and had no clue what I was looking for. They were all Poisk bottles exactly like we'd used until I stumbled upon one with an expiration date. Then I became a racoon scouring for fresh food. Examining forty bottles with my phone magnifier, I saw a pattern. Some had expiration dates, but most didn't."

Heath jumped up and went to the wooden railing. "Here he comes." He handed the chicken to Ryker. "You throw it to him."

Ryker shuddered. "Uhh, no."

"Toss it before he reaches the house and comes in."

"Oh, shit," Ryker muttered. He hurled the chicken with both hands. It smacked George square on the head. "Oops."

"No problem," said Heath, unfazed.

He resumed his seated position. "I took one of each to the owner and politely inquired about the difference. He stonewalled me, pretending not to speak English after having done so with another customer. My demeanor ruffles some folks. I decided to spook him further by standing tall right in his face, arms crossed, head tilted just slightly, and giving him a cold, reptilian stare until he confessed."

The veins in the back of Heath's hands bulged as his fingers locked in fists. "Newer bottles are labeled with expiration dates. The old, refilled ones aren't. Some trip leaders buy them to cut costs. I showed him Vance's photo and got a nod."

Heath's back stiffened from the waist to his shoulders. "We kept thinking it was our fault for not setting correct flows, and Vance had no issues since he'd used oxygen before."

"I doubt he had," said Sara. "Aconcagua in Argentina is the tallest mountain outside of the Himalayas and under twenty-three thousand feet. Most climbers don't need it there, at least not for an extended period."

"When did you tell Patrick and Tanner about the bottles?"

"Shortly after we got back."

"So all three of you have known for months that he screwed you for money and could have been responsible for your deaths."

"Yes, Vance needed the prize money and gambled with our lives to get it. I was lucky a Korean helped me, but Patrick lost the use of three fingers. Tanner returned with constant headaches, unable to sleep or think straight."

"Could be the lingering effects of mild cerebral edema," said Sara. "What about his wife?"

"Never got to know her. She stayed in Kathmandu while we climbed and hardly spoke to anyone on the way home."

"Thank you for leveling with us," said Ryker. "We'll report your findings to our boss." He stood and slowly backed away from Paco, hands in front of his head and palms facing outward.

"Quit with all the drama," Sara teased. "Admit you bonded with a bird."

"We all have our hang-ups."

And hers was Michael. She secretly checked her phone and saw no new messages. Had her abrupt end of the conversation turned him off? If so, there was too much past to overcome. She couldn't deal with it any better than Ryker could a bird flapping in his face.

When they arrived at McBride's, he was sitting on the couch in a terrycloth robe, watching TV and munching hot-air popcorn. He offered them some. "It's supposed to be good fiber."

"Thanks, but I filled up on sunflower seeds," said Ryker.

McBride muted the switch. "What did you get for me?"

Ryker winked at Sara. "A plethora of motives."

"Five, to be more precise," she added. "Jason and Celia are brazenly seeking the second key to a safe containing over a two-hundred-grand prize, which he won only because his opponent ended up dead in a freezer."

Sara waited for Ryker to chime in, but he was busy texting. "They're suspects one and two. Three, four, and five are climbers and have the same motive. Vance gave them defective bottles that almost cost their lives."

"Did one kill him or all three working together?"

"We have no verifiable proof on a single member. We're set to trace a call and locate Tanner Monay morning."

"Then take Sunday off and report back afterward."

Ryker's fingers were still tapping on the phone as they left the house." Are you texting your daughter?" Sara asked.

His mouth spread into a grin. "No, with a gorgeous woman on the dating site. We're meeting for dinner tomorrow."

"Be wary. Things aren't always what they seem."

"You forget. I read people."

"But your desire for a woman may override that."

"And yours for ghosts," he shot back.

Sara's phone buzzed. A sharp inhale. Michael calling?

No, McBride. "A hysterical woman named Celia Miller just called me. A voicemail message from a man with a foreign accent said he was at the bus station and would be at her house by noon.

"Name? Accent?"

"She doesn't know but feels certain it's someone's coming to collect Vance's gambling debts and will kill her if she doesn't pay."

"Assign a guard to her house."

"Budget's shot. You know accents. Go there and identify the caller."

"How? Stand in the middle of the bus station and yell, 'This is the police. Will the man who left a voicemail for Celia Miller please stand up?'"

Chapter 22

The downtown bus sat beside a homeless shelter that opened only at night. The air reeked of diesel, sweat, and fast food. About sixty people were waiting: teens slumped over phones, families sprawled across benches, businessmen snatching sleep. Not one face said *hired killer*. Sara made a slow sweep down each aisle, cataloging posture, listening for an accent that might have rattled Celia. Skin tones ranged from pale to coffee to bronze, the mix of a country in motion: migrant workers and tourists. Any one of them could have left that voicemail. If she stood in the middle of the room and shouted, "Who called Celia Miller?", half might not have understood the words.

She'd search by eliminating families, women, six teenagers, the elderly man in a wheelchair, a young athlete on crutches. That left five men who might speak with an accent. Four shared the facial structure and hair color of those from Latin America. That left only a man with thick, dark hair and yellow-brownish skin, his eyes closed, lips moving in a silent rhythm as if chanting. The Mongoloid cheeks gave him a distinctive Asian appearance. She paused. Unaware of Vance's death, a Sherpa had phoned his widow.

Sara bowed slightly, pressing her palms together, fingertips upright, thumbs close to her chest. "Namaste."

He opened his eyes and returned the gesture. "Namaste."

"Have you come to see Vance Miller?"

"I worked as his sirdar last spring. He invited me to stay at his home if I ever came to America."

Sara smiled. "And here you are. Welcome, Pemba."

"You know my name?"

"I've spoken with everyone you helped on Everest. But I'm sorry to tell you Vance died a week ago. His widow lives alone and is in mourning. My home is open to you."

She stepped back to make room as his body unfolded in sections. "I am honored to meet you."

Pemba shouldered a gray backpack and rolled a suitcase to her car. "Visitors told me many stories about beautiful America. I have always wanted to see it. I saved for three years. Patrick, Heath, Zoey, and Tanner were generous with tips. There is no work during the monsoon season. I flew to Los Angeles in June and have taken a journey by bus all the way across your country."

Sara hoped her fellow Americans had been as gracious to him as Sherpas had been to her and Michael. She broached the subject of Vance carefully. "You didn't mention Vance's tip."

"He said staying in his house was more valuable."

She doubted that miser ever imagined Pemba would come.

"I texted him three weeks ago that I want to come and return home before the tourist season begins in mid-September. I texted twice again this week and called today."

"His wife heard your voicemail, misinterpreted it, and was afraid of a strange man's voice. She called my boss, the chief of police. He asked me to pick you up."

Pemba's face went blank. "Then who are you, and why are police involved?"

"It's hard saying this, but last Sunday someone murdered Vance. I'm Detective Sara Lansing. My partner, Ryker, and I are in charge of the case. I spent three months in Nepal six years ago but didn't make the summit. We can talk of that later. Right now, you must be hungry. What would you like for lunch?"

"I love American cheeseburgers more than anything I have ever tasted. I wish to eat as many as possible before leaving."

Sara concealed a smile. "Cheeseburgers it is."

She took him to a more upscale restaurant than the fast-food places he could afford. He asked for water instead of the cola she suspected he also liked. "Please order anything you want. My boss is paying."

While waiting for the food, Sara said, "Patrick, Heath, and Zoey told us disturbing stories about what occurred on Everest."

Pemba stared at the cola glass, rotating it between his hands. "I worked on Everest for ten years and could feel when a storm was coming. I told Vance we must turn back. Heavy wind and snow would stop the summit attempt that night. Remaining in the Death Zone an extra twenty-four hours risked all their lives."

Sara ordered a salad with the dressing on the side. When his double-decker cheeseburger arrived, she chuckled at the sight of him trying to fit his mouth around it.

"But Vance wouldn't listen," she said.

Pemba swallowed and shook his head. "I was helpless to stop him. My soul has been crying for the men. They could have died on the mountain."

"Nobody blames you for what happened," Sara said softly. "Heath just told us a deadly secret he discovered in Kathmandu after the climb. To cut costs, Vance had purchased used, faulty bottles for the team and kept new ones for himself."

Revulsion spread across Pemba's face as he set the burger down. "Is everyone okay?"

"All but Vance and we're trying to find out who killed him. You were there; you saw them all. Do you believe any of the climbers is capable of murder?"

Pemba pressed the palms of his hands together, the thumbs resting against his chest. "The first of five rules that Buddhists live by is not to injure or kill any living being, including animals. Harmful acts create obstacles on the path to spiritual freedom. I cannot put myself in the mind of someone who would murder."

"That's hard for me too. Let's finish and go home."

Sara rarely ate anything sweet, but the one dessert she could not resist was carrot cake. She bought two slices for later. Her second bedroom doubled as an office; its small loveseat would suit him fine. Like most Sherpa men, he was about five-foot-four and solidly built, no fat anywhere. She'd seen men like him carry more than their body weight across swaying suspension bridges and up ladders on a steep ice wall.

Once he'd unpacked and appeared comfortable, she served carrot cake and green tea in the living room. "It's not as flavorful as your Tibetan salt tea, but yak butter's in short supply here."

He smiled. "I've grown used to American tea and coffee."

"Would you like to see the team members?"

In a somber voice, he said, "In truth, I came to see how they are doing." He looked up at Sara. "Patrick's hand? When I saw early signs of frostbite, I got him down to the emergency medical tent in base camp as quickly as I could. They warmed it slowly but said he needed to go to the hospital in Kathmandu. I helped him into a helicopter but heard nothing more."

"Patrick said the doctor here delayed amputation, hoping some tissue would heal in time." Sara shifted to face him fully. With downward folds along her mouth, she said, "He still lost parts of three fingers. It limits what he can do now.

"This saddens me," Pemba said quietly. "The fourth rule is to refrain from false speech or deception. The expedition began on a lie." Pemba squared his shoulders and straightened. "The third rule is to refrain from sexual misconduct, lustful looks, or adultery. Many nights in base camp, I saw Vance enter Zoey's tent after everyone had gone to bed and not leave until dawn."

An explosive breath choked Sara. This backed speculation that Zoey was the mystery woman at the Havenwood Motel. Her husband's unbridled fury at the pirate party vaulted him to the top of the suspect list right below Jason.

"Thank you for telling me," she said. "More tea?"

"Yes, and with sugar if you have it."

Rarely using sweeteners, she had to dig through the pantry to find an old bag. She set both cups on the coffee table and curled up on the couch, hugging her knees to her chest. "I haven't met Tanner. He and his wife left their house before six the morning after the murder."

"Where did they go?"

"Nobody knows," she said in a whisper as if revealing a secret. "It's a mystery. He calls his office every Monday. We'll trace the call tomorrow."

A faint smile crossed Pemba's lips. "Tanner and I often spoke. He had many questions about Buddhism. While he was on the mountain, his wife went to the Kopan Monastery that sits on a hill above Kathmandu. She took meditation classes and a seven-day retreat."

"Were the others aware of this?"

"I don't think so. He's a very private man and asked me not to share our conversations."

"We heard that very private man lost control and slugged Vance in the face for urinating on prayer walls."

Pemba closed his eyes and slowly rocked his head side to side. "We believe every action, good or bad, creates karma that affects this life and the next one. Careless acts of disrespecting the mountain can bring misfortune."

"Like frostbite and mountain sickness."

"Vance dishonored our beliefs by disrupting the puja prayer given before beginning a climb. He refused to remove his shoes when entering a temple and made burping noises while monks chanted the teachings of Buddha. He called prayer flags childish superstitions but then stole one to take home."

"The man had no moral ethics," said Sara. "Did he also take thangkas home?"

Pemba leaned forward to stir the sugar in his tea. "No, but

Tanner did. He bought two very delicate, expensive ones painted on silk. Vance was broke and borrowed from Heath, who seemed the least likely to have money."

"Why least likely?"

"His gloves didn't match, and he wore funny hats. One had a propeller on top; another had a duck bill with streaked purple hair. But he connected with porters even though they spoke different languages. He tried to get up off the ground with one of their loads on his back and fell over. When they helped him up, he staggered, waving his arms like a drunk and made them break out laughing after a tiring day. He'd brought five yo-yos and taught them how to do the sleeper and round the world. They practiced until the strings tangled and their delight spilled across base camp."

"He's one of a kind," said Sara.

"And the smartest. He asked me how much porters earned. When I told him, his face turned red, and he ground his teeth so tight the veins in his neck stood out. He went after Vance that night and hauled him to a private spot. He jabbed him hard in the chest and accused him of charging climbers double and keeping the rest for himself. Heath told him to pay them now or the expedition was over, and he wouldn't get his seventh summit."

Sara felt a chill. "I didn't think he had that kind of anger."

"We all saw him blow up when Vance ate the bird."

Sara went to reheat her tea in the microwave and absorb the news. No one had mentioned it, not even Heath. Returning to the living room, she asked, on "Did Vance pay?"

"He swore he had no money."

"And was telling the truth. He went to Western Union our first day in Kathmandu."

His hands folded in his lap, Pemba settled against the back cushion. "Heath must be rich. He paid the porters himself and tipped them and me."

"And just let Vance off?"

"No. Heath told him he would cover the costs only if he promised to repay as soon as they arrived in the US."

A nervous tingle crawled over Sara's skin as her gut said Vance reneged, moving Heath higher on a crowded suspect list. She thanked Pemba for confiding in her and explained the basics of the house: washer, dryer, TV remote, and garage keypad to come and go at leisure. I'll be gone a couple of hours tomorrow tracing Tanner's call."

"Do you think he killed Vance?" Pemba asked.

"He raised suspicion, leaving at six a.m. the morning after the murder and not telling anyone where he was going.

Chapter 23

Saturday night, Ryker dozed off in front of the TV and woke in a nervous sweat from a nightmare where he bombed his first online date. To embellish his profile, he'd claimed he goes on nature hikes and plays pickleball. He could bluff his way through a hike, but not the game. He swung his legs off the bed, feet flat on the cold linoleum. Shoes. Real shoes, non-slip soles. And for clothing, he needed something vaguely athletic. He hit the mall before closing with a detective's focus and the desperation of a man who feared failing.

Back in the motel, he lined up his new gear on the bedsheet like evidence in a case file and set the alarm for 6:30 a.m. Able to bend the will of male bullies, he feared arriving late and faltering in the face of three women.

At six sharp, a thud on the window jolted him out of bed. Instinctively, he grabbed his gun, inched to the glass, and peered out. A dead cardinal lay on the third-floor walkway. "You stupid birds," he muttered, pulse still racing.

Too wired to go back to sleep, he flipped on the news and watched an anchor lament police failure to solve a second murder in less than a month. "Give us a break," he muttered. "We have lives too. It's Sunday morning."

By the time he reached the courts, the sun was glaring off the asphalt. The ladies were on court five, their laughter echoing through the chain-link fence. He chose a paddle from the lost-and-found box and waited by the bleachers like a nervous recruit before inspection.

"Look who's here," said Judy. "He ditched the Oxfords."

"And wore better clothes," said Margie. "Our detective has come to play."

Ryker looked at each lady in turn. "You offered to teach me. I need to learn how today."

Roxie giggled. "He wants to become a pro in one lesson."

"No, I just want to hit a ball without falling flat on my face and disgracing myself."

Judy took his paddle and dropped it in the fourth slot with theirs. Waiting on the bleachers, Ryker felt his pulse climbing.

"Courts!"

"We're next," said Judy. "I'll be your partner."

Ryker's breathing became panic gasps as he stepped behind a line seven feet from the net called the kitchen.

"We dink to warm up," said Judy. "Let the ball bounce and then lightly tap it back into their kitchen."

He managed five dinks in a row without hitting the ball into the net. Not so bad until they moved to groundstrokes, where he had to drive the ball from his back line to theirs. His body was under siege. The first six shots hit the net or flew onto another court. Ball number seven, though, landed squarely in front of Roxie, and she had the nerve to drive it low right back at him. White-knuckling the paddle, he smacked it so hard neither she nor Margie could return it. He did a little victory dance, grinning like a schoolboy who'd just pulled off the impossible. But after an hour, sweat dripped from his chin and plastered his shirt. His calves were on fire. He'd made one great hit that felt good. Truth was he'd never be a great player, but Dulce might approve of him trying something other than work. They could build from there.

Tonight, he'd play Casanova, another awkward role. Not in a relationship since his wife, his fingers trembled trying to lace the Oxfords. He'd met his wife, Lily, by serendipity and was wary of this computer stranger. Holding every shirt up to his chin in the mirror, he chose the blue one and trimmed his beard fuller on the chin to emphasize a jawline that once drew compliments.

Strike one. Lottie arrived twenty-five minutes late with no excuse and no apology. Strike two. She looked ten years older than her profile, had a brown stain on her blouse, and blabbed nonstop about herself with food in her mouth. Strike three. She was too blotto to drive, so he made sure she reached her front door safely—another failed match in a long day.

**

Sunday, the misty rays of dawn stole through the blinds, slid across the floor, and spilled over Sara listening to mockingbirds outside her window. Nature had always been her most constant companion, and she'd shared it with Michael for seven years, racing in faraway places experienced by few. His leaving slashed a deep wound she bandaged with work until a hard scab formed. But his pulling it off now would start the bleeding again. And she hated the sight of blood. She told herself to quit reminiscing. Get back to work and find Tanner.

Curious about locating him from a single phone call, Pemba went with Sara to Tanner's office. "We're thirty minutes early," she said. "My partner better be . . . " Her words stuttered to a halt.

Ryker swaggered in, wearing court shoes, navy shorts, and a blue T-shirt reeking of sweat.

"Did you wake up in a Kafka metamorphosis?"

"I am not a cockroach," he said, brushing damp hair off his forehead. "I've been trying to play pickleball"

Sara's laughter quotient doubled. Miracles do happen, but a giant bug would not have surprised her more than seeing his bare legs for the first time. And they were decent looking, muscular calves, not too hairy. "What on earth have you been up to?"

"Getting ready for my first online date tonight. I said I play pickleball. You told me not to lie."

144

Sara just shook her head.

"What is this meta word you are using?" Pemba asked.

"Sorry, I had to tease him. It means a complete change. My partner usually wears very expensive shoes, long pants, and long-sleeved shirts. Kafka wrote a story about a man who wakes up one morning changed into a giant bug."

A bewildered look crossed Pemba's face. He retreated to the IT table, perhaps in search of something that made more sense.

"Who is that?" Ryker asked, still glistening with sweat.

"Pemba."

His forehead scrunched, solving an unexpected riddle. "*The* Pemba from Everest?

"Yep, showed up at the bus station yesterday and is staying with me. He divulged some dirty little secrets."

"You sharing or planning to gloat?"

"The seductress invited Vance to her tent in base camp."

"That's gossip."

"That's fact. Pemba saw him enter her tent in the dark and exit before sunrise."

Ryker gave a low whistle. "Can't say I blame him. Zoey's not like other women. She's a dark chocolate you want to wrap up in your pocket and keep forever. For her, I bet Heath would wear matching socks."

"He's not the wacky character we presumed."

The IT tech hushed everyone. "He'll be on speaker phone. It will only take seconds to triangulate which cell towers were pinged and get his position."

Looking at Sara, Ryker mouthed *Really? Zoey and Vance?*

She raised and lowered her head in a definitive nod.

A ringing phone captured everyone's breath and held it. As Tanner's secretary took updates, the IT tech drew a circle on a table map and pointed to a town four hours away.

When the call ended, Sara asked his secretary, "What does he drive?"

"A 2022 blue Mercedes-Benz, I think."

"License number?"

"All I know is there's a black bear on the bottom."

"Thanks, that's perfect."

As they walked to Ryker's car, he stepped beside her and lowered his voice, "McBride know Pemba's here?"

"Of course, I had to report back to him. He sent me to the bus station to pick him up."

"But you didn't bother to tell your partner?"

"I knew I'd see you today."

"So what's the second dirty little secret?"

"Ask him yourself. The Sherpa's going with us."

**

Once again, the New York cop felt like an odd man out. During the Renaissance case, Sara had moved easily among the rennie nomads, reading their quirks and secrets while he stood outside their circle. Now she glided through the climbers' world with the same fluency. Their words; crevasses, crampons, glaciers, death zone, were a foreign language.

"He opened the front passenger door for Pemba, leaving Sara to sit in the back. "Welcome to America. How long have you been here?"

"More than three months. There is no work for most of us from June to mid-September. Monsoon rains keep tourists away. Canceled flights, floods, washed-out bridges and roads, muddy trails, and leeches."

"It must be a hard time for you."

"Yes, and in winter also. It's too cold for most foreigners."

Ryker frowned. "How do you feed a family on six months' income?"

"We work very hard in the spring and fall and don't see our families much." A sly curve tugged at his cheek. "But soon I will have one."

He opened a photo on his phone and passed it back to Sara.

"When I get home, I will marry this beautiful girl. My parents' marriage was arranged. We are young and don't want that now."

Sara studied the screen. "Her smile lights the photo with a sweetness that caught my breath. She's lovely, and I'm excited to see young love beginning to build a life together. Cherish what you have and don't lose the one closest to you, as I did. Is she also a Sherpa?"

"Yes, and Shanti's not only beautiful but smart. She went to school two years in Kathmandu and speaks good English."

"So do you."

"A sirdar must know words in many languages, but English is most important. We study it in elementary school."

Ryker risked a look at the photo. "She's not beautiful. She's gorgeous. You're a very lucky man."

A hot flush billowed in his cheeks. "I know and love her so."

"Where were you born?" Ryker asked.

"In Namche Bazaar. It's my tribe's biggest village."

Tribe. Sherpa meant tribe, not porter. Ryker felt foolish for not knowing.

Pemba must have sensed Ryker's discomfort and continued kindly. "All expeditions stop in Namche for two days to rest and get used to breathing thinner air. Her father owns a good lodge there. He is growing old and wants Shanti and me to take care of it for him."

"Patrick, Heath, and Zoey will be happy to see you," Ryker said.

"And I will them. Their climb had many difficulties. I was worried about them. They are one reason I came to America."

"We'll get everybody together tonight or tomorrow," said Sara. "Before then, Ryker should hear what happened in Nepal."

As Pemba repeated all he'd told her, the words were like cut glass. Ryker's jaw slackened. He caught Sara's eye in the mirror. Her small nod confirmed all.

Silence settled over the car. The road narrowed, winding

through a cluster of small houses and shops in a town of three thousand souls. Tanner could have called from anywhere.

Riding quietly staring out the window, Pemba turned in his seat, meeting their eyes with quiet certainty.

"I know why Tanner is here. And I will find him.

Ryker's hands tightened on the wheel. The car rolled on, but the air had changed.

Chapter 24

Stuck in the back, Sara grabbed the front seat and leaned closer to Pemba. "Wait. Did I hear you right? You know where to find Tanner?"

"He'll be gone at least thirty days?"

"Yes . . . and?"

"His wife went on a seven-day Buddhist retreat at the Kopan Monastery and could now be on a thirty-day one."

Ryker snorted. "Monastery, Buddhist retreat. None of that's in my realm. I'll drive. You two look."

He parked on Main Street. "Go ahead. I'll wait here."

"The hell you will." Sara opened the door. "You can ask questions as well as I can. Get out."

Pemba went one direction; Sara and Ryker, the other. They ducked into every store, restaurant, barber shop, and gas station, pointing to Tanner in a team picture and asking if anyone there had ever seen this man in town.

No one had until the manager of a health food store, forty minutes later. "He came in two hours ago with a list of vegetarian items, and said he'll be back every Monday with a similar one."

"Which way did he go?" Sara asked.

"I was too busy with another customer to notice."

"Know where he's staying?"

"No idea. We're a small town but serve hundreds of homes

and motels within fifty miles."

Ryker shook his hair out. "Fifty square miles and a no-show till next Monday? We can't hang around here for a week. I'm going back to the car."

Pemba came racing down the block, an irresistible smile. "I know where he is."

One brow raised. "How'd you find him?"

"I asked locals for a small cabin in a private, natural setting."

"And you got one?"

"Yes, put this area in your Google Maps and let's go."

Thirty minutes later, they traded the asphalt for a winding, gravel road that snaked through a pine forest, the sound of their tires crunching on gravel, and passed cabins tucked away among the trees. Most structures appeared derelict, weeds pushing up through porch cracks, missing roof shingles and broken stairs.

Pemba lowered his window and pointed excitedly. "There's a blue car parked near that old cabin."

Ryker screeched to a stop. "I'll check the plate," said Sara. She jumped out and ran toward the car. Sudden movement twenty feet ahead. Tanner had spotted her, turned, and fled deeper into the woods.

"Tanner! Stop. Police," she yelled, picking up speed.

After a quick look back, Tanner sprinted faster, dodging low branches, kicking up sand, leaping over a pile of rotten wood.

"We only want to talk."

Pine needles and grasses crackled underfoot as Sara ran over patches of exposed roots on uneven ground. The adrenaline of her racing days kicking in, she warned him to stop one last time.

He didn't. She lunged, tackled him from behind, drove him into the dirt, and saddled him until Ryker got there.

Pulling Tanner up, he laughed under his breath. "Idiot, you should've stopped the first time she shouted. Now we've got a problem."

One on each side, they escorted him from the woods.

"Why'd you run?" she asked.

"Saw you coming. Didn't know who you were."

"I yelled, stop, police."

"No police car, no uniform. You could have been anybody."

"Who are you afraid of hiding out here?" Sara asked.

Tanner stiffened at the question. "Nobody, and I don't have to answer to you."

Ryker's jaw locked so hard it looked ready to crack. "We can talk here or at the Reunion Heights station."

"On what grounds?"

"The murder of Vance Miller."

"Good riddance, but I didn't do it," he said with no alteration in expression or attitude.

They'd reached Ryker's car. Tanner jerked free. "I'm done."

"Not until you answer a few questions," said Ryker. "Where were you the afternoon and evening after Vance's slideshow?"

"At home with my wife preparing for my next job. I'm an architect and work on site designing homes that incorporate a natural landscape."

Ryker surveyed the area. "Then what are you doing here?"

"Just taking a break to go hiking in the woods."

"And where's your wife?" Sara asked.

"She was too tired this morning." Tanner turned and headed for his car. "I have to get back to work."

Ryker caught him by the arm. "We're not done."

"Well, I am." He swung around and clipped Ryker in the mouth."

Ryker raised a fist, but Pemba's quiet voice cut heat from the air. "Peace."

In all the confusion, Sara hadn't noticed his absence and bowed to his calm presence.

He stepped from the cabin porch. "I've been sitting quietly beside a gracious woman in deep meditation. We did not speak, but I felt great sorrow surrounding her."

Seeing Pemba, Tanner buckled as if his mental scaffolding had given way. "Namaste. How have you come to me?"

"When I heard you were lost, I knew where to look."

"Sara and I are here because your skipping town at six a.m. the morning after Vance's murder set off an alarm that's louder now. Why's your wife out here alone in a shack?

Tanner fidgeted with his hands. "She unplugged from the outside world for a silent retreat."

Ryker huffed. "And what does that mean?"

"Monks in Kathmandu taught her that undisturbed by world activity, the mind could turn inward and develop the positive qualities within herself. And she was doing well after struggling for years with her father's sexual abuse."

Back rigid and eyes to the ground, Tanner paced in front of the cabin. "I'd been gone several days working on a difficult design. She came home, found Vance rolling up our beautiful silk thangkas, and rushed to phone the police. He caught her arm and killed the call. With pent-up fury from the time she was eight, she kneed him hard in the groin."

Tanner's nostrils flared as his hand curled into a fist. "He called her an obscene name, knocked her to the floor, and raped her. It brought back all the horror of her childhood and regressed her to those moments. That afternoon, Vance stole my wife from me and their mother from our children."

Tanner folded his arms tight as if they were the only thing holding him together.

"Why here? Why this cabin?" Ryker asked.

"For months, she's been seeking forgiveness to free herself from anger and resentment to move forward. Buddha says that holding on to anger is like grasping a hot coal with the intent of throwing it at someone else; you are the one who gets burned. It has been a hard lesson to learn. "This long retreat is my only shot at pulling her out of the darkness that has taken hold of her."

"A darkness precipitated by a man now dead," said Ryker.

"We get all that," said Sara. "But what are you doing here?"

"Sunday night, she places a list for the following week in a sheltered place under some boulders. It may be toiletries, food, water, medications, toilet paper. I pick it up, fill it by afternoon, and leave everything by the same rock."

"You never stay the night?" Ryker asked.

"No, this is her spiritual journey. She won't see anyone for a month, but I'll remain nearby in case of an emergency."

"The timing of your departure remains in question. Your neighbor told us you set the date and time prematurely."

"I wanted to be there to support my teammates at Vance's slideshow. Can we finish this discussion somewhere else?"

"Yes, at the Reunion Heights station for further questioning and for striking a police officer," said Ryker.

"I won't leave. Somebody has to watch."

"No, you *will* go, and someone from the local station can be on call. Go bring your car around."

"I'll ride with Tanner, giving you time alone with Pemba," said Sara. "Did you notice how Tanner never blinked when we said Vance was murdered. It wasn't public when he left at six."

"If somebody raped my wife, I'd kill him," Ryker muttered.

"But his performance was sharp, pulling all the right strings. Tanner's as clever as a crow laying walnuts in the street for traffic to crack its shells."

Ryker gave a quiet applause. "I would have gone with smart as a fox."

Tanner pulled up next to Ryker's car. Before Sara got in, Ryker whispered, "Check the hands. See if they burned holding hot coals or if he threw them."

Chapter 25

Sara climbed into Tanner's blue Mercedes with a dashboard like an airplane cockpit. "Business must be good."

"I have a select clientele."

"Who paid you enough for a lawyer at the court hearing."

"What court hearing?"

A crease puckered on Sara's forehead. "For the rape charges filed against Vance."

"There was no trial. We didn't report it."

Sara threw her head back, mouth agape. "Why not?"

"A hearing requires testimony. Karamia wouldn't survive." Tanner slowed and stopped for three white-tailed deer to cross. "And our girls would be as helpless as these deer in headlights."

"Wait, pieces are missing from this puzzle."

Tanner's chest sank. "Vance and I shared a tent. He'd sneak out to Zoey's and not return until dawn. When I learned how he'd conned us, I told him to ante up a hundred grand or I'd tell her husband he'd slept with his wife. We'd all witnessed Daniel's seething jealousy and knew what he was capable of."

"You blackmailed him."

Tanner white-knuckled the wheel, leaving the gravel road back onto asphalt. "He threatened my family if I ever said a word. He knew my children's names, their school. The pompous ass picked them up one day and said I had asked him to give their mommy a rest. He called my wife, cheerful as hell, said he had the kids for a fun boat ride and would drop them off by dinner. She called me, hysterical."

Sara's stomach churned at the image of two little girls on a lake with a soulless man. "You should have called us."

"And say what? The town hero, the leader of my expedition, gave my kids a boat ride?"

Sara tented her fingers and tapped them on her lips. Vance dead. Tanner skips town to a wooded retreat. Make room Patrick, Heath, Daniel, Jeffrey, Jason, and Celia. Tanner has crawled up your list.

Heartened by what Tanner had revealed, Sara texted Ryker to have Heath and Zoey at Patrick's, but to not let on that Pemba and Tanner would arrive with them.

A silent man drove the next three hours. Was he trying to find inner peace or plotting ways to avoid a murder arrest?

As they pulled into Patrick's driveway, Heath was inside the fenced area holding and petting a goose. He waved to Tanner and gently set the bird down. "Where'd you disappear to?"

"I took my wife to a private place for a Buddhist retreat."

"I'm glad for her and you. Everybody's on the patio."

Zoey gave him a cooler greeting, "Hello, Tanner."

Patrick rushed over and put an arm around his back. "Good to see you. We need to stick together through this tragedy."

Entering alone, Ryker moved to the nearest cocktail table and quickly tapped a pinky to thumb drum roll. "Presenting the world's number one, most gifted sirdar brought to you live from Nepal." He quickened the beat to a crescendo. "Pemba Sherpa."

A collective gasp and then laughter broke through choked voices. Emotions swinging from joy to disbelief, they rushed to him. Handshakes turned into hugs, shoulders clasped, cheeks pressed together. Sara's eyes glistened with tears.

Ashley had ordered trays of lasagna, meatballs, garlic bread, salad, and tiramisu. When the excitement ebbed, she called, "Eat before the food gets cold. Beck will serve drinks at the bar. Garlic bread is on the table."

Their plates heaped, everyone took a seat at a table for eight. Patrick raised his glass in a toast to Pemba, without whom they would not have made the summit and then be safely back here to celebrate this evening. All cheered and touched glasses.

"How long have you been in the US?" Ashley asked.

"I arrived in Los Angeles in June and have been traveling by bus and hitchhiking across your beautiful country. My favorite stops were canyons in Arizona, deserts in Nevada, and geysers in Yellowstone Park. We have nothing like those in Nepal."

"Las Vegas?" Zoey asked, twining her hair. "That's my kind of vacation."

Pemba raised his shoulders almost to his ears like a turtle hiding in its shell. "I did not enjoy that place. But I want to see the famous Disney World before going home."

"We have season tickets," said Ashley. Looking at Patrick. "Can we afford a couple of days off and take Pemba?"

"I'd love to but must get that large order out on Thursday."

"How about you, Heath?"

"I'm doing a piece on commission that's due this week."

"I need to get back to Karamia," said Tanner.

Ashley's face lit up. "How about Beck? Have you been there before?"

"No, we had a six-day reservation for last Christmas, but I lost my family the week before."

"Then you and Pemba must go," said Patrick. "It's a three-hour drive. Check in this evening and stay two more days and nights. I'll make a reservation at our favorite hotel and text the address. But you must return by ten to help package and load violins, cellos, and double basses."

Heath opened his wallet and handed Pemba a credit card. "Buy whatever tickets you want for both of you and have one hell of a good time. He gave Zoey and Tanner the stink eye until they forked over some cash for food and gas.

Patrick and Ashley dug out brochures and described their favorite rides to Pemba and Beck.

"That was kind of you," Sara told Heath.

"Money is meant to be spent. They deserve it. Pemba had to put up with Vance's shit. The accident killing Beck's wife and kid mucked up his life. A gorgeous piece of metal is beckoning to me. Gotta go now."

Left alone with Tanner and Zoey, Sara and Ryker wanted to question them together. She asked Zoey, "Does your husband know you slept with Vance in base camp"?

Zoey tilted her chin upward and stated with unwavering certainty that it was an outright lie, as if the power of her voice outweighed the truth.

"I shared his tent and watched him sneak into yours every night after he thought I'd fallen asleep," said Tanner.

Her face jerked into a contemptuous smile. "What did you tell Daniel?"

"Nothing. That conniving Vance threatened my family."

Zoey picked at a cuticle on her thumb. "It wouldn't have mattered anyway. He followed me one night when I told him I was going to a club member's baby shower."

"But you were meeting Vance at the Havenwood Motel," said Sara.

Zoey's eyes shot open in a double-take. "How'd you—?"

"We watched you exit the back door on CCTV the night Vance was murdered. But back to the night Daniel followed you, what happened?"

"Nothing." She closed her eyes and slowly shook her head. "I didn't know he had until a week later when I gave another lame excuse for going out. He grabbed my shoulders and shook me hard, shouting he'd divorce me if I ever let another man touch me."

"Yet you still entice male attention," said Sara.

She raised an indifferent shoulder. "Daniel will never leave. He can't admit failing at anything. He also knows I'll take him for everything I can get, and the man loves his money."

"That he works his butt off to earn, and you spend freely."

Ryker took Sara's arm to defuse her. "We need to leave. Thanks for cooperating in these difficult times."

After they left, Sara said, "You can let loose now. I wanted to slap her but have more decorum than to obey every impulse."

He breathed in tremors. "She could drive a man crazy."

Sara smiled. "I think you're safe." She craned her neck to see around the pirate sign still at the patio entrance. "It appears Pemba and Beck are about to leave."

Pemba bowed. "Thank you, everyone. I am excited to go and will see you in three days, proud to have been to America's Disney World."

Everyone bowed in return. "Namaste."

"Have a great time," said Sara.

On their way down the driveway, Sara told Ryker, "It's a rout. They trounced us."

He jerked back. "Who?"

"The cabal. Remember me saying if it takes a village to raise a child, maybe it takes a cabal to commit a murder?"

With a quirky look, he asked, "You truly believe they're all in this together?"

"Who knows? We've hit a brick wall. Six to eight suspects with motives, means, and opportunity but not enough proof to nail any one of them."

Ryker said, "Motive, they all hated him. Means, only men are strong enough to haul a sedated body. Opportunity, all had an equal chance after the slideshow."

"We've got to be missing something."

He leaned on the car, feet crossed and arms folded. "How do we tell McBride without inciting another heart attack?"

"Don't even go there. I hope Bonnie put him to bed early in a good mood. We just got the Daniel bonus. Another surprise may wait us tomorrow?"

Ryker's phone rang. Caller ID, the police station. "Or maybe tonight."

His brows lowered as he mouthed, *What the eff??*

Sara gasped. "Please don't say it's another murder."

"Worse. Jason is in the hospital. Somebody beat the shit out of him. He asked for me."

Chapter 26

Visiting hours were over and Jason was asleep when Ryker arrived. Sensing no imminent danger, he returned the next day. Jason was propped up against a pillow on an elevated bed. His right eye was purple, swollen shut, oozing. Dried blood caked lacerations on the orbital bone, cheeks, upper and lower lips. A wide bandage wrapped around his head.

Ryker sat beside the bed and asked in a compassionate tone, "Who did this?"

Jason winced. "The syndicate."

Ryker moved closer. "You're a gambler?"

"No, but Vance was and owed them a barrel of money. In an alley two days before the show, they threatened pay or die. He handed over his key and promised the second upon collecting the prize. I knew nothing of this."

"How'd they find you?

"Someone at the party saw me searching."

"Why'd you summon me?"

"To crack down on the syndicate and take my keys back."

Irritated, Ryker pushed away from the bed and stood. "Did you file a police report?"

"Yes, when they admitted me."

"Officers will question you about the assault but don't have the authority to chase down your keys. And I don't either."

"Syndicate doesn't know where the safe is. I refused to tell, but they could come after me again."

"So cut a deal. Show them the stash and split it."

"No, it's all mine."

And none goes to Celia. On a jaunty walk down the hall, he laughed at the irony of a possible scenario. Jason kills Vance, proclaims himself winner of a quarter million. Jason has one key; Vance, the other but uses it to save his skin. Syndicate takes Jason's. He's left with nothing but a murder conviction. Ryker loved his job on days like this.

And it was about to get better with a second online date but for coffee only. The first one stiffed him with a big dinner bill.

He watched Mia stroll across the parking lot with the grace of a white swan. As she brushed his shoulder in passing, his muscles melted.

"Your mellifluous voice could charm a wild boar."

She tilted her head slightly. "What do you mean?"

"That it flows like honey."

A smile curved her lips, and Ryker was doomed. Being on time canceled not knowing what mellifluous means.

The espresso hissed. His pulse thudded louder than the grinder. The discussion moved to travel. Attempting to appear worldly, he said his partner insists he see Iguazu Falls in Brazil. She felt Africa was too dangerous for her. Correcting that Brazil was in South America could put her off. He kept his mouth shut.

Asked about her free time, Mia said, "I'm a very romantic person." She gently traced the back of his hand, making his pants uncomfortable. "I've always wondered how sex would be with a policeman. Would you handcuff me?"

Ryker's loins and brain locked in battle.

Loins. "Look at that body. It's been a long dry spell."

Brain. "Barnyard sex. She doesn't know where Brazil is or what mellifluous means."

Loins. "We're getting hard down here and need action."

Brain. "Can't do it. An affront to my wife."

Loins. "She's been dead three years."

Brain. "Not to me."

Ryker slowly removed his hand from Mia's and checked his watch. "Oh, it's later than I thought. I'm meeting my partner at noon to review evidence. I enjoyed meeting you but must go."

Telling loins to cool it, he walked to the car without too much embarrassment.

**

Ryker phoned Sara. "Here's my day so far. Gambling syndicate versus Vance. Pay or die. They got his key and beat the shit out of Jason for his. But they don't know where the quarter million dollars is hiding. It all began with Vance's murder. I moved Jason up the top-heavy suspect list. He wants us to crack down on the syndicate and get both keys back."

Sara scrunched her face. "You told him no."

"Of course. I'm no fool," he paused, "except when it comes to women. Second online date was as bad as the first. Gorgeous but dumb as a doorstop. Boing! She thought Brazil was in Africa and doesn't know what mellifluous means.

"Who cares if you're out to get laid?"

"She touched my hand, wondering what sex is like with a cop. Would I cuff her?"

"And did you?"

"No! I want my wife's beauty and brains."

"Good luck. It's impossible to replace someone you loved. A cartoon shows a skeleton waiting for the perfect match."

"Good news is I called my daughter, and she may come see me in two weeks."

"Congratulations."

"I hope we're out of this morass by then."

Ryker searched for love. Sara longed for it too, the warmth of Michael wrapped around her while sleeping. To be in his arms again, even if for one night, would be worth the risk of a broken heart. She reached for her phone, clicked WhatsApp, drafted a message, and then deleted it before finishing the last word. On the tenth try, she wrote, "I remember hearing your voice for the first time. 'On your left,' you warned before riding past me on a hiking trail. No one has filled your void. I too am willing to gamble on love." The phone lay on the table before her, thumb hovering but resisting. Holding her breath, she kept telling herself, It's only a message. Only a message. On a whoosh exhale, she tapped Send. Done. No idea where he is or if he'll read it.

To get Michael out of her head, she'd jog. Sara sipped last night's coffee and was out the door at seven, her father's voice forever echoing his disappointment that a killer eluded her.

Running in place while waiting for the red light to change, she reviewed every suspect's motives and concluded they were all guilty. Across on the green, she stopped. Or none were. In narrowing their search, could they have missed an anonymous psychopath still at large?

This called for a new strategy requiring a half marathon. She called Ryker.

"You okay? Sounds like you're having trouble breathing."

"I'm jogging."

"Still going for that runner's high and endorphins?"

"No, to clear my brain and wing it with ideas such as none of our suspects murdered Vance."

"You're effing kidding me. We've got six strong ones with motives, means, and opportunities."

"So which one did it?"

"Slow down. Nobody's absconding. We keep making them sweat, somebody will commit a fateful error. They always do."

"While you wait for their perspiration, I'll keep running and theorizing."

She raced down three more blocks and into the city park past families with no more imminent decisions than where to lay the picnic blanket. Teens hitting a volleyball at random over the net needed a setter. She could ramp up their game, but the feet and mind had to keep runnin' and strummin'. Sweat stung her eyes. Each step pounded the mantra. All guilty, or none.

Motives. Dissect each one. Power. Money. Jealousy. Sex. Vengeance.

Sara slowed under sweet magnolias, inhaling their lemony aroma. She had an epiphany—a new strategy for finding the killer. But it would take hours of meticulous research and phone calls. Her father's voice in her head yelled, "Don't stop now. Go get the bastard."

Chapter 27

Sara came home and let the shower wash the brainstorming from her head. The steady white noise allowed her to clarify her thoughts. Someone had killed Vance the night of the slideshow. Not an accident. Not a coincidence. It had to be a mountain thing. Jason said Vance was nobody's hero. Climbers on other summits had grievances. But which peaks and when?

She toweled off and looked at herself in the mirror. Was she about to embark on some far-fetched tangent that would make Ryker and McBride roll their eyes? There was no other recourse. She couldn't stop digging even if the trail led far from home.

But where to begin this wild-goose chase? Vance had done the Seven Summits. To learn when he climbed them, Sara needed the woman she'd called a lying murder suspect and whose partner lay in a hospital bed. That could be an obstacle. She went to Celia's house, swaying a moment to relax, and then rang the bell.

Celia answered, took one look at Sara, and slammed it. "I want nothing to do with you pigs."

"This is the police. I request permission to enter."

"Not without a warrant. I know my rights."

"Bring what I want to the door. It may remove you and Jason from suspicion."

"You know what's worse than a pig? A lying pig."

This two-timing prima donna was getting on Sara's nerves.

"I want Vance's passport and the year he climbed Denali."

"Why the Denali's date?"

"He didn't need a passport for Alaska." Irritation crept into Sara's voice. "I need that date now. Check your calendar."

"I don't have to look. That egomaniac departed for Denali two days before the grand opening of my first gallery."

Sara shouted through the door. "Maybe because he knew you were cheating on him with his rival, Jason."

Minutes later, Celia opened it a crack and shoved a blue US passport and a newspaper clipping of her opening date. Then she slammed it in Sara's face, an excellent way to secure a spot on the suspect list.

She called Ryker. "Meet me at the station. While running, I had an epiphany on how to track down our killer."

It felt strange walking into the building without McBride's two-finger signal to his office. She missed it oddly. Sara poured coffee, sat at the computer, and listed the issuing country for each of the summits.

Ryker arrived, rolled his chair over to her desk, and set a bag on it. "Here, I brought one for you too." He bit a bear claw and tucked a flake of pastry in his cheek with an errant raisin on his lower lip. Like a naughty cat, she pushed the bag off the counter into a wastebasket.

Keeping his back straight, Ryker bent his knees enough to lower himself close to the floor. He was about to reach inside when Sara yanked the basket under her desk and held it hostage between her feet.

He groaned and pushed upright. "What's this harebrained scheme you conjured up while jogging?"

"Jason said other climbers had grievances. What if someone from another summit hated him enough to kill him?"

"Possible, I suppose. But how do we find who was on seven or eight mountains with him?"

"We only need to look at four. We know the Everest crowd;

they trained with Vance on Kilimanjaro. Australia is a day hike, and Vance didn't climb Carstensz. Fifty percent of murders go unsolved. Not this one."

"How do we—?"

"Internet research and phone calls. I have a plan."

He stuffed another bite into his cheek and asked, "Are we abandoning the investigation of our five suspects?"

"No, just working until something breaks." Sara slid dates from Vance's passport across the desk.

"I'll do Vinson and Denali. You do Elbrus and Aconcagua. First, find out who issues the permit. Second, request a list of expeditions matching Vance's dates. Third, search each one for his name."

Ryker glared at Sara, his foot tapping an angry rhythm. "This is not my expertise."

"It's a good mental exercise to keep your brain sharp."

"Quid pro quo. I glue myself to a mind-numbing computer for interminable hours in exchange for you helping me find and furnish a better place for my daughter's visit, an awe-inspiring one she won't want to leave." He rolled back to his desk. "Put me to work."

Ten minutes later, Ryker reported, "Elbrus only needs a national park permit. I've got the phone number. Country code seven." He tipped back in the chair and crossed his feet on the desk with a cocky smile. "I did a little side research. Code seven is only used by Russia and Kazakhstan."

"Check the time zone before calling."

He dropped back down. "Like they'll answer in English?"

"No, but if you keep saying *English* to an office that serves climbers from all over the world, they'll find somebody." With a wiggle in her walk, she said, "My country code for Antarctica is better than yours for Russia."

"Do they even have phones down there?"

"Yes, satellite ones. But to climb Vinson, you must register with a monopoly, Antarctic Logistics and Expeditions. Guess the country code."

He grimaced. "How the hell would I know?"

She burst out, "Dial number one for the US. The company is in Utah. That blew my mind."

"You've already lost yours with this scatterbrained scheme, but I'll keep searching and turn up an Aconcagua list of climbers before you do Denali."

"I win. Since 1979, the Denali National Park and Preserve has compiled mountaineering summaries. Every climber had to file an application for a special use permit. Alaska's accessible and the mountain's cheaper to climb. It will have four times the number of names than Vinson due to the costs and logistics of getting to Antarctica."

She slapped a paper on his desk. "Here's the Utah number and passport date for Vinson. I'll tackle Denali."

She pushed off to roll back to hers and spoke to Vance in her head. "You must have really pissed somebody off to end up naked in a freezer. Meet the bloodhound about to track him down."

Chapter 28

Sara emailed the Talkeetna office in Alaska, underscoring the urgency of her request. First thing the next morning, the list of 152 expeditions with 978 climbers arrived. She took a sixteen-ounce cup of coffee to her computer and began the monumental task of scrolling through each folder. One proviso. After every four, she'd check WhatsApp.

Three hours later, she rubbed her eyes and went to the break room for a cherry yogurt. She passed Ryker, hunched forward, his palms pressing his temples, eyes squeezed shut.

"Find Vance?" Sara asked quietly.

He perked up. "Huh? No. This is too far-fetched. It'll never work. Even if we find his name, what do we do with it?"

"To be determined. My gut says there's more to this case."

"Your gut has indigestion."

Sara finished the yogurt and poured another coffee. Back to the doldrums. Every team had five or six members, nine at most. She'd found no mention of Vance and only ten expeditions to go. Had Celia given her a bogus date as retribution for questioning about Ganesha, the thangkas, her relationship with Jason, her alibi the night of Vance's death?

"I've got them," shouted Ryker. "Five certifiably-disturbed people climbed Vinson the year matching Vance's passport. His name's on there."

"Plan A worked. Plan B is to get their contact information."

"They all have names I can't begin to pronounce. So no, not until some quid pro quo." He raised his nose in the air. "You owe me three hours."

"And I'll pay with interest when done with Denali names."

Forty minutes later, Cory Williams came up. A common last name, same as Beck's. It wouldn't hurt to see if any of his family members were mountaineers.

She called Pemba's number. "Hi, it's Sara, just checking to see if you're having fun."

"Yes, the best time of my life. A legend in my village. I've been to Disneyland in America."

"What's your favorite ride?"

"Expedition Everest. It's so scary in the dark."

Sara cracked up. "You've been in storms on Everest."

"But not going so fast!"

"If Beck's there, I'd like to speak to him."

"Hello, Pemba's a sheer delight. He sees everything through unspoiled eyes."

"I called to ask if you know anyone named Cory Williams."

"Not that I remember. Why do you ask?"

"A Cory Williams was on Denali at the same time as Vance but on another team. Sorry for interrupting your day. What's your next ride?"

"Tron, a motorbike-style ride. Pemba's revved up."

Pemba's excitement eclipsed the murder, lies, a gathering storm. "He'll tell me all about it on Thursday."

"Have to go now," said Beck. "We're next in line."

Ryker tapped a pen on the desk. "You done chatting with the amusement park crowd?"

"Just checking on Pemba."

"Well, I need a new place, now. Dulce may come. She and my wife gone, I had sold the New York house and rented. You were on R & R. I flew back, ended my lease, shipped clothes and a few things, donated the rest."

"Look in Zillow for rentals. I'll run through the last teams."

On fourth from the last of 152 expeditions, Vance Miller's name flashed like a neon sign. Plan B. Sara emailed the Talkeetna office and thanked them for sending the information so readily. She now needed contact information for all six members on the Vance Miller expedition.

Eyes blurry, she turned to Ryker. "What did you find?"

"Four two-bedroom houses with yards in case Dulce wants a dog. We have an appointment in two hours and three later on."

She exhaled like a slow-leaking balloon. "Mister efficient, don't get so far ahead of yourself that you'll be disappointed."

"Fair warning. But right now, we're going for pizza."

To laud Ryker's efforts, she agreed to a cheesy, pepperoni pizza for dinner. The phone open to WhatsApp in her lap, Sara glanced down every five minutes. Set on silent, it vibrated on her leg. Startled, she grabbed it but saw it was McBride calling, not Michael. She updated him, explaining the logic of her strategy and touting their success in gaining access to information for each summit. Sitting across from her, Ryker stared at the ceiling and blinked at each hyperbole.

"I was trying to bolster his recovery with good news. You'll quit making faces when we nab the killer. Now finish your pizza so we can go look at that house."

Ryker was driving when *Ding* came from Sara's phone. Not used to this sound, she stared at it until another *Ding* notified her of a WhatsApp message. Heat flushed her face at Michael's name and then drained away cold as she wavered between eagerness to open it and fear of what it might say.

"Dear Sara, I got your message. I'm sorry for not replying sooner. I'm in India and was in bed when it arrived. I am greatly relieved you're willing to give us another chance. That first day biking up a winding mountain trail, my heart was already racing. Then I watched the confident rhythm of your stride ahead of me mixed with a warm and inviting aura. Sunlight touching your hair has been forever etched in my memory. I never stopped loving you. I wanted to be your hero forever and you my celestial being.

"But driven to demonstrate my strength and courage, I raced to the Everest summit, abandoning reason and ignoring the rules of safe climbing. That reckless choice nearly cost us our lives. And giving up your chance of summiting to save me deepened the rift between you and your father. I was too ashamed to look in the mirror or face you. If you have forgiven me, I'm done proving to myself that I can be the hero I promised. I'll return having climbed all fourteen of the eight-thousand-meter peaks. Love, Michael."

"We're here," said Ryker, drawing her back into the present with no time to reflect on Michael's letter. But right now, Ryker needed help, and she couldn't renege on their quid pro quo.

They kept his appointment at a two-bedroom house built in the nineties. The instant Sara walked in, she smelled dog urine in the carpeting. "Don't even consider it," she whispered to Ryker, "unless the landlord agrees in writing to replace all the carpeting and eliminate the odor in the wood floor."

He surveyed every room as thoroughly as a CSI agent. "This place isn't worthy of my daughter. On to the next one."

The townhouse was a maze of rooms, each a different color. Grease smell in the kitchen; mildew in the bathroom. Slanted ceilings upstairs made Ryker feel boxed in, the small windows denying enough natural light to suit Sara.

They didn't go inside the third. Location alone eliminated it. The yard backed onto an industrial lot with the sound of trucks and machinery at all hours. Streetlights were scarce, making the neighborhood unsafe after dark.

Ryker rubbed his temples. "I can't do this. I'm going to my motel room which, compared to these, is a luxurious escape."

"Sleep on it. Things may look better tomorrow. I'm still waiting for Alaska to send contact information on the men who climbed Denali. I hope I didn't press my luck by asking."

Sara went home and crawled into the comfort of her bed before opening Michael's message and reading it again. Little shreds of uncertainty swarmed like gnats in her brain. Wanting to believe him, she snatched and squashed them.

"Dear Michael, I'd lived alone, shutting everyone out, until you got off your bike and walked it beside me up a mountain trail. You touched a place inside me no one else had reached, and I had no GPS to guide me. You swore a love so strong you'd take me to the ends of the earth, and you did on a boat to the end of the world at Cape Horn. You wrapped your arms around me in the freezing cold and pledged to grow old together for an eternity. Come home. I'll be waiting. Love, Sara."

Without hesitation, she pressed Send.

An hour later, six applications arrived from Alaska. All were US residents. Back at the station, she created a new folder, The Denali Six, and filed them alphabetically by first name.

Donald Wilson was at the top, and a storm was brewing on the horizon.

Chapter 29

Thoughts of Michael made it hard to concentrate on the present moment. She had to brush them aside like dust motes in the air. A faint quickening stirred in Sara's chest as she called Donald's home in Wisconsin.

"Hello," a woman answered.

"Mrs. Wilson?"

"Yes."

"May I speak to Donald, please?

"Who's calling?"

"My name is Detective Sara Lansing from Reunion Heights, Florida. I'm investigating the murder of someone who was on the Mount Denali expedition with him."

Her voice was muted, almost indistinct. "I lost my husband three years ago."

"I'm so sorry to hear. That must have been very difficult for you. Had he been in poor health?"

"No, he was very robust and proud of reaching the summit, but he came back a different man from the husband who'd left six weeks earlier."

Sara's pulse rose. Did he share his discomfort with you?"

"No, he wouldn't talk about it."

"Please excuse me for bothering you. I wish you a calm and peaceful heart."

A millisecond from Sara hanging up, Mrs. Wilson said, "I will never find peace until I know who murdered him."

The news jolted Sara as if shot at close range with a taser. "Your husband was murdered?"

A disconcerting silence.

"I know this is hard, but please tell me what happened."

Then, with an unsettling current in her voice, she said, "He went ice fishing at the lake every Sunday and would bring home a perch or bluegill for dinner. It was dark, and I hadn't heard from him. I called a neighbor who'd often gone with Donald. He drove to the lake and found our car but not him. An hour later, police pulled his frozen body from the ice hole."

Every nerve in her body firing at once, Sara asked, "Could he not have slipped and fallen in?"

Tears slurred her speech. "I'm sorry. I can't do this again." An instant later, Sara's screen turned black, and the widowed Mrs. Wilson was gone.

Two frozen bodies from the same team? Sara didn't believe in coincidences. At the local station, detectives admitted all leads were exhausted. CSI had found no witnesses, tire marks near the lake, no footprints on the ice, no fingerprints on the body, fishing gear, or ice shanty. They hadn't actively pursued the killer for over two years. It was a cold case.

She told them, "I have a similar situation and connection to yours. If you send all the relevant information, I may offer a new perspective."

The station shared a large Dropbox folder. Sara sipped a can of Ginger Ale to settle a nervous stomach as she opened the files and stared in disbelief at dozens of sources covering the unsolved murder of Donald Wilson. Her eyes blinked fast, struggling to process photos of fishing rods, lines, lures, buckets, and a life jacket methodically laid out beside an ice shanty. The murderer had not attempted to disguise it as an accident. He flaunted the kill. Subsequent pictures showed the shanty removed from the fishing hole and rescuers pulling Donald's body onto the surface. The cause of death was hypothermia and drowning. Detectives had determined the killer pushed him into the ice hole and covered it with the hut staked to the ground to prevent his escape.

Two frozen bodies from Florida to Wisconsin baffled Sara. Was this a quirk of fate, random occurrences, or malicious acts? She left her desk and circled the room several times to quell the rumbling before opening Mason's folder. His living in Akron, Ohio, rubber capital of the world, mollified her uneasiness. She phoned his home using the same introduction. His wife's voice broke as she replied that her husband was no longer with them. He'd died two years ago.

"I am so sorry."

"And my two children are without their father."

"I hate having to ask intimate questions, but this is pertinent. Was Mason a changed man after Denali?"

"Yes, and he kept everything to himself."

A rapid heartbeat thudded in Sara's chest as if protesting the question she had to ask. "I'll understand if it's too hard to answer, but how did he die?"

"Police found him two days after I reported him missing in January. They explained he'd been forced over the railing above Niagara Falls and fell onto the unstable ice formations and spray-chilled rocks below." Her voice seemed to drown inside, fading to a mere whisper. "Even if he'd survived the fall, the freezing mist and hypothermia would have killed him within minutes."

The scene blurred and made no sense. "Akron's about three hours from Niagara. Did your husband often go there in winter?"

"No, he said all waterfalls are the same. It's water; it falls. His death wasn't an accident. His hands and feet were bound. A witness passing by reported a blurry vision of two men on the walkway at midnight."

"Did CSI find any physical evidence: scuff marks on the walkway, fingerprints on the railing, or the killer's DNA on his body or clothing?"

"None anywhere. Everything had been wiped clean. They shelved it as a cold case."

Next was Colorado, its Rocky Mountains were her anchor in life and where she met Michael. Two climbers shared the same last name and phone number. A cold draft trickled down her spine and spread into the extremities as she introduced herself and gave the reason for her call.

The mother's voice faltered, fitting words in between gasps as she said her twin sons, Owen and Paul, had been inseparable since birth. They'd played Little League baseball, bought a car together, skied, and dated the same girls at different times. A year ago, they entered the Breckenridge International Snow Sculpture Championship. In below-freezing temperatures, they had ninety-four hours to hand-carve a 25-ton block of snow into a gravity-defying masterpiece. Their theme was the creation of Denali, the Great One. It depicted Raven Chief hurling his spear at a giant wave that turned to stone.

When her voice broke in an explosion of air and she began sobbing, Sara awaited the unspeakable. The morning after a six-day viewing period, snowplows level the sculptures. Operators found their frozen bodies strapped to the Raven Chief, water having been poured over them, their hands and feet bound.

Once again, CSI had found no evidence and labeled it a cold case. A sickening horror overcame Sara. Not accidents. Not coincidences. A harebrained strategy had surpassed expectations but dumped her in a quagmire. She and Ryker weren't equipped to hunt a serial killer across state lines. McBride would have to call in the FBI, and that was not a good omen.

She shuddered at the idea of making the last call and putting another wife or mother through the needless agony of dredging up painful memories. In Nepal, Sara had read some of Buddha's teachings and thought of one. *Have compassion for all beings, rich and poor alike; each has their suffering.* Tonight's women had suffered enough.

Time to go home. She packed her notes, washed the coffee cup in the break room, and said goodbye to the staff. Seated in the car with her belt buckled, she was about to start the engine but couldn't. The last folder sat inside on the computer, chiding Sara for not finishing something she'd begun. It would keep her awake all night. She rationalized her fixation with a fear that the killer may have made a careless mistake but would still escape a murder charge. She marched back into the station, plopped down in front of the monitor, and opened the file to call Reed Adams.

A woman answered.

"Mrs. Adams?"

"Yes."

"May I speak to Reed, please?

"Who is this?"

"My name is Detective Sara Lansing in Reunion Heights, Florida. I'm investigating the murder of someone who was on the Mount Denali expedition with your husband."

Her voice sounded remote, thin as thread. "My dear husband lies in a snowy grave on Denali."

Jolted out of her seat, Sara took a few steps to mellow her response. "I'm sorry. Are you saying he never returned?"

"Yes, his teammates were beside themselves when they all came to comfort me. I saw the despair in their eyes as they spoke of losing a member of what had become a family during eighteen days on the mountain."

Sara could hear her voice fluttering in her throat, each word straining to get out. "Everyone made the summit, but sixty-mile-per-hour winds and blinding snow struck as they were going back down. Reed had become separated. Visibility less than five feet. Temperature minus fifty. It was impossible to search for him. Others helped the next morning, but they never found his body. They concluded he'd lost his way and fallen in a crevasse."

She paused as if gathering her breath. "Leukemia took his

father when Reed was five."

"I'm sorry life's been so unkind to you. I know what it's like to lose a father." Sara didn't need Reed's life story but listened to a mother in mourning who wanted to tell it.

"I remarried a year later to a special forces Marine who took good care of us. His son, four years older than Reed, helped him adapt to the frequent moves and always watched over him. He was strong and determined, like his dad who'd raised him to be a Marine. But Beck wanted a home and family grounded in one place. He developed an online company selling military and outdoor gear."

The call struck like a gut punch. "Beck!" The name burst from her lips before she could stop it.

Every detail—the discipline, the precision, the survival skills—snapped into place.

He hadn't vanished. He'd been trained to disappear.

Chapter 30

Sara needed to know the instant Beck and Pemba returned to the hobby farm but couldn't phone now. Patrick and Ashley were early-to-bed, early-to-rise types. By eight, the lights were out; by six thirty, the animals needed feeding. Outside, rain whispered through the trees, and somewhere in the dark, a frog croaked as if mocking insomnia.

The prospect of his daughter coming had buoyed Ryker like sunlight through a fog. Sara couldn't crush that hope with the truth that a serial killer had been sleeping under their noses and outsmarting a seasoned detective who prided himself on reading people. She wondered if Beck had lingered long after the other murders to savor suffering. Or were detectives Sara and Ryker his final trophies, and he liked the power of orchestrating them?

She'd let Ryker have a last night of peace and sweet dreams before tomorrow's reckoning. Beck disgusted her, a rot beneath the skin of humanity, a maggot that fed on other people's pain. She swore to exterminate him. Ramifications be damned.

But how? Every option felt like a trap. Call McBride at dawn and risk another heart attack. Bring in the FBI and watch the case dissolve in bureaucracy. Or go straight to the hobby farm, catch Beck off guard, and endanger the lives of everyone inside. All options were unpalatable.

Sleep never came. In a bone-weary exhaustion, she tossed,

turned, punched the pillow flat, trying to purge the chaos rattling in her brain. Behind her closed eyes, images flickered of frozen hands, ice-caked lips, the silence of death in ice and snow. She hated how Beck lived in her head, rearranging thoughts like furniture.

When the alarm screamed at seven, she felt scraped, raw. Yogurt, berries, and coffee steadied her hands. She stared into the mug, rehearsing how to break the news to Ryker.

"You know that list of suspects? Destroy it." Too blunt.

"Sorry, but I can't uphold my end of the quid pro quo. Turns out we're sharing our air with a serial killer." Too cruel.

Or maybe say, "Guess who murdered Vance and four Denali climbers by freezing them to death." Too much truth, too soon.

She waited until eight to call Patrick. "Have you heard from Beck or Pemba?"

"No, not yet," he said through a yawn. "Beck promised to be here by ten to get the shipment out."

Sara weighed each word carefully. "It's critical you notify me the second you hear from them or they arrive. I think you have my number."

"Yes, but what's the urgency?"

"I can't say now, but please be on alert."

One down. Ryker next. And that would be a battle.

When he answered, his voice was light, upbeat. "I was just about to call you. Three houses are ready for viewing."

"And I'm eager to help you find the perfect place for your daughter, but something's come up. My strategy paid off. Big time. We need to get on it right away."

"You're violating the quid pro quo bill of rights."

"I'll comply, but not today."

"What's going on?"

"I'd rather explain in person. Come pick me up."

She filled a thermos, grabbed a bag of nuts, fruit, and cheese and stepped outside. Fog ghosted through the trees, wrapping the street in a hush that felt almost funereal. When Ryker's SUV rumbled up, she was waiting on the porch, hair damp, jacket zipped, resolve hardening in her chest. She dropped the supplies in the backseat and buckled up in the front. They drove to the hobby farm and parked.

Ryker gave her a sidelong look. "You gonna tell me what's going on, or do I have to guess?"

"Drive to the hobby farm and park behind shrubs but close enough to see the gate."

"Yay, we're doing a stakeout," he shouted with a Cheshire Cat grin and drummed his fingers on the dashboard in a staccato beat. "I love spying on somebody unawares." He reached over the seat to retrieve her bag. "What'd you bring for sustenance."

"Coffee, fruit, nuts, and cheese."

He made a face. "You made me skip breakfast. Rabbit food won't fill my belly. Lucky for you, I keep stakeout provisions in the trunk." He returned with brownies and a bag of potato chips. "Now we're talking. So who's the target?

"Beck and Pemba."

The thin line of his brow jumped in surprise. "You can't be serious."

"Do I look like I'm joking?"

"Actually, you look like hell, gray around the gills. Did you even sleep?"

"No, I couldn't shut my head off."

"Now, you're scaring me. What happened?"

"My compulsion to finish anything once I start made me go through every Denali folder. Vance's was buried near the bottom. Brace yourself for what I'm about to say. It isn't pretty."

She swallowed hard. "I made heartbreaking phone calls to two grieving widows and a mother who'd lost both sons."

"Christ. Tell me."

"There were six in Vance's group. Donald Wilson's folder was on top. His wife said he loved ice fishing in a lake. Someone pushed him into the water and covered the hole with his shanty. He drowned frozen under the ice."

Shock rooted him to his seat. "A strong Denali climber was murdered under a shack?"

"Mason was next. Bound hand and foot, shoved over the rail at Niagara Falls during a freeze."

"That's two more frozen bodies from the same team. Why bind them and cover the hole?" Ryker asked.

"To make sure nobody mistook them for accidents. Then twin brothers, Owen and Paul, were found frozen stiff, strapped to their snow sculpture."

Ryker dropped his hands over his face. "I can't fathom that mother's grief. If something happened to Dulce . . . " His voice broke. "I'd have no reason to go on."

Sara's sinuses tingled, meaning tears weren't far behind. "I couldn't bear putting another wife or mother through a traumatic ordeal and had packed to go home. I made it as far as my car and buckled my belt, but that last folder sitting inside on the computer would haunt me all night long, harping, 'You didn't finish."

"The last name before Vance's was Reed Adams," she said.

"A sixth frosty corpse including Vance's?"

"Appears so. On the descent, Reed got separated from the team in a whiteout, and they never discovered his body."

"And you lost a night's sleep for nothing. We're no closer to solving the crime than before your grandiose scheme."

"Are we not on a stakeout?"

"Yes, but for who?"

"For the stepbrother of Reed Adams who goes by the name Beck Williams."

Ryker's eyes shot wide open. "Beck? Our Beck?"

"That's my conclusion."

"Oh, I did not see that coming. You're messing with me. I would have read it in his eyes and face."

"He played us beautifully."

"Have you told McBride?"

"I said we have a lead and are following up."

"You think two of us can waltz in and cuff a serial killer?"

She finger-tapped his chest. "You and I were both negligent not asking for back up on the Renaissance case. McBride already has men on hand waiting for our call."

Ryker unwrapped a brownie and held it out. "Sugar?"

"Not unless it's laced with caffeine."

He tilted the seat back and settled in.

"Comfy?" Sara asked in a sarcastic tone.

"Yes, considering I should be out there looking for a house instead of waiting for a serial killer."

"I wouldn't set your hopes too high. There's a chance Dulce won't show up or come and only stay a few days. The higher you hope, the harder you fall. I don't want that happening to you."

He tore the bag of chips open. "We share a quandary. Maybe Michael shows up; maybe he ghosts you again."

"I'll survive. I'm used to being alone. You're not."

He flapped his arms like a bird. "What about the falconer at the fair who wants you to run away to Argentina with him?"

"I'd never love him or anyone else the way I do Michael."

"My point exactly," he said, his voice dropping. "You don't get to love that deep twice."

"Maybe you could if you stopped measuring women against a ghost."

"I tried twice online and struck out. One more and I'm off that team."

He handed her the chips. "Go ahead. Be a daredevil."

"Did you not know that I'm a chip connoisseur? They're like a fine wine to be evaluated for quality in all aspects."

Sara picked one between two fingers and slowly held it to her nose as if discerning the nuances of an aromatic wine. "Hmm, this is delightfully light, thin, and crispy." She nibbled it. "Salty but not a sodium bomb. It has a satisfying crunch with a natural earthiness. I'll take another, please."

To keep from bursting out loud, Ryker slammed his mouth shut so tight his lips disappeared. He handed her the whole bag and asked how much longer they'd wait.

Minutes crawled. Sara's watch read 11:15. "Beck promised to be back by ten. He doesn't know we're onto him."

"Maybe Patrick's so busy packing he forgot to tell us."

Sara called Ashley. "Any word from Beck or Pemba?"

"No, and Patrick's furious. He may fire him."

"We're out in front. May we come look at his apartment?"

"I'll open the gate and unlock his door."

A honking goose erupted as they drove in. Dogs barked, zebus bellowed—a farmyard symphony in full discord.

Inside Beck's apartment, the bed was unmade, dishes in the sink, yesterday's newspaper open to the weather page. Ryker opened the closet, dresser, and medicine cabinet. "I don't see anything out of the ordinary."

They went to Patrick's workshop, a mind-boggling number of machines, tools, and tall ceiling-high shelves of shipping cases designed for string instruments. Ashley and Patrick were packing violins. A dozen more hung from a rack beside ten violas. A cello stood on a floor stand next to a double bass.

"I have zero musical talent," said Ryker, "but if I did, what would a double bass cost?"

"One of much lesser quality, about ten thousand. Mine earns forty to fifty."

Ryker bit his lips before *holy crap* could escape. "They're exquisite," slid out instead. "It's a shame Beck left you high and dry after graciously giving him two days off."

Patrick zipped a viola bag shut. "And free room and board in exchange for work."

"You're being too hard on him," said Ashley. "They're like two kids having so much fun they lost track of time. After all he's been through, Beck's been in good humor, hard-working, and respectful. He hasn't taken a day off in the months he's been here. He's become part of our family."

"Did he ever mention a brother?"

Ashley shook her head. "No, he was an only child."

"Did he ever mention a favorite place or special interest?"

"Not that I heard of."

Patrick asked Ryker for help lifting the cello onto a work table. "Why are you so interested in him?"

Sara shot a warning glance. "We just want to ask a couple of questions. Sorry to disturb your work, but please contact us immediately if you hear from him or Pemba."

As Sara and Ryker got back in the car, he said, "That didn't sound like a cold-blooded killer. You're condemning a man for having the same first name."

"You know I don't believe in coincidences."

Waving his hands around, gesturing at nothing, he shouted, "That doesn't mean it can't happen. You're too eager to prove your strategy. There are hundreds of men named Beck. Reed's brother could be any of them."

"You'll eat those words."

"His only sin is staying too long at Disney World. We blew an entire morning and raised McBride's blood pressure. Call him to stand down the cavalry." He turned the engine on, and they drove in silence.

Ten minutes from the farm, Sara's phone buzzed, a sharp, metallic ping that sliced through the air. "Stop the car!"

Ryker slammed the brakes, gravel spraying. "Christ, don't yell like that. I thought a truck was coming."

"Sorry, but look." Her screen glowed with a message from Pemba. Attached was a short video file. Denali. Day One.

She tapped it open and turned the phone toward Ryker.

In roaring wind, the Denali team appeared, grinning beneath goggles and hoods, voices rising above the gale. They waved to the camera, laughing about frozen noodles, their faces pink with cold and exhilaration.

Then the cameraman, Harry from Highland Trails, angled the lens for a selfie in the corner. "Base camp at last," he shouted.

Sara's breath hitched. Those same faces stared up from the case files she'd spent all night studying. Vance. Mason, Donald, the twin brothers. Beck's brother, Reed, stood front and center, his arm thrown around Vance's shoulder. The image crackled, flickered, and went black.

"That's old footage," said Ryker. "Why'd Pemba send it?"

A shiver rippled down her spine like a wire tightening. "He didn't. Beck did and chose a video that he knew I'd recognize. He's saying he still has Pemba and knows I've connected the dots. Now he's baiting us in a high-stakes pursuit game, but we don't know the rules yet."

Chapter 31

Beck's revelation sent a shockwave through Ryker in a chilling image of Dulce finding his lifeless body in a dingy motel. He'd go to any extreme to see this vermin rot away in a cold, sterile prison cell for life.

Ryker asked Sara, "Why send it to you? We never formally interrogated him or sought an alibi since he'd only been here four months and wasn't connected to the expedition."

"My mind's been wandering through the past twenty-four hours and stumbled on an answer. I may have accidentally alerted him when I phoned and asked if he knew anyone named Cory Williams."

"Who's that?"

"Nobody of interest. But adding I was searching for names with Vance on Denali must have slightly pinched a nerve."

"But he felt safe. Reed had a different last name."

"And would have gone scot-free if his mother hadn't said Beck looked after his younger stepbrother."

"Got it."

He pressed the call button. "It's detectives Sara and Ryker."

The metal gate slid open. They passed the barnyard choir on the way to Patrick's workshop.

"Back this soon, you must have urgent news," he said.

"Ten minutes ago, we received this video taken the eve of a

Denali climb."

"We should all sit down and watch together," said Sara.

Ashley's lips curved with delight. "They're all so eager to begin. Look, there's Vance, but it's sad seeing him so excited and then lying in a casket."

"Let me sit between you and play it again," said Sara.

She paused the video on each climber and described how he died. Ashley clutched her shirt tighter at each one.

"Five murdered in cold blood and the sixth died on Denali? I'm a violin maker, not a detective, but something happened on that mountain, and the killer is out for vengeance."

"That's our premise too," said Ryker. "Sara can clarify."

"Talking to wives and mothers, I drew a blank. The killer left no clues at any site. All are cold cases. I'd reached an impasse until Reed's mother, by a fluke, mentioned his stepbrother who had looked after him since they were kids."

"They went by different last names," said Ryker.

Sara took Ashley's hand, fingers interlacing softly with hers in silent support. Her legs gripped the edge of the chair to ground herself before she spoke. "Adams and Williams."

Ashley squeezed Sara's hand so tight it hurt, her eyelashes wet with tears. "Not Beck Williams."

Ryker intervened. "After hearing you speak so well of him, we decided it was just a coincidence, a common surname. But then the video arrived from Pemba's phone."

The muscles in Patrick's face had strained more with each photo. At Beck's name, the air crackled with tension as he leaped off the seat. "Are you telling me a serial killer has lied, shared meals, and lived rent-free for months using us as cover from the police?"

"He deceived us too and would have continued his charade, but Sara saw through the lies and exposed him."

"How'd you do that, and how can we help?" Patrick asked

"We're up against a pro. To execute four murders, he had to

be creative, pay precise attention to detail, and be diligent enough to carry through."

"I'm sure he's already designed an insidious escape plan," said Sara, "and I fear it involves Pemba. Beck used his phone for a reason."

Ashley drew her breath in sharply. "He wouldn't hurt him."

With an uncertain smile, Ryker said, "We hope not. Beck is vindictive, but you've both been nothing but kind and generous. I doubt you're in danger but be alert and notify us of any change."

"We need to apprise our boss of the situation," said Ryker. "We'll stay in touch."

He got behind the wheel. "Where to now?" he asked Sara.

"Every inch of my body sickens at the idea of calling Beck's mother again, but she may be our only hope of finding him."

"Better you than me."

Sara could barely control the shaking in her voice. "Hello, Mrs. Adams, this is Detective Lansing again. I'd like to ask Beck a couple of quick questions. Is there someplace I can reach him?"

"If it's about Denali, all he knows is his brother died there."

"Is there somewhere special he'd go?"

"He's a private person. Don't phone again." The call ended.

"You didn't tell her what he's done," said Ryker.

"How could I? The poor woman's left with a large hole in her chest where a mother's heart belongs."

"What's next in your master plan?"

"I'm stuck, like at a broken red light. Maybe we were better off not knowing."

"What's done is done. McBride's waiting for the report."

Bonnie answered the door and led them to the living room where McBride sat in a leather recliner with a lunch tray across his lap. "Greetings, my ace detectives. First you have him and then you don't."

"Beck was due at the hobby farm before ten. Everything was in place to nail the guy. But at eleven thirty, he was a no-show and sent this to me."

After watching the video, McBride leaned forward to give her the phone. "Just a bunch of smiling idiots trying to convince themselves that climbing a deadly mountain is a sane decision."

She pushed his hand away. "Take a closer look."

"For what?"

"Someone you might recognize."

Seeing Vance, he gawked in disbelief and clutched his chest as if to protect the sternum from breaking. "What's it mean?"

"Four of the others were murdered in ice and snow."

McBride fell back in the recliner. "By whom?"

"The brother of the fifth man. He sent the video to prove he knows we're coming for him," said Ryker.

Almost hyperventilating, McBride said, "And are you? Do you have any idea where he is?"

"No, he foiled us. The next move is his."

To keep McBride's health from spiraling downward, Ryker refrained from mentioning Pemba. In the following grim silence, Bonnie went to the kitchen to brew fresh coffee.

"Remaining faithful to you for years, she's a keeper," said Ryker. "Never let go of love when you find it."

McBride nodded.

A jarring ring seemed to suck the air from the room, making it hard to breathe. Sara steadied her voice before speaking.

"Hello."

"You stinking bitch, why'd you call my mother?"

Ryker's hand shot out to grab the phone and protect her from his rancor, but she stopped him with a shake of her head.

"You destroyed my life. I planned to live in paradise with Ashley and Patrick until you jammed your nose where it doesn't belong."

A gut-deep alarm ripped through Ryker. As an eleven-year-old, he couldn't protect his mother from a drunken father who killed her. Not again. Never. He'd give his life for Sara.

Beck's voice cracked like a whip. "Say something. Did you hear me?"

"I heard," she said evenly.

"Then listen well and put your phone on speaker for all to hear. I'm not the monster you paint. I learned the truth from the video camera man. My brother had acute high-altitude sickness. They left him to die on the mountain, freezing while they chased after their summit glory." Beck's words seethed with contempt. "I made them pay, and now so will you for wrecking my life."

Ryker grabbed the phone from Sara. "If you so much as breathe wrong near her, I'll put you down myself."

Beck chortled. "A New York cop threatening me? Both of you start packing for a long trip."

"Not happening," said Sara.

"Oh, my bad. Did I forget to mention Pemba? He's locked away. Enough food and water for ten years if he rations well. Once you personally cuff me, Patrick will get an address. Refuse, and Pemba rots like a decaying piece of wood."

"You despicable piece of shit," Ryker yelled.

"Save it. Blame her. If she hadn't called my mother, we'd all live happily ever after. Instead, you've signed onto my game. My plane's about to depart and will land in twenty-six hours. Detective Lansing, you're my worthy adversary. Find out where I'm going in the next five hours or Pemba's dead."

Call ended. A cold shiver tore through Ryker like ice water in his veins. He looked at Sara, her face drained as if an invisible coil were squeezing the life from her.

He broke an uncomfortable silence. "Sara, this isn't on you. Three police departments shelved the murders as cold cases. You were the only one capable of tracking him down."

"Only because I stayed on the phone long enough to hear a grieving mother's story and the word Beck." Her eyes lifted, raw with dread. "Do you have a passport?"

"Yes, thanks to my wife's lecture in London."

"Good. Beck didn't have time to secure Pemba and make it to an international airport other than Orlando. Check parking lots. We know his car and license. The GPS will show recent activity and lead us to Pemba."

"Twenty-six hours? He could be anywhere. How in the hell will you find him?"

"Leave that to me."

Ryker hoofed it up and down every aisle in the outlying lots for two hours and then requested four more officers to help with the airport surface and garage spaces. He called Sara.

"Patrick and Ashley have heard nothing. The population of Orlando's metro area is two and a half million. McBride's paying overtime to expand the police search of abandoned warehouses, restaurants, stores, gas stations, and houses. You name it, they've been there."

Four hours into the twenty-six, he spotted a Subaru Outback on a garage upper level. The license matched. CSI was on hold nearby. He emphasized the urgency in finding Pemba. Shining his flashlight through the passenger window, he spotted a single hair the color and length of Pemba's on the passenger headrest. If forced to fly to an unknown destination, putting work ahead of family again, Dulce would never forgive him. This was his last chance. They had to stop Beck.

When CSI arrived with a tow truck, Ryker said, "Check the GPS. Where's the car been today?"

"Owner disabled it. The tires may tell us."

His pulse raging in his temples, Ryker called Sara, "I found Beck's car. CSI is towing it. There's a black hair on the headrest. Could be Pemba's, but there's no time to prove it. He never left evidence before. Why slip up now?"

"To rattle us. That wasn't evidence. It's bait. He wants us to chase him, and I know where he's going."

Chapter 32

Sara had started her quest for Beck's mysterious landing with a court order for the manifest of today's international flights from Orlando with passenger names Williams or Adams. Only one Adams turned up, a woman, and a family of four Williams.

Next, a task as tedious as going through the Denali files. She searched forty-five pages of Orlando departures and arrivals and came up with nothing pointing to twenty-six hours in the air. The overseas destinations were unfathomable. Where would he go? Most of Europe travel time was ten to twelve hours. Argentia was an escape route in the past, thirteen hours. Australia, twenty-one, but Beck froze bodies not leave them on a desert. Not his MO. Somewhere cold. Greenland, Iceland.? Not far enough away. Antarctica, two days with stops.

Why'd Beck call her, not Ryker, his worthy adversary? She bounced the heel of her hand off her forehead. Because she knew Nepal where two hundred frozen bodies remain on Everest. No direct flights. Total travel time around twenty-six hours. He was going to Kathmandu. Let the hunter-and-hunted dance begin.

Ryker's response to Nepal carried more pain than defiance. "This has to end quickly. If I'm not here when Dulce arrives, she'll give up on me. I'll die an old man alone."

The mention of his daughter twisted inside Sara. She'd seen the longing in his eyes before. "Nonsense," she said more firmly than felt. "We'll be back. Did you warn of possibly being late a day or two?"

"No, I'm king of the shirkers and didn't even tell her I was leaving."

She bit back the urge to remind him that Dulce's grudge had deeper roots than this trip. Some wounds were his to mend, not hers.

Beck called five hours after his first provocation and seemed pleased Sara had done due diligence. He would phone again after landing to text the plane reservations. They should begin packing warm clothes and comfortable walking shoes.

At hour twenty-five, Sara met with the station's IT team to trace the call. Pacing, she said, "Locate him to prove he's not sending us on a snipe hunt."

"I'll do my best."

McBride surprised everyone as he entered the room, stiff but determined. "Aren't you supposed to be in bed?" Sara asked.

"Not if there's a chance to notify three police departments that my detectives solved their cases. This will verify."

She admired McBride's grit. "Maybe I can goad his ego into confessing."

Ryker ambled in carrying a long, heavy coat. When Sara's chest rose and fell in a deep sigh, he said, "What? You told me to bring something warm."

"Not Antarctica warm."

Silence stretched through the twenty-fifth hour. Music and phone games preoccupied them through twenty-six and twenty-seven. At eighteen, an IT tech rose and shoved back his chair. He leaned across the table, hovering over Sara. "That maggot's never going to call. He's played you. I'm going home to my wife."

"Me too," said another, standing up.

"No one's leaving unless you no longer care to work here," McBride cut in sharply. He turned to Ryker. "Order three large pizzas and drinks."

Eating smoothed the frayed edges and spurred debates about which was better pepperoni or sausage and what plebeian added pineapple to pizza? When the last boxes and cups were cleared, Ryker dropped his head onto folded arms. Sara fought the pull of exhaustion but clung to wakefulness.

At loud ring knifed through the room. Nearly falling off her chair, Sara snatched the receiver and yelled to IT, McBride, and Ryker, a finger pressed to her lips.

"Hello, Beck. How gracious of you to call so many hours after landing."

"And good morning to you too," he said with a low chuckle. "It's almost noon. Ready for lunch? Oh, wait, that's right. It's only two in the morning there, eleven forty-five in Kathmandu. You'll have to hop on over for a free trip. I bought you and your fat friend one-way tickets. Plane leaves at eleven tonight. Do not miss your flight."

"I'm not coming," Ryker muttered.

"I'll be watching every passenger who disembarks. If I don't see you both . . . " He paused. "Well, it would be a pity to let young Pemba endure a long, painful death."

"You bastard!" Ryker erupted.

"Now, now. Patience please. I've booked you a room at the Kathmandu Guest House. Our game begins there, Sara. I chose Nepal because you know the ground. I want a capable opponent."

"Just use me," she said quickly. You don't need Ryker."

A soft laugh. "Oh, but I do for the sheer pleasure of watching him stumble on foreign soil. And you IT guys trying to trace my call, don't bother. I'm in Kathmandu on narrow winding streets. You'll never pinpoint me."

A ping on her phone. Flight details. Another ping—room confirmation. "How do I know this isn't a fraudulent scheme?" Sara asked. "I need proof Pemba is alive and well with adequate food and water."

"Thought you'd never ask. Here's a video."

She opened it. Pemba, alive, but trapped in a bare room with only a bed, sink, fridge, microwave. His eyes held more fear than any words could carry. Sara felt as if a bag of cut onions had been shoved into her head. She had no choice but to enter into this dogfight and win.

"Satisfied?" Beck asked.

"Yes."

"As an incentive to do precisely what I say, I'll share murder details only I know. And in good faith, I'll contact Patrick when you land. Oh, and leave your guns at home. Nepal bans firearms."

The line clicked dead. Even the seasoned IT men sat mute, stripped of answers.

Ryker's cheeks twitched as he fired a scathing look. "Nepal is the last place on earth I want to be. I can't do this."

She wanted to steady him, but her own stomach dropped. Nepal, the place she loved, now twisted into Beck's playground.

"You have to," McBride said. "There's more at stake than a Sherpa. Four stations will close cold cases. You're on your own. The FBI won't step in without invitation. There's no extradition."

A fevered look swept across Ryker's face. "What about exotic diseases? Do I need a load of shots?"

"Not for a short trip," Sara said, "but your basics should be up to date."

He gave a small, almost boyish nod. "That, I do right."

Sara checked the itinerary. "Twenty-four hours including layovers. The departure's at eleven. I'll pick you up at seven thirty. We need to be there three hours early."

**

While watching a sci-fi flick, Ryker dozed off at three a.m., snoring softly, his head bobbing. He'd have a stiff neck when he woke, but Sara didn't want to disturb him. During their racing days, she and Michael had flown to distant horizons most people would never see. That was part of the allure."

Upon landing in Kathmandu, Ryker checked his watch. "It

says eight at night. I'm dead tired and ready for bed."

"Turn off airplane mode and look again. In Kathmandu, it's five forty-five the next morning."

"Forty-five is a weird time zone change."

"India chose a half-hour zone. Nepal refused to be like its neighbor. Our bodies are confused and out of sync. We have to stay awake, keep active, and eat when Nepalis do. But first, we need to get fifteen-day visas and go through customs."

At baggage claim, Ryker insisted on lifting her suitcase off the carousel. She restrained her independent impulse and allowed him to be a gentleman.

Outside the airport curb was a storm of noise, taxis honking in frantic bursts and tour buses idling with doors flung wide. Dozens of tour guides stood clustered along the curb. Their signs bearing client names bobbed above weary-eyed travelers lugging baggage and patrolling the lines in search of their group.

"Beck demanded both of us show up," said Sara. "He'll be watching to confirm we followed orders. Act like we're looking for our tour guide as we move through the chaos."

"Look there at the far end," said Ryker, averting his eyes to conceal discovery. "He's hunched down behind a tour placard as if we wouldn't spot a six-foot, long-haired Caucasian among the shorter, browner Nepalese."

Beck raised his head and locked his gaze on Sara's. For a heartbeat, the roar of traffic and chatter dulled to a hollow hum. Then he bolted and darted across the loading lane, horns erupting as a cab braked hard to avoid hitting him and plowing into the sea of visitors.

Sara's pulse quickened. "Wait here with the luggage."

Her shoes slapping the pavement, she elbowed past a porter wrangling a cart stacked high with bananas and apples, dodged a child dragging a stuffed yak, and slid between two idling buses belching exhaust.

A driver leaned on his horn as she darted across a lane of

honking taxis. People cursed, spun around, and stared, but she didn't care. Adrenaline sharpened, she quickened her stride and closed the gap, yards shrinking to feet. She stretched forward and caught his sleeve. He twisted, slipped from her grasp, and shoved a cart loaded with luggage into her path. Bags toppled, blocking the way. Sara vaulted them, nearly colliding with a grandmother clutching a child. Beck used the chaos as camouflage behind a lumbering tour group and hopped onto a rickshaw.

By the time Sara shouldered her way through, he was gone.

Ryker stumbled up at last, sweat dripping, duffels weighing him down. "Tell me you didn't just chase him into a parking lot full of taxis."

"No, a lot full of rickshaws." She gave a swift kick to a littered cup. "Damn, I almost had him in my grasp, but he slipped away. The arrogant turd knew I couldn't catch him here. Let's get a cab to the hotel."

Agreeing on a price before stepping in, she told the driver, "Kathmandu Guest House."

"Did you give an address?" Ryker asked.

"Don't need to. It's in the Thamel tourist district. Relax and enjoy the view."

They rode down narrow, winding streets choked with cars, trucks, taxis, rickshaws, and stray animals. A man on a bicycle sped toward them, a small goat tucked under his arm. In the split second before the bike swerved, the goat bleated *Maaaa*.

Ryker shrank back. "I'm not sure who was more startled, it or me.

"Assuredly, you," said Sara.

They passed ancient, elaborately carved wooden windows and doorways where the decaying figures of gods and goddesses quietly guarded the homes. Simple household altars and Hindu shrines filled every niche with the images of deities and colorful offerings of fruit and flowers. The scent of aromatic spices, street food, and incense mixed with exhaust fumes and dust permeated the air. Sounds everywhere: honking cars, barking dogs, crying babies, Hindus praying, and vendors hawking their wares.

Ryker threw his hands up. "Sensory overload. I need to get out of here and into a comfortable bed."

"Too much even for a New Yorker?"

"A myriad of unfamiliar sights, smells, and sounds."

Traffic slowed behind a herd of goats and three cows.

"Can't the driver honk them out of the way?" he asked.

"Cows are sacred and free to roam the streets."

"And shit everywhere?"

"Yes, they're a symbol of purity and nonviolence."

He folded his arms and slunk in the seat. "Then I'm hiding behind a cow when Beck charges me with a knife."

Checking into the hotel, they found. Beck had reserved only one room. Sara wanted another, but none were available. Riding the elevator to the third floor, Ryker said, "Even if I wanted to jump your bones, you'd be safe tonight. My body's spent."

The room was clean and spacious, twin beds separated by a nightstand. Sara flopped backward onto one and spread her arms. "It feels so good to lie down."

Ryker's finger darted toward her pillow. "What's that?"

She picked up a torn piece of paper. Her eyes slid past faint bookstore lettering visible at the edge as she read jagged ink lettering that made her pulse spike. *Welcome to Nepal. You can't arrest me if you don't find me.* She crushed the note in her hand and hurled it aside.

It was 9:30 p.m. yesterday in Orlando, not too late to call Patrick. He answered and put it on speaker phone. "Thank god, you made it. Are you both all right?"

"Just tired. Beck saw us outside the airport and should have contacted you."

"Not a word yet and we've been keeping the line open. He may think it's too late and will call in our morning."

"You're implying the man has a soul. Text me the minute

you hear anything."

"Seeing your expression," said Ryker, "I gather Beck didn't keep his end of the deal."

Sara's mouth jerked into a contemptuous smile. "He broke his word. I'll drag his noxious body through the cow dung of Kathmandu."

Ryker shuddered. "You're giving me the creeps. I'm going to shower the odors and dust from our sweaty jaunt across town."

Sara's body unfolded in sections as she rose and said, "Rule one—no nudity. Rule two—bathroom door stays shut."

"Got it, Mademoiselle. He snagged a towel and disappeared inside.

"She called after him. Most of the water is contaminated with fecal bacteria. Drink only bottled or boiled, and do not wet your toothbrush in the sink. In the shower, keep your mouth shut tight. You'll wish you were dead if you don't. I'm coming next. Is there hot water?"

"Was cold when I reached inside the door and turned it on."

She heard water running and him rustling around with his clothes, brushing his teeth, and claiming space for his toiletries.

"I'm ready to step into the tub for my first Nepal shower."

She heard the scrape of the sliding door.

Then a scream, sudden and sharp, tore through the room like glass shattering.

Chapter 33

Ryker bolted from the bathroom stark naked, one hand clawing for a towel, the other pointing back inside.

Sara arched an eyebrow. "A Nepalese spider frighten you?"

"Hell no." His voice cracked. "There's a snake in the tub!"

Sara inched forward, eyes sweeping left and right to see if it was on the move. From a safe distance, she saw coiled in the corner of the tub a bluish-black snake with narrow white bands gleaming under the light. She sucked in a breath. "Himalayan Krait. I saw one when racing in India."

"Poisonous?"

"One of the four deadliest in the world." For Ryker's sake, her tone remained cool despite the riot in her stomach. Beck. He'd thrown the glove down in a silent challenge. His message couldn't be clearer. *I can reach you anywhere.*

"Get dressed," she told Ryker. "Go to the rooftop bar, relax, and take in the view while I find someone to trap Mr. Krait."

Sara had attempted to appear unperturbed in front of Ryker, but not to the manager. "Explain how a venomous snake got into our bathroom. It didn't slither up a drainpipe to the third floor."

Beads of sweat dotted his forehead. "I . . . I'm at a loss. I have no explanation."

"Who had a key?"

"The man who reserved the room. He stayed last night."

Sara tensed to the point of an uncontrollable shudder. "And your housekeeper? She didn't notice a snake in the shower?"

"She never entered. He'd hung a Do Not Disturb sign."

"But the room was spotless when we arrived."

"He must have cleaned it himself." The manager cleared his throat and tugged on the collar of his shirt as if it were choking him. "How can I make this situation right for you?"

Sara's voice dropped to a blade's edge. "Move us to your best suite. Tonight. Two queen beds, balcony, and garden view. After traveling halfway around the world for twenty-four hours, my patience is thinner than rice paper."

He wiped sweaty hands on his trousers and cleared his throat for the third time. "I'll see to it immediately. Meanwhile, please enjoy the complimentary buffet."

**

On the rooftop bar, Ryker folded his arms under his head like a makeshift pillow. He could have slept twenty hours right there, but his Amazon partner would not be curtailed. He pretended to be asleep when she laid her hand on his shoulder.

"Hey, Jet-lagged. Stay awake or your clock will never reset."

He cracked one eye. "I can't go back to that room."

"Don't have to." She sat across from him. "We've got the luxury suite now with two queens, a balcony, and garden view."

Ryker's brows rose half an inch. "You threaten a one-star review?"

"No, I explained my current low tolerance. He blinked and handed me the keys." She tugged on his arm. "Come on, Sleepy. Complimentary breakfast buffet. Food always perks you up."

He shuffled after her. "Beck planted that snake, didn't he?"

"Yes."

No questions about how, when, or why? The scent of bacon possessed his brain. He was quite content lifting six pieces from a chafing dish until she spouted, "Think about how you want to look when your daughter arrives."

Too late. Once bacon hits the plate, it's a binding contract. He shot her a look. "I've barely traveled farther than London, and may not walk out of this country alive. Forgive me if I indulge."

"Don't be so morbid." She buttered toast as if discussing the weather. "I know why Beck chose this guest house."

"Tidings from your gut?"

"No, hard-earned experience. I'll show you when done."

"Done taking naps?"

"No, after breakfast. There's a travelers' message board not far from here. Beck would have left something."

"Like a cordial dinner invitation?"

"Sure. For filet Mignon and lobster."

At the board, Sara planted her hands on her hips. "Take the right side. Search for a clue."

"As in his mother's maiden name, favorite pet, first car?"

She gave him a stink eye. "You're incorrigible. Just look."

Eager to prove his worth to a woman who didn't freak out over a venomous snake, he bent, scanning scrawled notes and doodles, grumbling under his breath until he straightened back up and reported, "Nothing here."

To his relief, she hadn't found anything either but insisted there was a clue or Beck wouldn't have booked them at the guest house. "Look again for anything unusual, no matter how bizarre or obscure."

Mumbling to himself about the futility of going over every word again, he finished his half and threw both hands in the air. "Still nothing other than some kid's scribbled spider."

"Spider? Show me."

He pointed to the lower corner. She squatted, then recoiled, eyes sharp. "That's no spider. It's a yeti."

Ryker laugh. "As in abominable snowman? If you think I'm chasing some hairy ape into the mountains, count me out."

"I'll show you its footprints."

She hailed a tricycle rickshaw and climbed in, waving him after her. Ryker wedged into the cramped space, yanking a blue fold-down canopy over their heads. "This isn't transportation. It's punishment. Why not take a taxi?"

"Many streets are too narrow. Besides, this way you get to see how people really live."

"Where are we going?"

"To Rum Doodle."

His eyes narrowed. "That better not be your idea of a joke. I'm running on fumes."

She laid her hand over the back of his for the first time since he'd known her. This woman, who faced down a krait and bullied a hotel manager, could also melt him.

"I'm not teasing," she said. "I know all this has rattled you—strange streets, shrines, animals in traffic, a lunatic hunting us, and the chance you'll miss your daughter."

Ryker swatted at a persistent, buzzing fly, missing it twice. "I just want to bag this psychopath and get home in one piece."

"We will. But first, your yeti."

Ryker bounced the heel of his hand off his forehead. "Ah, yes, the omniscient yeti scrawled on a message board."

Sara smiled. "Smart-ass."

The rickshaw arrived at Rum Doodle Bar and Restaurant.

Ryker stepped inside and gawked at hundreds of paper yeti footprints dangling from the ceiling and plastering every wall. His brow wrinkled. "What the hell is this place?"

"The go-to place for climbers, rafters, cyclists, adrenaline junkies. Every footprint tells a story. You sign one and recount your experience."

"Did you and Michael write one?"

"Yes, but I have no idea where they put it among thousands. The boxes on the walls contain signatures of Everest summiteers. Edmund Hillary signed the first. Free meals for life to anyone who can prove they stood on the roof of the world."

"Fascinating trivia," Ryker said, "but why are we here?"

"Beck would've left a message. Start looking."

Ryker gestured at the avalanche of paper overhead. "With what? A cherry picker?"

"Improvise. Presidents Carter and Hashimoto signed one, if that motivates you to start looking."

"For what?"

"You'll know when you see it."

Ryker rubbed his eyes, struggling to stay awake, as he stared at a wall stampeded by yetis. Sara said he'd know it when he sees it. Names, dates, quirky drawings and quotes were scribbled on footprints across an endless surface. He craved a cold beer, but Sara's crusade to improve his health would clamor in his brain. Miss perfect. Who was she to lecture him when she couldn't even make peace with her father?

He stepped five feet further down the wall, scanning every yeti footprint. Searching in the opposite direction, Sara could dredge up painful memories of the failed Everest episode. If so, he needed to find the right antidote.

Forty minutes of futile squinting later, something thumped the back of his neck. He whirled. Nothing. Another strike, then a third—this time wet on his cheek.

A spit wad.

Across the room with a straw poised at his lips, Beck jabbed a finger upward toward the ceiling and then fired a fourth. Livid at being treated like a third grader, Ryker wanted to rip his throat out. He bulldozed through tables and chairs, but Beck slipped out the door, gone before Ryker could lay hands on him.

Sara maneuvered her way to Ryker, boxed in by a crowd, his face ablaze. "What's going on?"

"Beck humiliated me shooting spit wads like we were grade schoolers. He pointed to the yeti footprint over my head."

"It's too high to reach."

"Not when rage energizes you to do the impossible, like you saved me from that charging elephant."

Ryker squatted and then sprang off the floor, pushing with the strength of his quads. His fingertips grazed empty air.

Sara borrowed a chair from a stunned diner in the front row and braced it. "Here, try again."

She steadied his wobbling legs as he stood tiptoe, reached, and grabbed the cord suspending the line of footprints, yanking the entire row loose. Gasps erupted as the chain of yetis swung wildly. Sara and a few quick diners caught it before it smashed into tables.

"Sorry, folks," Ryker muttered, flashing his badge. Sara did the same. "Police business. Serial killer."

They spread the captured footprint on a table and studied the blood-red scrawl. Each toe bore the name of a victim. Vance's loomed in all caps across the big toe. The arch spelled *Ryker* and *Sara* in two neat lines. An ice axe slashed across the heel.

Ryker's jaw locked. "So Beck thinks we're tiresome and leaves us this charming souvenir."

"He wanted to confirm we got his message."

"Oh, we got it, loud and clear. This endless duel of pursuit and evasion only ends one way."

Chapter 34

Sara replayed Beck's earlier taunt, the yeti footprint. Unbidden, another image surfaced—the torn scrap on her pillow, Beck's jagged scrawl, and the faint edge of bookstore lettering she had dismissed. Her nerves stood on end. Not random. A pointer. She wouldn't tell Ryker. Not yet. If Beck wanted her at Pilgrims, she needed to see why on her own terms.

Outside, they stepped into a chaos of honking horns, exhaust fumes, and rickshaws jostling with motorcycles and taxis. He rubbed a hand over his face. "Screw jet lag. I'm heading back to the guest house to sleep."

"You even know how to get there?"

"Just give the driver the name." He fished a crumpled five-dollar bill from his pocket. "And pay."

"Sorry, dollars won't work. You need rupees."

He pulled a sad puppy face, lips pushed out, chin quivering. "Take me home."

Sara hailed the next rickshaw and whispered to the driver, "Pilgrims Book House."

Between souvenir stalls and restaurants rose a blue-fronted building draped with colorful prayer flags. "We're here."

"Pilgrims Book House?" His brows knit.

"You read the sign. It's a landmark. Guidebooks rave about the ambience, classical music, and scented oils. It's our best place to stay awake and reset our clocks."

A woman was standing at the information desk, dark hair swept into a simple twist, asking in careful English about a book on Himalayan folklore.

Ryker noticed confidence in her voice, too calm for a tourist. Her eyes met his, and something flickered: interest, recognition?

"You're American?" she asked, as if confirming a hunch.

"Detective on temporary loan," he said, flashing a grin.

"Then maybe you can help me solve a mystery." She slid a small book to him. "The author claims gods still walk among us.

Her smile was wistful, but behind it Sara sensed exhaustion, a woman who'd been rehearsing calm too long.

Assured Ryker would remain awake in the presence of a beautiful woman, Sara drifted into her comfort zone: mountains and eastern religions. Settling in with a book on Hindu deities, she absorbed the balance of Brahma, Vishnu, and Shiva until drowsiness closed her eyes. Jolted awake four hours later, her insides trembled. Where was Ryker?

She went to an empty counter where he and the woman had been chatting. Where'd they go? Had he done a disappearing act with no money? She asked another employee whose smile moved from her lips to the corners of her eyes as she directed Sara to a restaurant two doors down the street.

Ryker and the woman were seated in a cozy corner booth sharing deep-fried, pretzel-shaped loops dipped in warm saffron syrup. He didn't notice Sara until she stood a foot from him.

"Have you finished reading already?" he asked, dropping a piece. "Sara, this is Isha. Her name means protector."

Sara noted her calm eyes and even tone, too studied to be a tourist, and that made her uneasy.

Isha rose smoothly and offered her hand. "You must be the famous Detective Lansing."

"Not that famous," Sara said, grip firm, smile absent.

The moment stretched taut, a current passing between two women. As they spoke over coffee and deep-fried loops, Isha listened, attentive but guarded. She glanced at the door and then steered the conversation toward Ryker's family, his daughter, his ex-wife—never herself.

Isha offered to show Ryker the temples in Durbar Square where kings had been crowned and ruled for centuries. Sara tried reading her intentions but found nothing there.

Ryker's glance begged her approval.

Sara smirked inwardly. Like you're such a devout student of history and religion. Will she lead you to erotic carvings on roof struts?

"How will you get back?" Sara asked.

"Isha took me to an ATM. We're going to dinner and then she'll arrange the rickshaw."

While trying to get your rupees. How gullible you are.

Sara said, "Keep a hand firmly on your wallet. Pickpockets roam the square looking for distracted tourists."

As they all got up to leave, she murmured, "Be wary. Don't go down any deserted alleys."

"I can handle myself."

"Not on their turf."

Sara returned to the guest house and went to the front desk. The manager's smile was tight lipped; the crinkling around his eyes spoke of stress as he handed her a key. "The suite is ready and includes twenty-four-hour room service."

"Thank you for being so obliging. I'm sure all will be fine."

Sara took the stairs to the third floor to energize herself. The luxury suite far exceeded her usual budget. What the heck. Enjoy it. She ordered eight momos and checked her phone for news of Pemba. Still nothing.

Sara settled on the couch with the steamed dumplings and watched an old western on the sole English TV channel until a knock on the door at eight.

"It's me," said Ryker.

Her glowing partner sauntered in and threw himself on the bed. "It was the best day of my life since my wife died," he said, half laughing at himself. "After those two disastrous online dates, Isha kindled something in me that lay buried in the dark too long. I can't remember the last time a woman looked at me the way she does, interested and engaged. She's not only stunningly beautiful but absolutely brilliant. She speaks fluent English and can quote Shakespeare."

Sara raised an eyebrow. "Uh-huh, because Shakespeare is every Nepali girl's dream? Do you not see the con?"

"She didn't ask me for anything."

"Other than to see you again and tighten the collar."

Lying there quietly staring at the ceiling, Ryker skewed his mouth and laughed with a slight edge of malice. "I think you're just jealous because I connected with the woman of my dreams while Michael walked out on you."

Sara's rebuke lodged in her throat. The man claiming to be an expert at reading people had surrendered reason to emotions. Any words from her would be twisted into reproach when unity was essential.

"We're having lunch tomorrow," Ryker said.

"Then get some sleep."

He was swinging his legs off the bed when a knock rattled the door. "Room service."

"We ordered nothing," Sara called.

"Sara Lansing and Ryker Harris?"

"Yes."

"I have a package delivery for you."

"I don't trust him," said Ryker.

She nodded.

"Leave it outside," he said.

Footsteps retreated.

"Could Beck be so diabolical he'd risk innocent lives with a bomb or gas?" Ryker asked Sara.

"Yes, he's vindictive but so far has played personal, not indiscriminate."

"He's willing to let Pemba starve to death."

"Only if we don't follow his orders. He put that onus on us."

"Then *you* be the one to retrieve our mysterious package."

Her stomach inching toward her throat, Sara found a small box in wrapping paper. Shaking it slightly, she determined it was a solid object weighing about a pound but had no notion beyond that. She locked the doorknob and deadbolt behind her.

"I brought it in. You open it."

Ryker carefully removed the wrapping paper and opened the lid. A loud whoosh of air escaped him as he removed a cylindrical stone with a rounded top sitting on a disc-shaped platform. "What the—?"

A ripple of humor creased her face. "A lingam."

"Eh?"

"The phallic symbol of the god Shiva."

He rotated the object in his hand. "Phallic as in penis, right?"

"Yes, it represents his power for creation and destruction. The flat disk is his consort Yoni, the divine feminine energy."

"I know nothing about all this . . . " Ryker's eyelids lowered, and he folded on his side, out cold. Total exhaustion had taken its toll.

"Here you go, big boy." Sara lifted his legs onto the bed and straightened his body to a more comfortable position.

A letter lay in the bottom. "See you at eight in the morning." She knew exactly where, the bank of the holy Bagmati River across from Nepal's largest cremation site.

Chapter 35

Sara's alarm rang at 7:00 a.m. "Shut that thing off. I need more rest." Ryker buried his head under a pillow and clung to the sides when she tried pulling him off the bed.

"Get with the agenda. A note in the box said to meet Beck at eight."

He peeked from under the pillow. "Where'd he set a trap?"

"Among eleven lingam."

He yanked the pillow off and sat up. "That phallic symbol?"

"Yep. Hit the breakfast buffet first and then head down to the Pashupatinath Temple, devoted to the god Shiva."

"I wish someone worshipped my phallic symbol that much."

A hint of a smile crossed her face. "Masses will bow before your altar one day."

He smirked. "Despite your sarcasm, I'm still going to lunch with Isha."

"Why don't you try thinking with your big head instead of that little one and focus on nabbing Beck to get home in time to see your daughter?

"That's cruel."

"But realistic about our endless circle of stalk and escape. Beck's a feral, dirty alley cat, not a fluffy Persian."

Ryker puffed out his chest and struck a mock bodybuilder pose. "But I'm a lion, fast, fierce, and hungry for justice."

Sara and Ryker strolled down the alley. Holy men in saffron and yellow robes sat cross-legged in shrine doorways, murmuring chants as their fingers ticked mantras on mala beads. Some wore tangled dreadlocks piled high, their faces smeared with paint, and necklaces dangling with bones. Others sat almost naked, dusted in gray ash, and folded into impossible yoga poses.

Ryker slowed. "Who are these men?"

"Sadhus. They gave up everything to dedicate their lives to seeking an inner truth. They depend upon the kindness of others. For a few rupees, they'll bless you or let you take their picture."

Ryker's jaw hitched to one side. "What's with the ash?"

"Shiva wore it. Purity is what remains when all else burns."

"And the locks?"

"Vanity's opposite."

Ryker shook his head. "Beck's going to recycle me before I figure all this out."

"That's not happening. Eyes ahead, play tourist and marvel at fifth-century Pashupatinath."

They stepped into the shadow of a pagoda-style temple, its copper roof layered in gold, doors faced in silver sheets.

"Can we go inside?" he asked.

"Not unless you're Hindu. But the grounds are free and open to the public with hundreds of shrines along the Bagmati River."

A heavy, brownish smoke hung in the air like a dense veil. "Where's that coming from?" Ryker asked.

"Cremation pyres on the ghat's stairway."

He stopped. "Bodies? Burning out in the open?"

"Yes. The eldest son usually lights the fire." Sara tilted her chin. "Look, one's about to."

From a long row of bodies shrouded in white on the plateau, a man carried one around a pyre with a lighted piece of wood and then touched its flame to the mouth.

Ryker's jaw hung loose, unmoving. "Why there?"

"They believe that's where the spirit leaves."

The man then dipped the body three times in the river before immersing it in fire with a hissing sound next to three corpses engulfed in flames.

"I'll never get my head around watching human bonfires as if it's normal," said Ryker.

"Hindus see it as a transition, not an end. The soul's cycle of birth, death, rebirth until reaching enlightenment."

"In that case, I've got a hundred lives left to go."

"Or maybe only one."

"Huh, don't count on it."

She tugged Ryker's sleeve. "Come over here."

At a smoldering pyre, an attendant swept charred wood and a partially decomposed body into the Bagmati River.

About to gag, Ryker asked, "Why?"

"The family didn't have enough wood."

The mourners stepped down into the water, chanting, their arms raised in prayer.

Ryker's eyes widened. "That water's foul, gray sludge."

"It's sacred, not sanitary. Bathing in the holy river cleanses sins, but they keep their heads above water away from disease."

Ryker gagged at the stench. "I'd need a hazmat suit."

Downstream, monkeys played and searched for food in the river. Women and children waded in knee-deep, sorting through Bagmati mud as bodies burned not fifteen feet away.

"What are they looking for?" Ryker asked.

"Rings, necklaces, brooches, gold fillings to sell for food."

He canvassed the crowd. Too many pilgrims and mourners. Any of the tourists clicking cameras like gunfire could be Beck. Smoke stung his eyes; he blinked hard, scanning the faces again. A man lingered too long and then slipped around a temple corner. Ryker's pulse leaped.

"Relax," Sara murmured. "Not every shadow is him."

Easy for her to say. His neck prickled the way it used to on a stakeout, that gut-hunch when trouble was close. He shifted his weight, hand twitching toward a holster that wasn't there.

Sara's stare fixed, unblinking, on the other side of the river. Through drifting smoke, she followed it to the narrow bridge. And there, dead center, stood Beck.

He tapped his wrist as though checking an invisible watch. Eight o'clock sharp. They'd received his message. A polite smile collapsed at the edges, leaving a taunting mask that wouldn't fool anyone. He raised a hand in a mock greeting.

You son of a bitch, Ryker cursed under his breath, fighting the urge to charge after him.

Sara's hand rested on his sleeve, grounding him. "Not here. He just put peanut butter in a trap and is daring us to cross.

"Then let's end this endless duel."

When they reached the other side, Beck had already turned and was gone, swallowed by smoke and stone among hundreds of shrines and mini temples dedicated to various deities.

"We're mice in a maze of red-roofed buildings," said Ryker.

Sara shook her head. "He calculated and sent us the lingam to direct us to a specific spot, and I know where it is."

Eleven stone shrines stood like sentinels, each with a lingam on a stone pedestal in the center of a small interior. Shiva, holding writhing snakes, adorned an arched doorway on all four sides.

Sara studied the embellishment, searching for a code she couldn't crack, and then suddenly laughed at herself. "I've got it. Shiva is associated with snakes and their symbolism."

"So that's why that sleaze put one in our bathroom."

"The workings of an egomaniac's mind."

Sara signaled Ryker over to stand at the front and look down a line of eleven lingams. "Stone pornography."

A flicker of movement. Beck darted across between shrines, disappeared. Bouncing back and forth and hiding behind walls, he was playing hide-and-seek among the gods.

"He could lurk inside any corner," said Sara.

On both sides of the small cubical buildings, they moved in unison, signaling *clear* between each one. Suddenly, Beck darted to the right from the tenth shrine before they reached it.

"Cat on the loose," she yelled and took off after him.

They burst into a maze of clustered temples, stone statues, and prayer wheels. The place swarmed with pilgrims, their chants and bells mingling into a restless hum. Sara caught Ryker's eye over the crowd. He pointed left. She nodded and veered right. Zigzagging forty minutes through shrines, sadhus, tourists, dogs, cows, kids, and monkeys without a glimpse of him, she stopped and heard Ryker calling her name.

"I'm here with sweat running down my face."

After three more calls, he found her, his chest heaving with each ragged breath. "I spotted Beck but couldn't catch him."

"Woods ahead. Split to cover more ground."

She filled her lungs and eased the air out slowly. Be vigilant. You can do this with the stealth of a hungry lioness.

She came upon a family under a banyan tree, swatting at the gray shapes lunging for their bag of cinnamon rolls. The youngest child squealed as one monkey clutched the prize and scurried off, shrieking triumphantly. Sara sided with the monkeys not having enough food and clean water for the hundreds romping around the temples and ghats.

She pressed on and then froze.

Ahead, a baby monkey sat tethered to a stake, its rope too short for escape. The little creature tugged and whimpered.

She kneeled to untie the knot. "You poor, hungry baby. Did those children do this?" As soon as she freed him, the monkey scampered off on all four feet.

"No, I did," said Beck as he stepped from behind a tree, his eyes burning. His hand clamped her wrist; the other flashed a knife. She twisted his arm, trying to drive her knee upward, but he jerked her off balance. The cold steel blade pressed against her throat. A rising panic, one wrong move, and he'd slit her open.

"The little fellow was my cheese, and you took the bait. The bill for wrecking the entire rest of my life is long overdue. It's time to settle your debt."

A wave of terror choked her, but she wasn't giving up. "You did that to yourself, leaving a trail of five bodies."

"They deserved to die in freezing cold the way they left my brother. I designed a personal death scenario for each one just as I have for you near your beloved Everest."

Sara saw Ryker slinking toward Beck without snapping a twig or bumping a pebble. Suddenly, children's laughter from the family picnic alerted Beck. He turned as Ryker crashed into him.

Beck swung at him. His arched body jumped out of reach, the knife striking empty air. The blade swept toward him again. Ryker seized Beck's arm with his right hand while his left pushed down on the forearm, forcing Beck to the ground.

Ryker kicked the knife away, but Beck was wiry, fast, and fought like a cornered rat. He rolled over and scrambled to his feet. "Neither of you will leave this country alive."

"Nothing will stop us from forcing your sorry ass to release Pemba and pay for six murders."

Beck lunged and head-butted Ryker's nose. He stumbled as if unprepared for the hit and struck back with a fist to Beck's jaw. Blood dripping from his mouth, he swung in a blind fury. Then in a whirlwind of motion, Ryker and Beck grappled, their bodies a tangle of limbs and sweat, their boots scraping dangerously close to the edge. Locked in a death dance, both lost their footing in the crumbling gravel of a precipice that dropped fifty feet.

A wave of acid shot into Sara's throat. "Ryker!" Her piercing scream tore through the woods. Skidding on gravel to the rim, she flailed her arms to keep from falling over the edge. Below, she saw sluggish water, brown with silt, frothing with debris.

No sign of either man.

Chapter 36

The world tilted, and then there was only air. The fall ended in a bone-jarring splash, sinking Ryker in a debris-clogged mire. The river swallowed him. His mouth clamped tight and holding his breath, he struggled to break through a surface of cremation ash and bone pieces. Gagging and coughing, he fought for breath, but Beck was already on him, pushing his head back under. They rolled, half submerged, half thrashing in the shallow bed.

Ryker managed a wild punch, caught Beck's jaw, and broke the surface for half a breath before the younger, wiry form shoved him into a stone wall along the bank. His head hit.

Disoriented, barely conscious, he slid into the river's grasp. His lungs seized, a spasm of shock. He clawed upward, desperate for air, floundering in deep water too exhausted to free himself.

"Ryker!"

Sara plunged into the river, grabbed his arm, and hauled him onto the nearest stone step. He collapsed, retching, coughing up filthy river water. The ghats enveloped them: smoke curling into the air, temple bells ringing, monks chanting, axes splitting logs, bones crackling in fires, and flesh sliding off corpses in the heat.

Sara dropped to her knees and brushed ash and blood from his forehead. "Speak to me. The Bagmati's not powerful enough to take down a badass like you. The ten hours are clicking away, and I'm not flying solo."

Ryker's hand grabbed hers, smearing her wrist with mud and blood. "Where's Beck? Tell me you saw him go under."

"My eyes were only on you."

He sat up, still spitting river water. They scanned the river. Ryker thought he saw a shape move beneath the surface, but it was only the endless current of the Bagmati carrying its dead. He forced himself to his feet, every movement painful.

Together they trudged among families and visitors, asking if anyone had seen another man in the water. One saw him drown. Another pointed downstream. A third claimed he'd staggered to the east bank and vanished among the temples.

No dead body. No conclusion.

The admission hung between Sara and Ryker heavier than the river's stink. Beck could still be out there somewhere in the labyrinth of Kathmandu's alleys, plotting his next strike.

She gripped Ryker's shoulder. "We have to move. Now."

They turned away from the ghats with a chilling certainty.

This was not over yet.

**

Back at the guest house, they stepped into the elevator. When the door closed, Ryker's acrid bouquet of smoke, ash, and river debris filled the enclosed space.

Sara covered her nose. "Even though you valiantly rescued me, don't even think of coming within ten feet before a shower."

He bowed in a soggy flourish. "As you command."

"That's more like it, you dunderhead, taking on a man with a knife."

"Your job was to keep track of him while this embodiment of strength and intellect fought him in the Bagmati."

"Between us, we gained nothing and don't know if he's dead or alive."

"True, but the river bath cleansed me of all my sins."

"If only it were that easy."

She unlocked the suite and escorted him to the bathroom.

He exited twenty minutes later, his three-day stubble neatly trimmed and his hair having won the daily brush altercation."

Sara sat back, arms crossed, and reviewed him. "Well, aren't you Mister Debonair?"

He strutted around the room. "Lunch with Isha at one."

"Friend alert. She's beguiling you for cash or a green card."

"When did you become an expert on love?"

"I call it as I see it. You two do not a couple make."

"And I call it as I feel it. We had an immediate bond."

"Sara turned her eyes toward the ceiling."

He halted in front of her. "She initiated our conversation."

"My point exactly." Sara rose. "I'll peruse books nearby to save your skin."

Riding in the rickshaw, Ryker kept crossing and uncrossing his legs, rubbing his thighs."

"Settle down," she said.

He blew out a heavy breath. "Sorry, I'm just a bit nervous." A cigarette slipped out of his pocket.

Sara yanked it from his hand. "Cool it. No more smokes."

They arrived back at Pilgrims. The moment Ryker's eyes met Isha's, her lips curved into a teasing smile, promising untold possibilities. She pressed her palms. "Namaste once again."

His pulse quickened as he stammered, "Namaste, to you as well." A sidelong glance at Sara caught that suspicious attitude again, making him even more nervous. He had to get out of her purview.

Ryker's throat was taut and dry, his words escaping above a whisper, "Pick your favorite restaurant and we'll go now."

She chose one only half a block away but across a street with no lanes. Getting through what looked like a rugby scrum forbade a daunting challenge: rickshaws, motorcycles, bicycles, tuk-tuks, cows, women balancing loads, and mothers pushing strollers.

Ryker envisioned himself a hero carrying a beautiful damsel to a favorite place, but Isha boldly walked into the street, traffic swirling around her like rapids around a boulder. Ryker held his breath, stepped behind her, and followed.

The café welcomed them with a wave of spice and warmth. Fans ticked overhead, stirring the air heavy with cardamom and coffee. Waiting for their food, Ryker sat without a word traveling across his lips. It had been so easy the day before, but now the muscles in Isha's face strained to ward off tears.

Please don't cry. I don't know how to comfort you. His right knee was bouncing rapidly. Do something, you dunce. He leaned forward and gazed into her eyes. "Are you all right?"

When water rolled down her cheeks, he crumbled. "Tell me what's wrong."

She dabbed at the moisture with a napkin. Ryker placed his hand over hers and caressed it with his thumb. "I'll do anything you ask."

Isha sniffed the last tears. "I don't know where else to turn."

"From whom or what? I want to help."

"My father . . ."

Watching more water trickle down that beautiful, silky hair, Ryker gently squeezed her hand. "What about him?"

"He . . . he—"

"Yes?"

"In the casino, he won ninety thousand dollars at a poker table with high-stakes players. His luck seemed unstoppable."

"But it wasn't."

"He felt indomitable, but the lucky streak ended. He tried winning the money back by betting higher and higher."

"And didn't know when to stop."

Isha closed her eyes and slowly opened them as if trying to clear the blur. "Now he's so deeply in debt to those players that he'll never get out. They locked my father in a warehouse."

Blood slammed in Ryker's ears. He'd failed to protect his mother when his father killed. Failed to be there for his daughter. Now, Pemba and Isha's dad have been left to die. Was karma giving him another chance to make things right?

Barely able to keep his own eyes dry, he wiped the last tear from Isha's face. "Do you know the warehouse location?"

"In a row of buildings outside of town. I've been too afraid to go there alone."

Her eyes flickered toward the door. When she glanced back and smiled, he managed to return it. But the question stayed lodged like grit under his eyelid. Was Isha his ally or another trap he hadn't recognized?

"Don't wait for me if your lunch arrives," Ryker said. "I'll be right back

He stopped at the curb. If ladies pushing strollers could cross the scrum, so could he. Questioning his feelings, he marched to the bookstore, found Sara, and related Isha's teary story.

"Interesting account, but it has a monumental tell. Nepalese natives are barred from entering. Casinos open to international guests only."

Ryker slapped the sides of his head. "How could I have been duped so easily?"

Sara closed the book on Hindu gods and gave him a one-shoulder hug. "We're ace detectives. We'll unravel this."

Needing to bolster his ego, he strode into the traffic, forcing Sara to follow.

Isha's face and eyes were dry but quickly moistened when they slipped into the booth opposite her. Sara folded her hands and made direct eye contact. "I'm sorry to hear about your father. How long has he been held captive in a warehouse?"

"Uhm, five days. He owes some very dangerous men a lot of money and can't pay."

"The money he lost gambling in a casino," Ryker added.

Sara tilted her head at Isha. "Is this true?"

"Yes."

"But you and I both know your father couldn't have entered a casino."

Fingering the napkin, Isha glanced across the room. Setting it down again, she folded one corner with deliberate care. Ryker clocked it and stored it away without knowing why.

"Is someone watching us?" he murmured.

She blinked once.

He studied her slim, graceful fingers—a silver ring flashing when she gestured—and longed to embrace her. "Take my hand and act as if I don't know you lied to me."

Sara stole a few forbidden fries from his burger and smiled at Isha. "Don't look away. While giving us the truth, convince whoever's watching that we're buying his casino story."

Ryker held her hand and met her gaze. She described a tall man with long hair who approached her at work early yesterday morning and threatened never seeing her five-year-old son again unless she did exactly as he told.

Adverse to eating anything greasy, Sara chomped on a fry to appear casual. "And what were his instructions?"

"Play up to Ryker, win his confidence, and lead both of you to the warehouse."

"Our brawl and swim in the Bagmati forced him to kick his game up a notch," said Ryker.

"I have to protect my son."

"I'd do the same for my daughter."

Heat rose in Ryker's neck as she said, "It wasn't all a lie."

"Perfect," Sara whispered, "Keep holding hands and gazing at each other so our observer won't suspect we're on to him."

"He was watching from behind the stacks when we met. I asked a friend to follow him to my son. She handed Sara a slip of paper with an address. "He also stopped at this travel agency."

That jolted Sara upright, eager to be on the hunt again with the address."

Lunch over, Isha led them through a warren of alleys to a corrugated steel door half-hidden between shuttered shops. The whole block reeked of kerosene and dust. Too quiet.

Chapter 37

Ryker forced the door. Hinges shrieked as it swung inward, revealing a cavernous space crammed full of crates and sagging scaffolds. They stepped inside, and the door clanged shut.

A shadow dropped from the rafters. Knife in hand and teeth bared, Beck hit the ground between them. His voice echoed off the steel walls. "Looking for me?"

Ryker charged, but Beck's blade flashed across his shoulder and drew blood. Sara grabbed a pipe from the floor and swung. Beck caught it on his forearm, twisted, and sent her stumbling backward into a stack of crates. Wood splintered, boxes crashing down in a thunder of nails and dust.

The fight became a blur of metal and fists. Beck drove Ryker into a steel beam, then wheeled toward Sara, knife slicing close enough to snag her hair. She ducked and slammed the pipe into his ribs, but he absorbed it, grinning through the pain.

"Not good enough," he hissed.

Ryker crashed into him from the side. All three went down in a tangle, the knife skittering across the floor. Sara lunged for it. Too late. Beck's hand closed first. He sprang back, chest heaving with feral triumph. For a moment, he held them both in the knife's arc and then backed toward the shadows between the crates.

"You'll never leave this country alive."

And then he was gone.

Ryker held his shoulder to stop the bleeding. "It's only a surface wound, but dammit, he got away again.

Amid the clang of metal and the echo of retreating footsteps, Sara spun, but Isha was gone. Only her scarf lay twisted near a toppled crate.

"She ran?" Ryker asked, scanning the shadows.

"Or was taken. Either way, she knew this place too well to be innocent."

Minutes later, a boy on a bicycle brought Ryker a worn book and said a woman had paid him to deliver it to the detective. A note lay inside. He turned the paper over in his hand, the words smudged with sweat or tears, and read, "I tried to protect him. Forgive me."

He slipped the note into his jacket. He'd wanted to find her before they left Kathmandu, to ask what was real and what was survival. But part of him knew better. Some people stayed alive by vanishing. Others by letting them.

"You okay?" Sara asked.

"I will be. But for now, Beck's a predator; we're the prey. What's his next plan?"

"I don't know, but we'll need a plane to get there."

His brows dipped unevenly. "Your gut talking again?"

"No, but the travel agency address is shouting."

They flagged a taxi and jolted through Kathmandu traffic. Motorbikes wove past the dented yellow cab, horns blaring. Dust hung in the air like a curtain, catching sunlight in a haze. Signs in English and Nepali competed for space on crumbling walls: Best Deals for Lukla! The streets smelled of fried dough, incense, and exhaust.

Sara showed Beck's photo at the travel agency counter. "Did this man come here this morning?"

The woman studied his face. "Yes, for a plane to Lukla."

"When does his flight leave?"

"There are no planes to Lukla."

Sara leaned across the counter, her voice sharp. "I just had a brutal fight with this man and have zero patience. There are planes to Lukla. I've flown in and out of there from here. Now give me the flight."

"Hiking trails were becoming too crowded. Since 2022, all planes to Lukla have been shut down during peak season."

Sara shook her head. "That's inconceivable. Trekkers going to Everest base camp?"

"Start from the airport in Ramechhap, a mountainous four-to-five-hour drive from here."

"But we know a team that climbed last May," said Ryker.

"And either made the drive or took a helicopter as your man plans to. Here's the card I gave him."

"Thank you, and I apologize for being irritable."

A slight smile. "You're not the first."

Outside, the hot sun pressed down through smog. The street noise felt like a physical weight. Sara said, "Choppers are not the cheapest way out of town."

"You've flown in one?"

She opened her hands and shrugged. "What do you think?"

"That I do not want to fly into mountains in a whirlybird."

"And I do not want to waste precious time on a long drive."

The address on the card was six doors down. They stepped past a man selling oranges from a pushcart and then into another shop where faded trekking posters curled on the walls. Sara laid Beck's photo on the counter. "Did he come in here today?"

"Yes, wanting a Lukla flight for this afternoon."

"Which would cost?"

"It's $500 American dollars per person for a shared ride and $2,700 for a single."

"And by plane from Ramechhap?" Ryker asked.

"Only $180 and planes depart early in the morning."

Ryker pulled Sara aside. "For $180, we go to Rame . . . whatever it's called, and fly out tomorrow morning."

"Get there by taxi and have to pay for a roundtrip? Uh-uh. We're taking the whirlybird."

Resting against the counter, she scanned a wall of helicopter ads, each with glossy peaks and smiling trekkers. "Which one did he buy?"

"None, like everyone, he wanted to reach Lukla and begin hiking toward Everest. We were sold out yesterday and today." He gave Sara a card. "I referred him to this company."

"Thanks. We'll inquire there."

"On the way, Ryker asked, "Why Lukla?"

"It's the fastest way to get into the mountains, but it's one of the most dangerous airports in the world. Short, steep runway, unpredictable weather, thin air, surrounded by mountain ranges, pockets of clouds, difficult to navigate without radar."

"Okay, okay. Enough. I get it."

She enjoyed rattling his cage too much to stop. "Its history of multiple accidents and fatalities gives passengers the heebie-jeebies."

"You trying to frighten me?"

She grinned. "Yeah, and I succeeded."

At the next helicopter shop, Ryker said with an impatient edge, "Hand me your phone. I will do the questioning this time."

As he approached the counter, Sara folded her arms, half amused, half wary. She watched him turn on the grin that worked on suspects and waitresses, his voice lowering into its smooth register. She hated to admit it, but he was good at this.

"What did you find?" she asked when he swaggered back.

"They're also fully booked to Lukla."

She opened her hands again. "And?"

"Beck knows your mastermind identified him as the killer, and he recognizes I'm not afraid to challenge him in a fight. He's upped his game. No more obscure clues, he's daring us to locate him using only our wits."

"What are you babbling about?"

"Beck chartered a $3,500 helicopter to Namche and left an hour ago."

A broad smile burst across Sara's face. "Yes! We got him!"

Ryker thrust his head forward as if not comprehending what he'd just heard.

She sashayed to the desk and asked the clerk, "Do you have a flight to Namche today?"

"No, but if you don't mind sharing, two members in a party of five became ill and canceled for tomorrow."

"Great, we'll take it."

Ryker pulled her aside. "We don't have that kind of money."

"The shared ride to Lukla was $500 compared to $2,700 for a single. Namche's not that much further." She whipped out her credit card and paid.

"Your fifty-minute flight departs at four tomorrow. Come fifteen minutes early to weigh in. No hard-sided luggage, weight limit is thirty-three pounds each."

On the ride to the guest house, Ryker said, "I've never seen you this pumped up. Why are you so cocksure we've got him?"

"Not knowing Isha's friend ratted on him, his guard will be down, but he'll have a slight altitude advantage getting there earlier."

His knee bouncing like a snare drum, he said, "I heard you guys talking about oxygen. Patrick and Heath could've died."

Sara slowed his bouncing knee. "Relax. They were higher on Everest."

"I understand, but why're you telling me this?"

"Because we'll go from four thousand to eleven thousand three hundred feet too fast instead of hiking two days in from Lukla. You need to rest and hydrate, but no alcohol. If not, expect dizziness, insomnia, headache, and nausea."

"Uh-hu, and a good time will be had by all."

"But rejoice. You burn more calories at altitude."

"So I can eat as much as I want without you harping at me?"

"If you're eating the right kind. Sleep well tonight and shop tomorrow for duffels, refillable water bottles, sunscreen, warm clothes, Snickers, and Diamox."

"And what?"

"Altitude pills. They're a diuretic and make you pee a lot." Sara smiled. "That reminds me of Michael. We had to stay in a yak herder's hut at fifteen thousand feet one night and slept on a plywood plank with no mattress. Using Diamox, I needed to pee. Flashlight burned out, I groped my way down two dark staircases and opened the door. A herd of long-haired yaks with sharp horns stood between me and the only boulder to squat behind. They're notoriously ill tempered, but my bladder screamed emergency. I pushed through thousand-pound beasts, yelling to get outta my way."

Ryker laughed so hard his eyes watered. "Poor Beck doesn't stand a chance against the yak conqueror."

Chapter 38

Ryker skipped the buffet breakfast and lunch before having to weigh in at the helicopter. Looking at the slimmer couple on their honeymoon and an aging monk, he asked Sara, "What if I'm too heavy?"

"Don't worry. The pilot assigns seats. Time to board."

Crouched low to avoid the rotor blades chopping the air, the *whup-whup-whup* reverberating in Ryker's chest, they ran to the copter and climbed into the cramped, intimate cabin. The monk slid serenely into the copilot's seat. Behind him, two rows: the husband diagonal to Ryker; the bride to Sara.

Seated in front of Ryker, the bride trembled, knuckles white, clutching her husband's hands. Her wide eyes heightened Ryker's anxiety to panic. Sara looped her arm around his and whispered, "She's a beginner."

"So am I."

Her chin pointed toward the monk. "Chill like him and enjoy the most sublime views you'll ever see."

The copter lifted like a seed on the wind, light as a dandelion puff, before tilting forward and accelerating. Clouds rolled below like a white sea. Valleys unfurled beneath them, green ridges and canyons carved by glacial-fed rivers. The stone retaining walls on terraces looked ancient, wrinkled, like an old man's face.

As the copter pressed north toward Himalayan giants, peak after snowcapped peak reared into view, jagged teeth glittering in the sun.

Half an hour into the flight, Sara leaned close. "We'll soon pass over Lukla in a very narrow valley with no options for error. Look for the short landing strip and a sharp right turn to avoid crashing into a mountain."

Ryker's heart raced. Until now, he'd been afraid of falling. Now he was terrified of landing.

Laughing lightly at his expression, Sara pointed at Namche. "See how the village is cupped in a natural amphitheater shaped like a horseshoe. About sixty stone houses are stacked on terraces clinging to the steep slope."

The descent was abrupt, nothing like a plane landing. Rotor wash blasted the ground. The engine still shrieking, the crewman flung open the door, waving frantic hand signals to exit. Sara and Ryker ducked low and ran through the rotor wind to a safe zone.

The sudden quiet was startling. Thin mountain air pressed into Ryker's lungs, sharp and cold as ice water.

A young Sherpa approached and bowed, his palms together. "Namaste. My name is Mingma. Welcome to Namche Bazaar. I can carry your backpacks and duffels."

Seeing this wiry five-foot-six man with olive skin and high cheekbones, Ryker dismissed him. "Thanks, but we'll manage."

Sara pointed upward. "See those terraces? We have to find lodging and are not acclimatized to climb steep hills. Your body will go on strike."

Ryker's ego bristled. "I'll carry for both of us."

Sara bowed her head forward to Mingma. "Namaste, please put them in your dhoko and show my friend how to wear it."

With practiced ease, Mingma loaded the sixty-six pounds into a bamboo basket, sat in front of it, and placed a jute tumpline over his forehead. He then rose smoothly to his feet.

Ryker sniggered, sat in front of the loaded dhoko, and pulled the tumpline over his head.

"Very good," said Mingma. "Now stand up."

Ryker locked his teeth, face turning red, veins bulging in his neck. He leaned forward onto both hands and pushed with his arms and legs, grunting, but didn't budge an inch.

Mingma nodded to Sara, and together they pulled Ryker upright. "Congratulations," said Sara brightly just as he toppled backward onto the dhoko and yanked the strap off his head.

"No matter what he charges, pay him double."

"I am here to help," Mingma said graciously. "Do you need lodging? We have budget rooms with shared baths, medium-size hotels with private baths, and luxury ones."

Ryker's head was throbbing. "Two beds and a private bath."

"I will leave you and the dhoko at a café while I run to see what's available."

Sara's lips parted in a warm smile. "Much appreciated. By the way, your English is excellent."

"Thank you. We begin learning English very early in school. I was fortunate enough to study two extra years in Kathmandu. I also learn from English TV shows and speaking with tourists."

After he left, Ryker rubbed his shoulder. "I've dealt with his kind in New York. He'll return saying it's peak tourist season. No rooms are available, but he spoke to his uncle who is willing to let such nice people share a room in his house for a very small price."

Sara sighed and said, "I'll disregard that comment, chalking it up to altitude and humiliation. It's all on you."

Twenty minutes later, Mingma came jumping down stone stairs two at a time from the fifth terrace. He handed Ryker a list of four available hotels with private baths.

Huh, this Sherpa was not only strong but guileless. Ryker's stomach churned, his head buzzing with fatigue. All he wanted to do was lie down. "Take us to the best one."

After checking in, he and Sara spoke privately with Mingma and showed Beck's photo. "Have you seen this man?" she asked. "He chartered a private helicopter to Namche yesterday."

"I was working with a French tour and didn't meet arrivals."

"We've chased him all the way from the US. He murdered five climbers and kidnapped a Sherpa named Pemba who will die if we don't catch him in the next three days."

"There are many Pembas," Mingma said gently. "His name means he was born on Saturday."

Sara scrolled through her photos and stopped at the one with Pemba and Beck, raising Disneyland mugs in a toast. "That's the man we're after.

Mingma leaned closer, his fingers enlarging the photo. His face hardened. "That's Pemba Dawa. When his brother died on an expedition last spring, he traveled to America to overcome his grief. Pemba is a brother to all. Tell me how to get this evil man."

"We have to catch him ourselves," said Sara, "but we need help to make sure he doesn't slip out of Namche."

"I will print copies of your picture and give them to Sherpas to guard the trails leading in and out. They will spread them to porters carrying between villages."

"How much do we owe you and them?" Ryker asked.

"Nothing. We only want the safety of our brother. Try to rest well tonight in our thinner air. Tomorrow is the weekly Saturday market. Hundreds of traders from nearby and distant villages will sell their goods on open terraces. The man you seek may try to lose himself among them."

"Not expecting us to have tracked him here so easily, he may be less alert than in Kathmandu," said Sara. "Please don't make our presence known."

After Mingma left, Ryker's body slackened. "I feel like crap and don't want any dinner."

"You do look a bit gray around the edges like a potato head I carved and let dry until it hardened and turned leathery."

He glowered. "Thanks, like I needed that now?"

"Just checking to see if you're paying attention."

"I am and why aren't you sick?"

"People acclimatize differently. It's genetic." She refilled his water bottle from a large container at the front desk. "Drink only this, hot tea, or coffee. Staying hydrated is mandatory. Did you take the Diamox?"

"Uhm, I forgot and am a little woozy now."

"Go to the room, keep drinking water and take a Diamox. If you're not better by tomorrow, a Sherpa will take you lower to Monjo, three hours below."

**

Sara ordered momos and tea and then settled on the hotel patio facing a forested hill bordered by a rock wall. Memory tugged at her. Years ago on the expedition with Michael, they'd spent two days in Namche to acclimatize. Wanting time alone one night, they'd wandered up the terraces and discovered a monastery. Laughing like children, they spun a row of two-foot-tall prayer wheels for good karma.

Behind the monastery, two massive boulders jutted from the forest floor and captured their interest. They sneaked over a wall and wound their way through the dense pines with flashlights. She could still feel Michael's fingers wrapping around hers, their bodies moving in unison as he lifted her onto one of the rocks.

They sat under a full moon ringed by an orange halo, a pale haze softening its edges. The snow-clad peaks loomed like silent sentinels over the village, prayer flags fluttering in the breeze, the only sound apart from her heart beat. His gentle hand caressed her lips. No words spoken, no longing whispers. Their bodies said it all.

Now after six years of silence, he was coming back to her. But if Beck snares his prey, she'll never know love again,

Chapter 39

Sara rolled over and looked at Ryker, still asleep in the other bed. She pulled a string of dental floss from her toilet kit and dangled the tip on his ear. Eyes closed, he swiped at it. The floss tickled his nose, and he brushed it off twice. When it danced along his cheek, Ryker woke and slapped the damn fly.

"Good morning. It's five thirty, time to rise and shine."

He yanked the floss from her hand. "Are you nuts? Sun's not even up yet."

"That's why you'll get up, dress, and go outdoors."

"Huh?"

"Do it now. We're losing time."

Grumbling, he dragged his pants and shirt into the bathroom and slammed the door. He emerged moments later like a pouting child whose parents had eaten all his Halloween candy.

"Where are we going?"

"Up a hill."

She took him on a fifteen-minute hike to a flat ridge above the village. "I couldn't let you come this far and not see Everest."

He gasped and began rubbing his arms. "You're giving me goosebumps."

The sun's first rim below the horizon set clouds aflame in orange with purple. Slowly, light spilled across serrated ridges, painting them copper, then gold.

Everest's triangle rose above the Nuptse wall, while Lhotse loomed to the right, immense and forbidding.

Ryker stood in silence, unwilling to interrupt this coveted moment. He slowly released a deep breath. "I . . . I'm guilty of unabashed staring. After hearing so much about Everest, I can't find words to describe it, but New York's skyline suddenly feels very small."

"I first laid eyes on it with Michael. Reaching the roof of the world was to be our final challenge after seven years of adventure racing." Her voice snagged on itself. "Who knows? We might have settled down and had a family."

She jerked and straightened herself up. "So what do you think? Worth getting out of bed for?"

He nodded in mute bewilderment that she asked.

Heading back down, Sara and Ryker met four of the Sherpa Squad monitoring three trails converging from the north. Nima said they took turns during the night, and all four had been there this morning as crowds arrived for the market. The man had not passed from the south trail, the north one, or from the helipad.

Back in Namche, the terraces had transformed into a sea of bodies. The Saturday market pulsed with life: yak cheese stacked like bricks, heaps of scarlet chilies, bolts of bright cloth, crude tools, candies wrapped in crinkled foil. Chickens squawked, goats bleated, and traders shouted prices. The press of bodies was suffocating, sweat and wood smoke mingling in the thin air. Packed tight, shoulder to shoulder, bartering and shouting, they made it hellishly difficult to search for Beck.

Sara and Ryker chose the two most crowded terraces. He took the upper one and she the one below. Their advantage was Beck's six-foot height towering over the five-foot-five Sherpas. The taller tourists wandering in the market posed the only visual impediment.

With frequent nods and Namastes, Sara carefully threaded her way among women selling vegetables from blankets, their hands worn and strong. The aroma of asters, chrysanthemums, and dahlias wafted in the air. Sara stepped wide of a butcher slicing yak meat for stew. Hammer blows rang as carpenters salvaged broken furniture. The air reeked of raw meat, butter, incense, and too many bodies in too little space.

She opened her arms wide, questioning Ryker on the terrace above. He shook his head. No sign of Beck up there either.

Continuing to squeeze between the mass of bodies, she came upon a tourist arguing with an elderly woman to shave a dollar off a beautiful hand-woven scarf worth twenty. "Shame on you," said Sara. "That dollar won't even pay for a cup of coffee at home but may mean the difference between dinner and going hungry for her children tonight."

"Bargaining is part of their culture. We're supposed to."

"But within the bounds of humanity."

He sneered and took the scarf anyway. Sara pressed two dollars into the woman's hand. She bowed, eyes grateful, before Sara plunged back into the crush.

Then Ryker cut through the din. "He's fifty feet ahead of me in a blue sweatshirt!

"Wait for me!" she shouted, shoving past vendors.

She raced up eight stone stairs. "Has he spotted you?"

"Must have. He quickened his pace."

Beck was fast. The crowd slowed them. Sara and Ryker shoved and elbowed their way, shouting, "Move," to non-English speakers who recognized the urgency and jumped aside. At the upper end of the market, four tourists blocked the path, fiddling with tomatoes as if the fruit held the fate of the world.

Ryker yelled, "Single file, guys, let us through!"

They were a clown act, jockeying to position themselves in a straight line and suck in their guts. By the time Ryker and Sara pushed past, Beck had vanished.

Ryker hurled a rock into the bushes, roaring, "We had him within yards. Four nitwits let a murderous fiend escape."

A sudden clamor rose near the yak pen. Beck, yelling and flailing, had sent the animals into a frenzy. Still riling them, he wrenched the gate open. Snorting beasts thundered forward, horns swinging, bells clanging, dust rising like smoke.

The ground trembled as lead yak's massive head and horns rammed Ryker, flipping him through the air and dropping him with a thud. The hooves of another clipped Sara's legs, pitching her to the ground. She curled tight to keep from being trampled in a yak stampede. Pain was irrelevant; failure wasn't an option.

An elderly Sherpani barked orders, and two teenage boys whistled and drove the yaks off with sticks. Then she knelt beside Sara, lifting her pant leg to reveal a bleeding gash. She pressed a scarf, still warm from her neck, against the wound, murmuring words Sara didn't understand but felt in her bones. Her eyes crinkled with kindness as she tied the scarf tight.

Ryker staggered up, clutching his side, face twisted in pain.

"You okay?" Sara gasped.

"I'll live."

The Sherpani tugged at his shirt, helping him ease one arm free. She inhaled sharply at the bruising, her gasp understood in any language.

"It hurts like hell. Sara, what do you see?"

"Not bleeding, just one hell of a bruise. Seems you're too tough to puncture." She bit her lip. "But it'll disrupt your sex life for months."

"What sex life?"

The Sherpani mimed putting ice on their wounds, helped Ryker back into his sleeve, and then pressed her palms together. "Namaste." She and the boys melted into the crowd.

"Well, well, well," a sardonic voice rang out. "You both got yak slapped. I wanted you trampled to death, but the day is young yet. However, Pemba's are running out."

Ryker bellowed, "We're your nemesis. There's no escape."

"I'm invincible."

Beck sprinted down two terraces and disappeared into the village maze

Sara limped down the irregular stone steps. "He could hide in any of two hundred businesses and sixty homes."

"We'll never catch him like this. I need food to heal after donating yesterday's meal to the throne. We had no breakfast."

She stopped and looked back. "How can you be thinking of your stomach right now?"

He jutted his lower lip like a sulky kid.

"Fine, but only after we get ice."

The Namche Bakery smelled of coffee and sugar the instant they stepped indoors, a shocking contrast to the chaos outside. They sank into a couch, ordered two bags of ice for their aching bodies. The menu boasted five different kinds of cakes, muffins, pies, brownies, and pizza.

"We're over eleven thousand feet. How do they bake here?"

"Be brave, my warrior."

She ordered a sandwich; Ryker, pizza and a chocolate-layered pastry with whipped buttercream. Sara noted the cruel irony of having pizza and pastry while Pemba was starving somewhere.

She logged onto the bakery's free internet and WhatsApp to contact McBride with an update. Beck is still loose, and Pemba's location is unknown."

"Well?" Ryker asked when the conversation ended.

"Not a trace of him anywhere."

On the off chance of a miracle, she tried Patrick and Ashley.

They picked up instantly, breathless. "Oh, thank god, did you catch him, get Pemba's location?"

"We were within a few feet of nabbing him an hour ago, but the bastard got away. He's somewhere in Namche. We'll keep knocking on doors until we find him."

After the call, Ryker ate with grim focus. Waiting for him, Sara scrolled a new message from Michael. "My sweet Sara, I admire your dedication and won't interfere until hearing from you. Every night, I dream of holding you in my arms and hope we'll be together again soon. Love, Michael."

Her phone rang less than a minute later. It had to be him. Almost hyperventilating, she answered in a passionate voice.

"Miss Sara?" said Mingma.

She wilted at the sound of his voice. "Yes."

"A porter raced down to tell me the man you seek passed him on the trail north to Tengboche. Bring warmer clothes and water. I can be your porter, but we must leave soon."

"Understood."

Bent forward, Sara stared into the depths of her coffee cup.

Ryker reached across the table and took her hand. "What's wrong?"

She straightened up. "Sherpa squad saw Beck heading to the Buddhist monastery six miles north of here."

He dabbed a drop of water at the corner of her eye. "Hmm, something more personal's going on."

"I thought it was Michael calling."

She caught a string of cheese hanging from his chin. "We have to leave now and get our duffels."

His eyes shot wide open. "You mean us walking that far?"

"Unless you hail an Uber." She snorted. "Let's go,"

Chapter 40

Duffels loaded and refillable bottles in each backpack, they met Mingma in the lobby. "Have everything you need?" he asked.

Ryker stood with arms akimbo, feet braced. "No, I'm going armed. Won't take long."

In a shop window two doors from the hotel, he showed them a large knife with a heavy curved blade sharp on the inward side.

"That's a kukri," Mingma explained. "Weapon of Gurkhas, the most skilled and feared soldiers in the world. See this notch? It keeps blood off the handle. Legend says once drawn, a kukri must taste blood before being sheathed again."

Ryker gave a short, hard laugh. "Good legend."

Sara's words spoke a restrained challenge. "Are you ready for that?"

He buckled the twelve-inch blade in its leather sheath onto his belt. "For Beck? I am now."

"Trail shouldn't be crowded," said Mingma. "Most trekkers leave early in the morning."

Their duffels and his gear loaded in the dhoko, they climbed to a sign for Tengboche. The trail following a mountain ridge was fairly flat and easy with a river flashing below. Embarrassment had gnawed at Ryker all night for giving in to altitude yesterday when he wanted to remain strong for Sara. Not going to happen today. He pushed ahead fast, legs pumping like he was chasing down a New York taxi.

"Bistari, bistari," Mingma called after him. "A slow, steady pace gets you there sooner than racing and stopping to breathe."

Sara chimed in, teasing, "Enjoy the view. Look for a danphe. Remember the pheasant crime scene?"

Crime scene. Everything circled back to murder. He set his jaw and kept moving.

For a mile, the trail cut into a hillside above a white river fed by melting glaciers. From a lookout, Mingma pointed straight across the valley to their destination high on another mountain.

Ryker checked their expressions. No alarm signal. "I don't need a guidebook to know if it's the same height on another damn mountain, we have to go down to the river and climb all the way back up."

Sara grinned. "Sherpas call that a level trail."

"Is there food between here and there?"

"Yes, at a riverfront restaurant in Phungi Tanga."

Ninety minutes in, they reached a whitewashed stupa flying prayer flags. "Tenzing Norgay memorial," said Mingma. "He and Hillary were the first to climb Everest."

A low rumble shivered through the ground. A crack, then a roar. Dirt poured from the slope above. Boulders ripped loose, bouncing and grinding against each other, kicking up a cloud of dust and small stones. One slammed down close enough that Ryker felt the gust of displaced air whip his face. Another spun Mingma sideways and spilled the dhoko before coming to a stop.

"Holy crap!" Ryker dove down the slope, cutting his palms. The basket teetered on the edge, seconds from tumbling into the river. He lunged and caught it. Breathing ragged, he crawled uphill with the duffels to Mingma's gear strewn across the trail.

Movement caught his eye. Beck jumped off the memorial's platform and hit the trail running.

Sara's fury ripped out louder than the landslide's echo. "If we'd gone five steps further, the boulders would have killed us.

He won't keep getting away with this."

The muscles in Ryker's neck pulled tight like a bowstring about to snap. "If it's the last thing I do on earth, I will kill him."

Beyond the stupa, the trail narrowed to single file: mountain wall on the left, thousand-foot drop on the right. Ryker's stomach curdled like sour milk. Every step carried the weight of the abyss.

Yak bells clanged from around the bend.

"Quick, climb up the hillside," Mingma ordered.

The dull, throbbing pain from his first encounter protested with every jarring scramble over rocks as Ryker grabbed a branch to keep from sliding. They watched a Sherpa pass, switching the animals. "Eee-yuk, eee-yuk."

The yaks raised massive back muscles and thrust themselves forward, heads lowered, long coats rippling as they moved. Their hooves scuffed trail dust in small clouds that stung Ryker's eyes.

"When their thick coats overheat," said Mingma, "they get in a nasty mood and may dump a load over a cliff or try to knock you off the path."

As if Ryker needed more reasons to hate this trail?

Yaks weren't the only heavy-load bearers. Bent forward and using single walking sticks, two five-foot-four porters followed in their dust. One carried a load wrapped in a blue tarp towering six feet over him and equally wide; the second, a cast-iron stove. Never again would Ryker complain about a bag of groceries.

They descended a steep hillside through blue pine and black juniper forests to Phunki Tenga, a small village on the banks of the Dudh Koshi River with prayer wheels powered by water.

"What are those?" Ryker asked.

"Prayers and mantras are inside," said Mingma. "Every turn recites them many times to purify karma and send blessings to all who pass by."

"I didn't see any in Kathmandu."

"Because most of Nepal is Hindu. We are Buddhists."

Ryker tugged at the knife on his belt. Blessings or not, he

wanted something sharp in reach.

**

A restaurant on the riverbank bustled with trekkers ordering cold drinks and refueling for the next leg of the trail. Sara, Mingma, and Ryker slipped between crowded tables, their eyes sweeping faces, their voices repeating the same question: had anyone seen the man in the photo? A young German couple nodded but said he'd left twenty minutes earlier.

Mingma asked Sara and Ryker, "Do you want to leave right now and try to overtake him?"

"My battery's low," said Ryker. "I need to recharge."

Sara had climbed the hill before on her way to Everest and knew he was already struggling with the altitude. "Beck's got a head start. We need to fortify ourselves with protein and rice."

The order turned in, Ryker pulled a photo from his wallet and showed Mingma. "This is my daughter."

"She's very pretty."

He put it back. "It's an older picture. I haven't seen Dulce for three years. She's coming to visit in about a week. If I'm over here chasing a ruthless killer instead of being at home for her, she'll never speak to me again."

He was sabotaging himself. Sara reached across and mussed his hair, trying to lighten him. "You don't know that."

She turned to Mingma. "Do you have children?"

"A five-year-old boy. In the spring and fall trekking season, I hardly see him but must work every day. Very few visitors come during the summer monsoon when it rains too much and washes out roads and bridges. In winter, it's too cold. Are you a mother?"

"No. Never had the chance." The ache of Michael flared, sharp and unwelcome. She twisted in her chair to distract herself. "You've been watching something ever since we sat down."

"A Sherpani with three small children owns this restaurant. I've stopped here often and spoken with Shanti. I know her well. Her expression and body language tell me something's not right."

"Then keep your eyes on her while Ryker and I babble like ordinary tourists about sensational panoramic views and porters carrying more than their own body weight."

Mingma tilted his head toward the next table where a server had given them three rice cones ringed with meat and vegetables.

"The plates are very appealing. What's your concern?"

"Shanti sprayed the cone molds, packed them with rice, and flipped them over on the plate. After serving that table, she went behind a back door and returned five minutes later wearing vinyl gloves to carry the plates herself. I think your lunch is about to arrive."

Not meeting Mingma's gaze, Shanti set the plates down and hurried back. Mingma's hand hovered low over the table, palm brushing side to side. "Touch nothing." He bent over the rice, drew in a shallow sniff, and closed his eyes.

"Everything's okay, right?" asked Ryker. "My stomach's making demands. It becomes very disruptive if not catered to."

Mingma sat back. "It has the earthy smell of a monkshood plant that grows in this area, extremely poisonous. You would start vomiting in ten to twenty minutes."

Ryker shoved the plate aside. "Lost my appetite."

Sara swallowed the bitter bile threatening her mouth. "How could Beck force Shanti to do something this vile, which would also destroy her business?"

"I cannot believe it myself. Discard the plates and move to another table while I talk to her."

Ryker's hands shook. "I wanna kill him."

"Not until we free Pemba," said Sara. "Look at Mingma. He knows Beck forced her."

"She needs a comforting hug."

"He can't. Not here. It's not proper for a man and woman to touch in public." Sara pressed a menu into Ryker's hands. "We still need to eat before the long climb. Choose something else."

"I want the cheeseburger with fries, but if Buddhists don't

kill animals, how's that on here?"

"Animals have a surprising number of accidents."

She ordered a chicken sandwich and allowed a smile to slip from her lips. "You realize it will be yak meat and yak cheese."

"You could've warned me."

"You expected Texas longhorn and Wisconsin cheddar?"

Mingma returned with dal bhat, the staple dish of steamed rice and lentils. His voice was grim. "He brought the monkshood from Namche and threatened to club her children and throw them into the river if she didn't obey."

Sara bit back a scream but said, "I want him cornered to feel the helplessness he inflicts. Every intimidation, blackmail, and smug look fuse into the one blinding truth. He wants us dead."

"We'll get him at the monastery," said Ryker. "There can't be too many places to hide."

"Tomorrow is the last day of the Mani Rimdu festival," said Mingma. "Hundreds of Sherpas and tourists will crowd into the courtyard to see monks dressed in costumes and masks as deities performing dances that symbolize the triumph of good over evil."

Sara's rage flared up. Beck would lose himself in a crowd again. Revulsion gripped her, festering into obsession. One way or another, she'd wipe that vermin from existence.

Chapter 41

Hiking past the restaurant, they reached two concrete supports anchoring a suspension bridge with steel planks on the walkway and a chain-link fence on the sides linked to steel cables along the top. Wind exaggerated the swaying, twisting, and creaking high above white-water rapids roaring, their echoes bouncing off tall mountain walls. Ryker stepped back to steady himself. "I can't go out there. It's too high. I'd stumble and fall, get blown off, get trapped halfway. The cables might break."

Anticipating a condescending remark from the woman with nerves of steel, he was surprised she took his hand and guided it to the cable. "Hold here, cross between us, and don't look down. Focus on the beautiful rhododendron ahead."

Heart slamming against his ribs, Ryker took a hesitant step and two more, building confidence until a gust whipped him. He grabbed tighter, held his breath, and then exhaled in rapid puffs. He'd survived the wind and now needed to get moving.

The deep, melodious chime of bells alerted them that three heavily loaded yaks had entered from the other end and occupied the entire width.

"Now what?" Ryker asked.

"Uhh, they're a bulldozer you don't play chicken with," said Sara. "Just turn around and get out of their way."

Waiting for the yaks to leave, Ryker asked about the prayer flags tied to the cable and flapping in the wind.

"Lungta, the wind horse, carries prayers written on them for all spirits, even a bird flying by," said Sara. "You've seen them everywhere since we arrived in Namche."

"Yeah, I did but was too hellbent on nabbing Beck to ask."

After crossing, Mingma said, "Now we'll climb straight up two thousand feet to 12,687, making it more difficult to breathe. Remember bistari, bistari. Hydrate and stop for brief rests."

They hiked through deep forests of rhododendron, birch, pine, and fir. The trail narrowed again between a mountain and a thousand-foot precipice. They met an old woman bent under the weight of a five-gallon container. Her gait was slow and heavy, the soles of her bare feet thick and cracked like aged leather."

"What's she carrying?" Ryker asked Mingma.

"Water from the river. She likely does it every day."

Ryker frowned. "She should be playing with her grandkids, not hauling back-breaking loads."

"They endure hardships we can't imagine," said Sara. "It's the luck of the draw where you're born. We were lucky."

An expanse of large flat rocks forced them to dodge slow-moving yaks, their heavy hooves thudding on the stone. Fresh yak dung patties the size of hockey pucks were plastered on walls to dry in the sun and be used as fuel.

They crested a hill and entered a wide arched gateway with brilliant images of Buddha and other gods embellishing the walls. Mingma explained that monks built it to cleanse people of evil spirits before entering the sacred grounds. Perched on a high hill, the monastery's whitewashed walls and red shutters were a striking contrast to the stark blue sky.

Guests for the Mani Rimdu dances the next day had secured all the lodging. "My uncle lives here," said Mingma. "While I go see if he has room for us, the monks welcome guests to observe afternoon prayers. Remove shoes before entering and sit quietly in the background. Their soft chanting soothes one's soul."

Sara and Ryker climbed stone steps to an inner yard and then a broad stairway leading to the main temple. They entered into a dimly lit room permeated with the aroma of butter lamps and a mixture of sweet and spicy incense. The ceiling and walls flamed with brilliant images of Buddha, gods, and mythological scenes. In the center, eight monks rocked forward and back reading aloud scriptures from low tables. Their deep-pitched monotone seemed to come from the depths of their souls, followed by an eight-foot horn sounding like a chorus of elephants in mourning. Focusing past the hypnotic rhythm, Sara scanned the monks in crimson robes and shaven heads. Her breath caught when their eyes met. Beck.

His jaw dropped, his face stark with shock.

Surprised we're still alive, you miserable creep?

She bumped Ryker's shoulder and nodded toward him.

A monk struck a five-foot gong. The deep, sonorous sound reverberating through the temple averted Sara's gaze the briefest instant. She twisted toward the doorway just in time to catch a blur of motion slipping into daylight. She grabbed Ryker's arm, whispering, "Outside. Now."

They padded across the temple floor, careful not to disturb the chanting monks, picked up their shoes, and then burst into the sunlit courtyard. The sudden glare off whitewashed walls made Sara squint. The chase began.

Beck was already halfway down the broad stone stairs. He cut left across hard-packed dirt and slipped behind a heap of mani stones. The carved Om *Mani Padme Hum* mantras, worn smooth by countless fingers, glowed white against the dark rock.

Beck glanced back with a lopsided, crooked grin, snatched a loose stone, and hurled it. The rock whistled past Sara's head.

"Coward," she shouted, dodging low. Her fists ached for the satisfaction of wiping that smirk off his face.

He'd used the distraction to dart around a large mani stone, leap over a low wall, and vanish into the shadow of pines.

"Don't lose him!" Ryker yelled.

They plunged into the forest. Resin and damp earth scented the air. Pine roots jutting from the soil, soft fallen needles, and rocks slick with moss made footing difficult. Though winded at 12,600 feet, Sara found her stride, her body remembering the Everest rhythm of hiking in thin air. Ryker was pushing hard, but his city-trained legs weakened in the altitude. His breathing became ragged and shallow. Beck turned suddenly, his shoulders puffed like a vulture ruffling its feathers, and flung a rock at Ryker. It struck his ear.

Beck turned and fled from the woods toward a whitewashed chorten. Its painted eyes seemed to watch the chaos unfold. He vaulted a low wall at the monastery's rear and pulled himself onto the sloping roof. Tiles clinked under his weight.

They scrambled after him, vaulted the same wall, and stood on the roof ten feet from him. As the monks chanted, incense smoke drifted from a burner, acrid and sweet all at once.

Beck's laugh was ragged, edged with hysteria. "Catch me, and maybe your Sherpa lives. Fail, and his bones will lie where no one finds them."

The words cut deeper than a mountain chill. Sara and Ryker surged forward, but Beck was already sliding down the far side of the roof. He dropped agile as a cat into the courtyard. By the time Sara and Ryker hit the flagstone yard, the space was alive with motion. The air thrummed with drums, monks moving in and out of side chambers, robes flashing crimson in the sunlight. Monks streamed past, some carrying demon masks, some hefting horns or cymbals for practice. Sara's gaze flicked wildly looking for Beck's face, physique, or stride.

"He's taunting us by hiding in plain sight," she told Ryker. "There!"

He lunged toward a monk adjusting a red and black mask, only to find a startled older man, staring back with clouded eyes.

A monk ducked behind a curtain; another hoisted a drum. The courtyard swirling in a blur of crimson and gold swallowed Beck in the tide.

"He'll disappear in the crowd," said Ryker.

Sara's throat tightened. "He already has."

**

Mingma met Sara and Ryker below the monastery. "Tengboche is a spiritual center, not like Namche with its restaurants, shops, and bars. Lodging is plain—two twin beds to a room, gear stowed beneath, and shared bathroom down the hall."

Bouncing from one foot to the other as if in urgent need of a toilet, Ryker asked, "Do we have a place to sleep?"

"My uncle found you a room one for tonight."

As they hurried toward a teahouse, Mingma added, "Yak-dung stoves heat the dining area, but bedrooms stay bitter cold."

Ryker exhaled a plume of mist. "That's just great since I'm already shivering and see my breath." His eyes stole toward Sara, wondering whether she'd cuddle for warmth.

Her furrowed brows replied, Don't even think about it.

**

By dawn, ice crystals had etched delicate patterns on the window. Bundled in two layers, Sara let Ryker sleep and crept outside. A cool morning breeze drifted across the clearing. At sunrise clouds with frayed crimson edges glowed against an inky sky. In the distance, a single cirrus cloud trailed from the foreboding face of Everest like a kite tail.

"Michael, we shared what could have been our last breaths up there, but our love was stronger than the will of the goddess of the mountain. Wherever you are, lift your eyes to a glorious sunrise and spend this moment with me."

Mingma startled her. "You're up early."

"Yes, I wanted to relish the view of Everest, Nuptse, Lhotse, and Ama Dablam in dawn's solitude."

"My cousins guarded the trail in and out of Tengboche all

night. Beck hasn't left. I showed his photo at every lodging. No one saw him."

Her arms flung wide, Sara turned in a circle. "He could hide anywhere in these forests." Air seemed to squeeze from her lungs as her arms fell limp at her sides. "Only two days left."

Ryker rambled out, his hair disheveled. "What now?"

Sara rubbed the tension in her neck. "Beck didn't take off on either trail but could hunker down in the woods."

"Or infiltrate the Mani Rimdu audience like he did among passengers at the airport."

"He enjoys teasing his prey and watching them flounder."

Mingma said, "Other Sherpas and I will sweep the forest while you hunt on the monastery grounds."

A queue of trekkers and villagers stretched along the path to Tengboche's main temple. Monks in burgundy robes filed past in solemn procession, their tall yellow hats crowned with plumes. Reed pipes wailed, drums boomed.

Sara and Ryker merged with the throng into the courtyard. Twelve-foot horns erupted, their copper tubes thundering a note so deep it felt as if the earth itself was groaning.

Spectators packed the perimeter, stairs, and balcony with no way for Sara and Ryker to move without drawing attention. They split, scanning from opposite sides, knowing Beck could crouch unseen among hundreds.

Two skeleton dancers bounded in, springing across the stone yard with sprightly leaps to the sound of horns, cymbals, and drums. A diadem of small skulls crowned macabre skull masks grinning with bloody gums. Hollow black eye sockets seemed to stare straight through the living. They trapped a dough effigy and set it aflame.

Ryker crossed to Sara's side and leaned toward her. "Any idea what that means?"

"Wrathful deities burning evil. The triumph of positive over negative energy."

"Not the way they taught religion in New York schools."

Perusing the crowd, they watched four more dances. Sara said, "We're wasting time. Beck's not in the temple or courtyard. Expand our search to the grounds and outer buildings."

In the outer yard, low chanting bled from an adjoining room. "The meditation chamber," said Sara. "If Beck stepped inside, his presence would ignite a spontaneous combustion."

They searched every corner—altar rooms, the library, even monks' private quarters. Sara dropped to her knees, checking under beds while Ryker reluctantly rifled closets. Nothing.

Slumped against a stone wall, arms folded, Sara said, "That went about as well as a yak on ice skates. We missed something. Where do they store items for the celebration? I can't give up, no matter what the cost."

They found a large outbuilding partially hidden by fifteen-foot rhododendrons. Inside, a room filled with gongs, horns, large drums, and rows of hanging costumes. An almost imperceptible noise came from behind a door.

"Listen," said Sara, "a faint sound in the next room."

"A monk having sex?" Ryker muttered with a wry grin and then yanked open a door. "Holy crap."

A monk wearing only a loincloth lay bound and gagged on the cold floor, shivering.

Sara hollered, "Untie and cover him. I'll text Mingma."

Pacing, she shook her phone. "Come on, answer me."

Five minutes later, he burst through the door, saw the monk, and threw his hands to his head. "What happened?"

The monk, wrapped in wool, stammered in Nepali. Mingma translated: "He came late to dress for a Mahakala dance. A tall foreigner held a knife to his throat, forced him to undress, then tied and gagged him. He fled when hearing you coming."

"So Beck's out there masked as Mahakala," said Ryker.

"Yes, look for a long gown with heavy layers of brocade, an angry red or green face with bulging eyes, bared fangs, a crown of skulls, and yak hair. Their terrifying faces are meant to frighten away evil forces."

Mingma nodded grimly. "And one more thing, Mahakala never appears without a sword."

A chill nipped the back of Sara's neck. Somewhere in the courtyard, Beck was among dancers, already armed and poised to kill.

Chapter 42

Ryker, Sara, and Mingma returned to the monastery courtyard. Twenty monks, clad in rustling silk gowns and wearing grotesque masks dwarfing their heads, danced with raised swords. All had bulging eyes and a wide fanged grin, the only slit for vision.

Moving in unison, the monks lunged and swung around in small circles, their swords raised as cymbals clanked and drums beat.

Spotting one turning in the wrong direction, Mingma said, "That's him. The one with a blue face and orange brow doesn't know traditional steps performed for decades."

Sara and Ryker approached from both sides. Beck swung in a wide arc, the sword whistling past Ryker's head. He ducked and snapped the kukri up, the curved spine ringing as it caught the blade. The shock numbed his arm, but the forward-weighted steel, curved like a predator's claw and bit into the sword's edge, locking it. They circled, sword against heavy knife, the festival crowd alarmed as the clash of metal rang through the courtyard.

Beck's next swing went too wide, leaving him open. Ryker pressed in, hooking the curve of the kukri into the brocade, and yanked him off balance. Beck stumbled, arms pinwheeling. The oversized mask bobbed with each blow, its fanged teeth grinning. The mouth's vision slot had diminished. Beck drove a boot into Ryker's thigh, freeing himself, and then swung a straight, killing thrust. Ryker twisted sideways.

Her heart hammering, Sara tracked every move in the battle of a wrathful deity versus Gurkha steel.

A guttural snarl burst from behind the mask as Beck ripped it off. Gasps rippled through the courtyard as his true face glared. Realizing he couldn't hide any longer, he smacked Ryker's face, staggering him, and then bolted.

The Mahakala dress bunching around his legs slowed him. Ryker caught the heavy silk neck and jerked him to a stop. "The chase is over."

Spinning around, Beck slammed an elbow at Ryker's nose. Blood dripping onto his chin, Ryker bared his teeth, narrowed his eyes. "You sleazy rodent." Barely avoiding a blow, he delivered a powerful uppercut to Beck's jaw, knocking his teeth and cutting his lip.

Beck stumbled back, staring at a handful of blood. "You'll pay for this just like all the others who deserved to die." In a blur of motion, he swung the sword and slashed Ryker's upper arm. Blood gushed.

As he was clamping his hand over the gash to stop the flow, Beck kneed him hard in the groin and sent him sprawling to the ground. His head hit with a thud. He lay motionless, his eyes closed. The impact jarred his hand loose, sending a fresh wave of blood spurting from his arm.

Sara rushed to Ryker and pressed with both hands to stop the bleeding. "Don't go dying on me. I would never forgive you." Still pressing on the wound, she looked for Beck. He'd dumped the cumbersome dress and fled.

She couldn't abandon Ryker to pursue him. Tearing a piece from the dress, she wrapped his arm.

Ryker moaned and slowly opened his eyes. "Where's Beck?

"He took off downhill. Without the awkward costume, he'll sprint full-out to Namche and charter another copter."

"Why didn't you go after him?"

With a long, slow exhale, Sara felt the knots in her shoulders and back melt away as her muscles relaxed. "Because you were bleeding too much."

"Means I've still got blood to spare."

"Well, don't get used to me saving your life."

"Too late, I'm planning on it being a habit."

He searched the area around him. "And where's Mingma?"

She shook her head. "Don't know. I was too focused on you lying there looking half dead."

"I'm still kicking but dizzy, and this arm's yelling at me."

"Rest, you're in no shape to chase. I'm on him." She picked up the kukri, sharper than any ice axe she'd swung, and twice as personal. "I've always wanted one of these. Now I have a target to practice."

"He has too large a lead."

"But I'm fast, a morning jogger. Follow slowly when you're able. A drop in elevation will enliven you."

She raced through rhododendrons, fir, and birch, slowing only when the trail narrowed on a thousand-foot precipice.

Reaching the bridge, she stepped onto the planks, the prayer flags whipping so hard it sounded as though the mountain itself was shouting a warning.

Beck was already halfway across, the sword flashing in the sun. Even without the Mahakala mask, the blade turned him into something subhuman. Spotting her, he spun on his heel, ran to the other end, and stopped short. Mingma and four yaks blocked his exit, their bells chiming in calm defiance. Sara smiled. What a delicious irony. His yak blitz at the Saturday market suckered him.

"End of the line, Beck," she called. "Nowhere left to run."

He sneered. "You'll never cage me."

They met three feet apart in the center of the bridge.

"You agreed to call Patrick when I caught you."

"I'm still a free man."

"Stop playing games. Where's Pemba?"

"Only one of us is going to leave this bridge alive."

Her voice came low and sharp, "Tell me where he is, or I swear you'll regret drawing another breath."

Even without the mask, Beck moved like a wrathful deity, sword flashing wildly. Sara thought of Hillary's legacy. A bridge built to save lives was now being defiled by a killer.

He raised his fist for a blow to her head but missed when she ducked and kneed him in the balls. "A gift from Ryker."

He doubled over and then knocked the kukri from her grasp, sending it clattering to the walkway. He whirled and pinned Sara against the railing. Her hands clawed at the cold steel cable as the rapids below snarled over jagged boulders, white water chewing everything in its path.

A gust of wind rocked the bridge. Seizing the moment, she booted Beck in the chest. He staggered, nearly pitching over the side. Twisting out of his grasp, she freed a hand and smacked his split lips. "Where's Pemba?"

The corners of his bleeding mouth turned up, mocking her. She hit him again. "Tell me!"

As they grappled, their linked bodies pressing against the railing, the sound of the bells grew louder. The bridge under the weight of loaded yaks swayed as a forceful wind gust tilted it precariously, sending Sara and Beck over the side and tumbling towards the rapids.

Arms flailing, she grabbed the steel cable with one hand but couldn't grasp the chain-link fence with the other. Hunter and hunted were dangling two feet apart. His face hovered inches from hers, eyes burning somewhere between rage and surrender. His grip faltered on the cable. "You'll never save him," he hissed.

His hand tore free. Arms stretched wide like broken wings, he laughed, blood on his teeth, and spat, "Yak," before plunging into the rapids below. The current smashed him into a boulder and then swallowed him with a roar. A churning mass of white water swept his body downstream.

"Help," Sara screamed.

"Coming," said Ryker, a hand clasped over his bloody arm.

The steel cable felt cold and smooth as her grip loosened and her hand began sliding. A hundred feet below, the rapids roared a terrifying prelude to falling and the chilling certainty of death.

At the last second, Ryker caught her by the wrist with one hand and grimaced while trying to grab the cable with the other. "I can't hold on. I'm losing you."

"Hang tight," Mingma yelled as he squeezed between yaks and the bridge fence to reach Ryker desperately leaning over the railing with Sara slipping from his fingers.

"Give me your other hand," Mingma shouted to her. "Ryker, together we lift."

The instant Sara fell, she'd felt as though her heart stopped beating. Now racing through her mind was the possibility of them not having the strength to haul her up. She reached for his hand, just to feel something solid and warm.

Her racing adrenaline must have flowed through their veins as they slowly lifted her over the steel railing.

Trembling, she fell onto the deck and closed her eyes as her ragged breaths slowed to normal and her pulse rate calmed. Then she stared at Mingma. "How are you even here?"

"I saw Beck take off for Namche and knew you weren't in condition to catch him. The bridge was the only way to stop him. We Sherpas can run down a mountain three times faster than you. I raced ahead and held some yaks traveling to Tengboche until I saw him enter the bridge."

"I owe my life to you."

"Everyone is interconnected. Buddha teaches us respect for all living things and to relieve their suffering."

"Well," she said, smiling, "we were both one step from the obituaries."

"Make sure mine reads I was handsome," said Ryker. He

reeled in a string of prayer flags. "Maybe these saved us."

"Or perhaps, we weren't meant to finish this here."

"Did you learn where our brother Pemba is?"

Her smile collapsed at the edges, leaving a mask that fooled no one. "Beck lied. Pemba's still lost, and tomorrow is day ten. I will not let him die but have nothing to go on except Beck spitting out a single word."

"And that is?" Ryker asked.

"Yak."

Chapter 43

Mingma looked at the sky. "It's getting late. Go back down to Namche. I'll return the Mahakala dress, mask, and sword to the monastery and then pick up your duffels."

"You've done enough for us already."

"It is my pleasure as your porter." He bowed slightly and led the yaks on across the bridge, their bells fading in the wind.

Ryker heaved a sigh, still holding his arm. "Well, we're on our own now with nothing more we can do about Pemba."

Sara's vision blurred at the edges as tears formed. "Beck lied to seek revenge on me for upsetting what he envisioned as a perfectly normal, happy life now that he'd murdered everyone responsible for his brother's death. And he derided me with one word, confident it would drive me crazy. In his mind, he won."

Sara picked up a stone and hurled it. "Sorry, Beck, but that's not how it works. You weren't dealt a Get out of Jail Free card. But at least, two wives and a mother finally have closure."

A crooked line of amusement slid across her face. "And so do I, knowing you slammed into rocks, and rapids dragged your body downstream, bouncing off fallen trees and sharp stones. I hope it was a long, painful death."

Her heart rate slowed. "Sadly, I haven't attained the level of forgiveness Tanner's wife seeks, but I'll try. For now, let's go. It's all downhill from here."

Ryker quickened his step. "Know what I'm looking forward to the most?"

"A large pizza dripping with cheese?"

"Nope, it's you buying me a stein of Guinness beer in the highest Irish Pub on the planet." With a jaunty air, "I want to sit on a porch gazing at snow-capped mountains while belting down long, tall ones."

"You know what I'm *not* looking forward to?"

"Hauling me to bed if I get wasted?"

"Well, that too, but calling McBride and Patrick for news on Pemba and then telling them what happened."

"You have to figure out what Beck meant."

"You think it hasn't occupied every cell in my entire body except when listening to your drivel?"

Twenty steps later, she stopped, hands on her hips. The sparkle had drained from his eyes, leaving only a dull weariness. "I'm sorry. I shouldn't have said that. I'm angry at myself for failing Pemba and took it out on my knight in shining armor who saved me."

Ryker hooked his thumbs in his pockets, rolling his jaw like a cowhand. "Aw shucks, ma'am. Tweren't nothin'."

Laughter came easy, but the idea of Pemba starving trailed them like a shadow. And Beck's last word, *yak*, pounded in Sara's skull as if the syllable carried a death sentence.

Sara and Ryker arrived in Namche midafternoon and rested in the suite, eager to shower and change clothes when Mingma arrived with their duffels.

"You go first and clean that wound," said Sara. "I'll wait and give Mingma rupees to spread among the Sherpa Squad."

He arrived just after four and bowed humbly. "You are too generous. We worked to save our Pemba, not for pay."

"I insist. We couldn't have found Beck without them. Don't lose hope. I'll decipher the clue and find him. Ryker wants to have dinner at the Irish Pub. Please join us at six."

Mingma arrived first at the bustling Irish Pub. Ryker strode in and announced, "I'm acclimated to Namche now and can drink as much Guinness as my stomach will hold."

"But you must also try some of our drinks." Mingma opened the menu to cocktails named Yak Attack, Dancing Yeti, and Sex on the Mountain.

"Exotic sounding," said Sara, "but iced tea for me. Guinness pint for my thirsty friend tapping the table."

The waiter set a bamboo container with a narrow neck and a bamboo straw with a perforated end in front of Mingma.

"My Guinness had better not come like that," said Ryker. "I want the perfect half-inch, creamy-white head."

"Chang is a traditional drink made from fermented barley." He slid the orange-colored liquid over to Ryker. "Have a sip."

Ryker glanced at Sara and got a thumbs-up.

"Hmm, smooth and fruity with a little bitterness. It's good, but I want my Guinness."

"Sop the alcohol up with food," Sara warned. "I'm going outside away from the music, laughter, and glasses clinking."

She stood outdoors watching the sky change from blue to purple and back to a deep shade of blue. With two dreaded calls looming, her heart felt heavy, each beat pumping like molasses. She opened WhatsApp and clicked McBride's name. "Hi, it's me at over eleven thousand feet in Namche. I booked a noon chopper for Kathmandu tomorrow. Any trace of Pemba?"

"Eight officers in the field have uncovered nothing. What about the killer?"

Unspeakable words stalled, too heavy to leave her tongue. "It's a long story best told in person. We caught him but got only one unintelligible utterance before he died."

"We thought by now—"

"Believe me, I did too. Our flight from Kathmanduu leaves at nine p.m. I'll text the Orlando arrival."

Sara watched the sky growing dark and weathered the same

discussion with Patrick and Ashley. She moved further from the raucous noise of the pub to make another call.

Their case closed and three others removed from the cold case file, Sara had run out of excuses. It would be easier here, halfway around the planet, giving each side time to reflect before meeting again. But what to say? Words spiraled around her in a whirlpool. Quit analyzing and just do it. He's your father. You're not preparing for a presidential address. Just open your mouth and let whatever comes out flow freely. She inhaled a lungful of dry air and exhaled to the count of six before tapping Dad in her contacts. A great sigh of relief when his voicemail answered.

"Hi, Dad, it's Sara calling from 11,400 feet in the foothills of Everest. It's chilly but so beautiful here. I'm sitting on a stone patio watching the moon rise among the stars. I remember sitting in your lap at five and memorizing the constellations. I meant to call you earlier, much earlier in fact. If you've been watching the news, you know Reunion Heights has had two murders in a few weeks. Thanks to the strength and perseverance you taught me, I was able to catch them both. The one here was a dangerous serial killer. His death brings closure for two wives and a mother and shelves their cold cases. We've been apart for too long. I want to be near you again. I need my father. I'll be home in a few days and call again." She paused and eased the fluttering in her heart before saying, "Love you," and ending the call.

Mingma found her watching a white aura crown the peaks as the moon crept over the mountains. "You will find the answer you need. Empty your mind of all distractions to make space for the truth; then, and only then, will it reveal itself."

She wanted to embrace him with gratitude but knew it was improper. "Thank you for being my spiritual guide."

"We are all one."

She turned back toward the pub. "And how's our one who's imbibing Guinness?"

"He made it halfway to the bathroom before gravity won. It

will take two of us to get him to bed."

"While you're there, I'd like to pack for our noon departure. Keep the sleeping bags, duffels, and warm clothing." She handed him an envelope. "And please accept this, enough for your son's schooling. You won't need to leave him for so many days. It's important to have your father close."

"Are you close with yours?"

"No, and that weighs heavily on me. I must reconcile with him when I return."

Mingma opened it, eyes widening. He handed the envelope to her. "I cannot. It is more than two years wages."

"But less than we earn in six months," she said. "Meeting you has changed our lives forever. I'll be very sad if you refuse a gift of love."

He pressed his palms together and bowed. "Namaste, my friend. My family will hold you in our hearts forever."

"As I will you. And perhaps one day, you will visit us in America."

***

Sara and Ryker arrived in Kathmandu at four and stored their gear in an airport locker. With three hours to spare before the flight, they plunged into the city's symphony of cars honking, dogs barking, and street merchants hawking. In the color and clamor of the Thamel's narrow lanes, shopkeepers were rolling out fresh flowers and pastries, hoping to catch the evening rush. The scent of roasted coffee, spices, and incense hung in the air.

They passed a tailor hunched behind an antique Singer, a boy polishing kukri blades, a woman arranging candles before a shrine. Prayer flags crisscrossed the alleys. Scooters brushed past baskets of marigolds and pashmina scarves.

Sara drifted past stalls draped with scarves and brass trinkets but hardly saw them. Her mind was on Pemba. His face pushed in: hollow cheeks, cracked lips, throat too dry to swallow. News from Patrick and McBride read the same. Still missing, maybe dying. Guilt pressed heavier than the humid air. She'd come to buy for suspects she and Ryker had harassed but should be decoding the killer's last word, *yak,* likely spoken since yaks were his demise. There was no more mystery to it than that, leaving her to wander the crowded alleys with her body present but dread consuming her heart.

On a street lined with tourist shops, a deep, sustained tone rolled out and wrapped around her. An old man with wrinkles etched in his aging skin held a brass bowl. He rubbed the rim with a wooden mallet until it hummed. The sound opened something in her: steady, insistent, calming. She bought the singing bowl for Jason and his wife on a thirty-day Buddhist retreat.

Sara got a kukri for McBride, making two Reunion Heights police officers daunting with Gurkha blades. In the next shop, Ryker was bartering so awkwardly for Dulce's gold necklace that vendors covered snickering behind their hands. He glanced at Sara for an approving nod after cutting the price in half.

They paused at a café for masala tea, the din of traffic rising like heat. Sara checked WhatsApp on their internet. Nothing from Michael. She'd left a note in Namche. Case solved. Home in two days. No answer. Had he died in India, found someone else, or decided she was too much a cop for a life with him?

"I hope Mingma will visit like Pemba did," she said.

Ryker smiled. "He'd hate the traffic but love the freedom."

Sara wiped a spill from the table and rose. "We're running out of time. You're the master bargainer. Use that talent to buy for Zoey and Heath while I shop for Patrick and my dad. You're an ace at hailing cabs now and have rupees. Meet at the airport lockers at seven. Do not be late. I have the only key."

Sara stopped at a stall with brass prayer wheels and bought one for her father. He wouldn't know what it means but might turn it once in a while. Then Patrick and Ashley. What do you get for someone who has everything plus forty to fifty animals? The jingle of yak bells hanging outside a shop sparked her to buy for three horned beasts with humps on their necks.

She stepped inside and bowed to the owner. "Namaste, I'd like three yak bells to take home to America."

He opened his arm toward a table of bells. "Handcrafted, each makes a different sound so herders can use them to track their animals. Listen to as many as you like."

The ringing was mesmerizing and mellowed her breathing and heart rate to normal. Large bells produced a deep, low pitch; small ones, a much higher, clearer one. After trying five or six sizes, she picked the two smallest and did a clumsy yak walk around the shop with uneven, intermittent clanging of the bells. Her hands fumbled for two more, and she gave them to the owner to walk with her.

Two laps, four bells jangling in a musical effect rather than a monotonous sound. The scene blurred as she tried to make sense of the images and sounds meandering in her head. Mingma said to empty her mind and make room for the truth. Only then, would it reveal itself.

Sitting by a small Ganesha shrine on a quiet side street, she breathed in the rhythm of the bells until the knot in her chest unraveled, leaving her light-headed and standing in the midst of similar high-pitched bells—a herd of sheep grazing near the abandoned belltower she often passed on a morning run. The image came back sharp now of sheep scattered in the grass above an underground burial chamber, the faintest cry easily swallowed by their clanging bells. That was it. Beck hadn't meant yaks. He was alluding to the common high-pitched jangling.

Knees unlocked, threatening collapse, she raced to a coffee shop, logged in to the internet, and opened WhatsApp. Fingers quivering, she could hardly tap McBride's name. Raw panic was in her voice. "Go ASAP to the abandoned bell tower near the burned church with sheep grazing there. Pemba could be in a basement burial chamber. Do it now. His time is up."

She texted Ryker. "I need the airport internet. Want your

bag? Be at the locker in twenty.

Still jittery, she paced, eager to hear from McBride and not planning to tell Ryker until then to avoid disappointment.

**

Sara paced at the gate, phone clamped in her palm. McBride had promised to dispatch police to the bell tower. If she was right, they'd find Pemba. If she was wrong, she'd crush Ryker's false hope. She kept it to herself, lips sealed.

Ryker made his own call to Dulce. Phone glued to his ear, his voice faltered and then rose with an ecstatic shout that carried across the boarding area. He was laughing, weeping, announcing to everyone who would listen, "My daughter's pregnant, and I'm going to be a grandpa."

His news heartened exhausted passengers who erupted with boisterous cheers and applause. But Sara's chest tightened as joy for him and agony for Pemba collided in her. Two lives hung in the balance, one just beginning, the other clinging by a thread.

When Sara congratulated Ryker with a hug, he winced. She stepped back, studied the rapture flooding his face, and laughed. He'd been acculturated. "It's all right. We're at departure gate heading toward America where public hugs are accepted."

The concourse buzzed with announcements of flight delays, gate changes, and passengers running to board. From kiosks, the smell of fried food, clinking glasses. To tame the storm brewing inside while waiting for McBride's call, Sara strolled back and forth from one end of the concourse to the other.

Behind her, a familiar voice spoke three words that jolted her to the core.

"On your left."

They pulled her back six years to a mountain trail, a bike rushing past, and the man who had changed her life with that simple warning.

Her heart stumbling over its own rhythm, she turned.

Michael stood a few paces behind, travel-worn, a duffel over his shoulder, his eyes locked on hers as though she were the only soul in the bustling terminal.

Memories swarmed so thick there was no room to breathe. It couldn't be him. Not here. Not now. Yet the grin that tugged at his mouth was his, the one she'd replayed on lonely nights.

"Michael." Her voice hitched in the middle of his name. She took a step, then another, disbelief giving way to relief so fierce it hurt.

He dropped the bag and caught her as she closed the gap. Her knees threatened to give way as she clung to him, six years of silence collapsing in the circle of his arms. The terminal noise fell away until it was only his heartbeat against her cheek.

"You came back," she whispered.

"I never really left," he said softly, his breath warm in her hair. "Not from here." He pressed her hand to his chest.

Tears blurred at the sight of him. She traced the familiar line of his jaw, rough with travel stubble, memorizing the face she'd feared never seeing again. "I doubted you," she confessed.

"You kept me alive on the mountain. I wasn't about to let you walk away without me now."

Her lips parted in a trembling laugh, half sob, half joy. And when he kissed her, it was not tentative but certain. Six years of distance, regret, and longing dissolved in one breathless moment. Everywhere around them, the airport bustled. But for Sara, time had narrowed to this embrace, this man, this second chance.

Past the initial shock, Sara asked, "How'd you find me?"

"I flew from India to Reunion Heights. You weren't home, working on a case. At the station, your boss remembered me and gave me your itinerary. I wanted to surprise you in Nepal where we have a history. I drove straight back to the airport and booked a plane arriving in time to join your return ticket. So here I am, weary-eyed and barely able to stay on my feet after forty-five hours in the air." He lightly kissed her cheek. "But eager to climb onto another plane with you."

"Group two," came over the PA.

"That's Ryker and me."

They boarded early, and he took the aisle. As he stuffed his carry-on into the overhead, she asked if he'd change seats with a friend she ran into on the concourse.

His hand still on the bag, he muttered, "My breath, my BO?"

"No, my ex in the blue shirt coming down the aisle."

"Hah, you wish."

A humorous pleat formed in the corner of her mouth as she said, "Ryker, meet Michael; Michael, Ryker."

He shook his head. "Uh-uh, No. Not possible."

"Later," said Michael. "I need to get out of the aisle."

Fumbling with the bag, Ryker pulled it down and gave up his seat. "Where's yours?"

"Thirty-eight E."

"Great. A middle seat between two portly hulks."

"I was lucky to get that at the last minute."

"I'll help find a new place for Dulce," Sara said after him.

Ryker's head bobbed as he moved to the rear.

Sara sat rigid as the plane taxied. Michael settled in on her left. The cabin buzzed with the shuffle of bags, the clipped voices of flight attendants, and the crackle of the PA. She kept her phone in her lap, screen dimmed but alive. McBride had promised to call the instant there was news of Pemba. She wasn't about to miss it, FAA rules be damned.

"Phones off now, please." The stewardess's smile was tight, already tired of noncompliance.

Sara nodded, thumb hovering over the power button when the phone vibrated in her hand. McBride.

She pressed it to her ear. "Yes?"

Static, then his voice, urgent. "Found—"

"Ma'am, I need that phone off now." The stewardess leaned in, palm out.

Sara hunched, desperate. "What did you find?"

"We cannot take off until every device is off. Hand it over."

"Pemba . . ." was cut short when the stewardess took the phone, snapped it dark, and dropped it on the seatback tray.

The unfinished words rattled in Sara's head. Found, Pemba. Alive? Dead? Barely hanging on?

The engines roared, drowning her question, and she was airborne without an answer.

Chapter 44

As they landed, Sara gripped Michael's hand as though letting go, she might lose him. Patrick's white van pulled to the arrival curb. He looked surprised to see a third passenger and extended his hand to shake. "I don't believe we've met."

"I'm Michael, Sara's former husband."

"You're welcome here." To Sara, "Everyone's gathered at the hobby farm."

"Pemba?"

"Alive and recovering. He's eager to see you."

Michael squeezed her hand as the air left her lungs in a rush she hadn't realized she'd been holding for days.

As soon as they reached Patrick's and stepped out of the van, four honking geese charged the fence, their necks outstretched and bills ready to strike. She smiled. Nothing had changed.

Tiki torches lit the patio, their flames bending in the evening breeze. The same space that rang with laughter and arguments at the pirate party now held a softer energy—muted, grateful, alive. Chairs scraped back as everyone turned toward the path.

They entered to whistles and clapping. Ryker smiled. "Now that's the reception I want. No need for a military parade in my honor, but Sara may demand a marching band."

She winked at Patrick. "A string concerto would do."

Pemba was leaning against the patio door, clothes loose on

a frame wasted by hunger and thirst, skin drawn tight over his cheekbones, but his eyes bright with recognition. For a breath, Sara couldn't move but then wrapped him in a hug that said what words couldn't.

"In America, this is how we greet those we care about."

He managed a thin smile. "Lying in the dark, I thought no one would ever find me. I prayed, then stopped praying. When the rock cracked and the light came through, I thought I'd died and doomed to a lesser incarnation without a lama's blessing."

Her eyes stung. "You're safe now."

"Yes, safe," he whispered, as if tasting an unfamiliar word.

"And here's someone else who's safe," said Sara, "after completing K2, his last of the fourteen 8,000 meter peaks." Her eyes foretold words she thought never to be spoken again. "Meet Michael, my former husband, who's come home again."

Everyone clapped a welcome.

"Thank you," he said with a warm smile. "I feel as though I know everyone. On a long flight, Sara wouldn't let me fall asleep until she'd told me all your life stories."

"Food and drinks," Ashley announced. "Fill your plates and glasses from the buffet and then take a seat in the circle to hear how our detectives captured a serial killer."

Ryker raised his glass. "To Sara, the brains of this outfit. Her research identified him and cracked his enigmatic clues."

Sara said, "And to Ryker, the brawn of this outfit. He saved my skin more than once. Every path has a few puddles. She raised her glass. "And a special toast to Mingma and the Sherpa squad who knew Pemba and loved him like a brother. Without them, we couldn't have captured Beck."

She turned to Ryker. "Don't you have an announcement?"

A very visible blush exploded on his face. He let out a slow, fluttering breath. "My daughter's coming home for my second chance at fatherhood." Sara gave him a gentle hip check. "And she'll also make me a grandpa."

A rousing cheer and jokes about him being awake all night, changing diapers, and teaching a baby to crawl resounded across the patio.

His expression turning brisk and business like, he waved his hand. "On a different note, we brought back souvenirs. Pemba's gift is money for his ticket home and a wedding to the beautiful woman in a photo."

Sara rang three yak bells. "Patrick and Ashley, these are for your zebus. They're more than tourist trinkets. Their jingling reminded me of bells worn by the goats grazing by the abandoned belltower where Pemba was held prisoner. So guard them well."

Jason bowed his head in reverence and played the singing bowl gift. "I'm grateful for the friendship here. The Bureau used my report to trap the men who beat me. They now face federal charges. Both keys were returned as evidence, and in time, so will the money. Justice, like interest, takes time to mature."

Heath lifted the carved danphe to his shoulder. Paco ruffled his feathers, squawking, "Dirty bird, dirty bird," and pecked at it.

Ryker cackled, "Naughty, jealous bird."

Zoey leaned close to Ryker as he lifted her hair to fasten the red-beaded necklace.

"And for you, my trusted detectives," said McBride, "the promised signed letter he left with Pemba containing information about the Denali deaths that only the murderer would know. I've sent copies to the other stations." He hugged Sara and shook hands with Ryker. "Thank you. I'm lucky to have you both."

Later, with lanterns burning low, Sara and Michael stood apart from the others, staring into the dark pasture. The weight of the past weeks showed in the set of her shoulders, but there was peace now. Michael looked at her, searching, but said nothing.

"Everest cost me you and my father. I need to mend things with him."

Michael brushed a tear forming in the corner of her eye. "Call him now."

Her heart thudding so hard she felt each beat in her throat, Sara pressed his number and got an answering machine. She glanced up at Michael who mouthed, *do it.*

"Hello, Dad, this is Sara. I'm here with Michael and want you with me too. It's been too long. I hope you'll be proud. Your code of never giving up moved me to the foothills of Everest to catch a serial killer and bring justice to those he harmed. I will be forever grateful to the strength you instilled in me." Her voice snagged. "We need to meet and begin anew. Love, Sara."

For a moment, neither Sara or Michael spoke, the weight of old wounds and new chances hanging between them. But for the first time in years, the path forward didn't look like a difficult climb but a bridge waiting to be crossed.

About the Author

Linda is an international traveler to seventy-four countries as of 2025. Her primary interests are the natural and cultural worlds of the regions visited. A Colorado native and mountain climber, she helped found the first lodge system in Nepal and later began a travel company, leading treks to the Everest base camp. Her close ties to the Sherpas inspired her to write the first book, and they have appeared in other works. Fascinated by solving mysteries, she has written the Sara/Ryker Mysteries series.

When not traveling to far-away places she plays pickleball every morning and walks every evening.

If you enjoyed *Revenge on Ice*, please tell your friends and post a review on Amazon.

Linda will meet with book clubs in person if within reasonable driving distance or via Zoom.

Website: lindaleblancauthor.com
Email: maa07yaa@gmail.com
Facebook: https://www.facebook.com/nepalwriter